the ARTIFACT HUNTERS

the ARTIFACT HUNTERS

Janet Fox

VIKING

VIKING
An imprint of Penguin Random House LLC, New York

First published in the United States of America by Viking,
an imprint of Penguin Random House LLC, 2020.

Visit us online at penguinrandomhouse.com

LIBRARY OF CONGRESS CATALOGING-IN-PUBLICATION DATA IS AVAILABLE

ISBN 9780451478696

Printed in the United States of America

1 3 5 7 9 10 8 6 4 2

Design by Kate Renner
Text set in Elysium Pro

*For all children who are thrust
into difficult circumstances,
and for Jeff and Kevin, always and forever*

CHAPTER 1

Guardian and Hunter

1942

At well past midnight, in the deep cold of winter, a man moved like a shadow through the snowy streets of Prague. He kept his head down and walked with a quick pace, finding his route over the slick cobbles of Josefov through old habit, trying not to stumble. Once, a cat startled him as it darted across the street—a black cat, of course, he noted with a brief, grim smile—and he paused for an instant.

Somewhere above him a window slid shut. Somewhere behind him his family slept.

His son slept, still oblivious.

The man passed the baroque facade of the church of Saint Nicholas, the stone statues of saints casting cold eyes downward. The great astronomical clock was silent at this hour, the apostles with their grave countenances hidden, the broad Old Town Square deserted. He crossed the space as quickly as he could, keeping to the edges, making for the House of the Stone Bell—a carved bell that was as silent as the saints and the clock—and the alley that ran between it and Our Lady Before Týn. He stopped only where he couldn't be seen from any direction and then faced the wall that was crowned by the arch of a filled-in remnant of a door, the plaster just inches from his nose. On that wall was a faint painted symbol. It looked like a looping vine.

He had to tug open the top button of his overcoat—it was frigid and the sudden chill penetrated to his bones—to draw out what he required. He placed his hand against the plaster and the air shimmered, the wall fading behind a watery veil, until a door appeared, a great carved oak door with no handle or lock, which swung open into darkness. He was through the door and gone, fading, as always, to nothing.

The prowling cat and the saints, had they been looking an instant later, would have seen no door, only the great blank wall and the cobbles of the empty alley glistening with icy snow.

In the dark, silent, frigid city, a hunter is looking, but not, in this moment, toward the square. This hunter, an Unseelie fae, perches on the pinnacle of the Charles Bridge's eastern tower, peering this way and that but missing what it wants by a breath. It can only sense the magic that whispers through the air, then vanishes.

If such a creature could feel disappointment, it would. Instead, it feels only anger and centuries-old resentment. It has been bidden by its master—Moloch, leader of a small band of miserable outcasts—to seek and find, and the hunter has missed its prey yet again.

The creature straightens with a barely audible snarl and stands for another moment before it lifts into the air on black wings that are each as big as a tall man, casting a chill shadow upon the city below.

The prowling cat, as it happens, crosses the Charles Bridge just as the great wings open. But even if the cat had lifted its head and looked all the way up to the top of the tower, it would have seen nothing but a mist. Nothing but a dark, evanescent blot against the starless sky.

Nothing.

Oh, except . . .

Except, had the hunter turned and looked down, the cat might have seen two red eyes, eyes as red as fire, as red as blood, as red as rage.

CHAPTER 2
Isaac

1942

Isaac Wolf lay on his stomach, propped on his elbows, book open before him. Shelley's *Frankenstein*.

Yes, he read it because it helped him with his English, but this story about a scientist who found the secret of creation and made a monster, that's what grabbed at Isaac's heart. It gave him shivers but also made him wonder: Why did he feel sorry for the monster? Would Isaac have acted differently from Victor—treated the monster differently—and so maybe saved his friends? Reading this book plunged Isaac into a realm so darkly magical he was lost inside it, and coming out, wanted to dive right back in.

He rolled over and sat up, rubbing his eyes, returning to the real world. The world of war.

It was an afternoon of filmy gray light.

Last night he'd heard a noise and was up like a shot. He'd

held his breath, straining to hear. The sound of a door closing? The distant, soft chime of a bell? But he heard no more in the deep and snowy silence, and he sank back into his bed, to his dreams of chasing strange creatures through shadowy forests.

A wolf should be a hero in a grand tale. That's what Isaac wanted to be. Was sure he could be, one day. Maybe he could become a spy and that would be his spy name. He traced the name *Wolf* with his finger in the air.

But Prague had been made fearful since the Nazis had come. People were anxious, secretive, huddled into themselves as they hastened through near-empty streets. His school was closed. His teacher's sister, Miss Rachel, sobbing, had shooed all the boys away, telling them to go, now, go straight home now, don't stop. He'd gone and he'd stayed put, because he was afraid of the Nazis, too.

One by one, his friends and neighbors had disappeared. Some had been "relocated." Isaac had guessed what being relocated meant—it meant that the forces of darkness were washing over all the world.

He lay back on his bed, staring at his ceiling, and became thinly aware that his parents were talking in their bedroom down the hall.

No.

Isaac sat up. They weren't talking.

They were arguing.

His father's voice was hard, his mother's pleading. He heard his name: They were arguing about him. Loud enough to be heard through his closed door.

". . . no time left"—he heard his father's muffled voice—"tonight . . ."

"But . . . haven't given him proper . . . should be trained . . ."

Isaac thought, *Should be trained?* He inched out of bed and opened his door, holding his breath.

". . . too young. In another few months," his father said, and Isaac could hear clearly now, "he'd be old enough. That's when his training would have begun. But it's too late, and for now, the less he knows, the safer he'll be. As soon as it's dark he must go."

The word *relocated* floated back into Isaac's brain.

"What about the others?"

A pause. His father said, "They've already gone into hiding. I haven't heard from anyone else on the team for months."

His mother, then. "Are you sure—"

"They know," his father interrupted, almost shouting.

"I'm sure. They know about me. They know where we are. If we stay, they'll find us, and then they'll find Isaac."

They? Who? The Nazis?

Isaac crept down the hallway toward their bedroom. The door to his parents' room was open a crack.

His father lowered his voice. "There's something else. I've heard that a mission is being planned by the resistance. Against the Reichsprotektor. Even if that mission goes well, it could mean reprisals. Upheaval. We'd all be in even greater danger."

"What if we all went together?" his mother asked.

"Impossible," his father answered. "They know about me, so I would draw them. They'd find us all. If he goes alone, he has a better chance."

"Perhaps I can fashion a disguise," his mother said. Her voice had risen in pitch, and she spoke faster. "Protective cover. I can make a shapeshift."

"That may well attract these hunters. But I do have an idea. One that might work." His father paused. "I hope."

Isaac found it hard to breathe.

His father went on. "In the archives, I've found—" And just then Isaac stepped on the hallway floorboard that creaked.

He froze, heart pounding in the silence that followed, and then his mother was standing in the doorframe, and she opened the door wide, the light from behind her shadowing her face.

"Isaac," she said. "We didn't mean to disturb you."

He wanted to yell, *Disturb me? What are you talking about?*

But he couldn't command the words to come. His tongue was as heavy as lead. He stuffed his clenched fists deep into his pockets and watched her, waiting for answers. She shifted her position, and Isaac could see that two spots of red colored her cheeks. Behind her, his father seemed to have aged a thousand years, his face thin and pale.

"We'll be out in a moment," his mother said. She closed the door with a soft *click*.

Isaac stayed in the hallway, but their voices were muffled and he couldn't make out words, even with his ear pressed against the wood.

A few minutes ago he'd wanted to be a spy. And now?

He tried to decipher what his mother had meant. Oh, he knew the word *shapeshift*. He knew it from fairy tales and the other stories he loved, of monsters and myths. A shapeshifter could change form as if changing a suit of clothes. But he wasn't at all sure he knew what she meant when she said she could *make* one.

Isaac didn't understand. Shapeshift, she'd said. Training, his father had said.

This was not what he thought would help them hide from what the Nazis were doing to his people. None of this—shapeshifting, training—made any sense whatsoever.

It happened quickly after that.

Isaac was told to pick out only a few items to take. "Just what will fit in this pack," his mother said, holding it up. "With your extra clothes."

He stood in his room as if struck by lightning. His mother bustled in and out. "Hurry, Isaac," she said, adding a sack full of sausage, bread, and cheese to his pack before leaving again.

Isaac chose two books from his shelf and stuffed them into the pack.

His father told Isaac that he was arranging to send him away with a total stranger, that they were smuggling him out of his homeland.

"But, wait," he said to his father. "You're not coming?" He couldn't decide which he felt more, frightened or angry or plain confused, especially when his father left the apartment without answering.

As the door closed, Isaac turned to his mother and asked, "Where am I going, Mama?"

"To Scotland," she said. "Away from the dangers of war. And other things."

"Scotland?" he echoed.

In his room he pulled out a map. Scotland was far, far away. Over a long stretch of land and then sea.

And what dangers were there other than war?

When his father came back, Isaac met him in the front room. "It's set," his father said.

"Papa, the Nazis don't scare me," Isaac lied. Then, "I can help you. With . . . whatever. I'm old enough."

"I know you can," his mother murmured, glancing at his father.

"You should come, too," Isaac said, trying to sound convincing.

"Too many people traveling together raises suspicion," his father said. "But we have a plan."

"When you reach Scotland," his mother said, "we'll find you."

They would find him in Scotland. Isaac bit his lip, reasoning, parsing it out. Maybe this is what had happened to his friends who'd been sent away. Maybe being relocated wasn't the bad thing he feared. He looked from his mother to his father, their expressions mingling worry with love, their eyes bright. He had to believe in them, in what they were telling him. He had to trust them.

"I know this is hard for you, but it will be all right," his mother said. "You're strong, Isaac. Stronger than you know."

"Try to stay low," his father said with a fleeting smile. "So tall for your age. You've grown these last few months. I should have noticed. I didn't see how much," he said, placing his hand on his son's shoulder, his eyes level with Isaac's.

Isaac straightened, bracing his legs. Then the reality of his departure made him feel small again and he slumped and rounded his back, swallowing hard. So many shifting emotions.

"Look for this in Scotland. It's a symbol. It will guide you," his mother said, and she pressed a folded piece of paper into his hand. He started to unfold the paper but his mother stopped him, her hands tight around his. "Look for it. This is all the information you'll need for now," and she squeezed the fist that held the paper.

Then came the knock on the door, and his father moved fast. "Yes?" he said, opening the door a crack.

"It's time," came the response. A woman in a large overcoat stepped inside. "We must hurry. Only ten minutes between patrols. Do you have it?"

Isaac's father placed a leather wallet in her hand. Money, Isaac thought.

His father tucked a similar wallet into Isaac's inside jacket pocket, and his mother folded his pack into his arms. His skin felt hot, then cold. If it was too dangerous for him to stay, what about them? When would they leave, if not now with him? He must stay with them, that was all there was to it. The shame of running away made his eyes burn.

"You're stronger than you know," his mother whispered as she held him tight.

"I—" he began, then stopped.

"Isaac," his father said. "You have what you need inside you. When we see you again, you'll begin to understand."

With that, his spirits lifted. He would see them again. He would understand. His parents believed in him.

He could rise to this challenge. Like his heroes in the old stories, Isaac could steel himself to move toward the unknown, not simply stay safe. Maybe it came from his longing to change. Maybe it came from being a Wolf.

He would own his name. He had to try. For the sake of his parents and their belief in him, if nothing else.

His mother pushed him through the door. The stranger

in the overcoat put her arm through his and pulled him into the darkened hallway, and the last he saw of his parents— his mother's hand covered her mouth, his father's hand on her shoulder.

Then the light from inside was extinguished.

CHAPTER 3
Josef, Anna, and Isaac Wolf

1942

Josef and Anna sat in their darkened apartment and listened. They had waited until Isaac was gone.

"We must leave," Josef said at last.

"I can sense it," Anna said. "The hunter. It's close and can smell us. Isaac left just in time." She added, "I will change us now, yes? I think it would be better, even if it gives us away."

Josef hesitated, then nodded. When she made the disguise, the shift to hide them as an old couple, he nodded again, approving. "We must hurry."

As they left the apartment for the last time, Anna paused and glanced back, wistful. "I loved it here."

Josef put his hand on her arm. He swallowed his own grief and worked to master his fear. They had to make it, for Isaac's sake. Yes. For Isaac's sake.

They slipped down the stairs slowly, cautiously,

haltingly—as suited the disguise—and out into the night.

The smell (an odor of rot, a stench as of meat left out too long) greeted them, and they stopped and pressed back against the wall of the building. Anna gripped her husband's arm tightly. Disguises really only helped against the Nazis. No disguise would fully shield them against the dark creature of the night—the fae hunter—who could see through almost anything and who might sense the shapeshift.

The cobbles were treacherously slick, especially for a couple who were to all outward appearances very old.

But it was only a short walk, a few blocks, and they would be in the Old Town Square. Just across the square they'd be safe inside. Anna could almost feel the vibrations of the magic locked inside the musty hidden space, so much magic, magic even greater than the fae that haunted and hunted them.

The odor of rot grew stronger as they approached the square, and Anna made a small noise in her throat, then stopped and pointed with an age-bent and trembling finger. There, at the top of the Saint Nicholas Church, was the hunter, poised like the statues that graced the facade. But this hunter was not carved of stone; this one, darker than the night, turned its head. Josef and Anna could see the dragon-like wings, the almost-too-beautiful face, the red eyes, eyes like fire.

They were all frozen for a moment, none of them moving. Anna was certain the fae smelled them. Josef stared across the square as if he could will himself and Anna to the Stone Bell and the wall with its painted symbol just beyond.

Then, from the far corner of the square, a rumble, and a car appeared, careening across the cobbles in mindless abandon, a black auto. Josef and Anna pressed even more deeply into the darkness below the church steps. The car screeched to a halt in the middle of the square, a door opened, and a Nazi soldier staggered out, his companions laughing behind him as he relieved himself right there, his gray hat cocked back on his head. Josef suppressed the anger that rose in his chest at this desecration.

He almost wished for the Unseelie fae to dive down from above onto the soldier's head, then checked that ugly wish. No one deserved such a fate.

But the Nazi car had startled the fae hunter. Anna felt it lift and drift on silent wings away toward the river and the Charles Bridge. The rot smell was gone and she could breathe again.

The soldier fell back into the auto, which turned and tore

away past the clock tower. As it disappeared, Josef whispered between his teeth, "Now."

They ran, no longer attempting to hide. They ran across the open space, making for the Stone Bell. Anna tripped on the cobbles and almost fell, and then she heard it, the fae, sensing them, the dark hunter screaming its deathly scream as it returned to the square, and Anna again smelled rot as the hunter bore down on them. "Hurry," she cried. "Please."

Josef pressed his hand against the wall, and they made it, they made it, disappearing through the door that vanished, leaving a blank plaster wall, and the angry fae hunter beat its leathery wings against the tower above the wall, sending a shower of broken tiles loose upon the cobbles below.

Isaac stumbled behind his guide while his heart tried to pound right out of his chest. But the woman was able to sense when a patrol car was coming, and she pressed Isaac back into the shadows until the taillights disappeared around a corner.

Then, without warning, Isaac heard from behind them a dreadful, piercing scream. He froze, clapping his hands over his ears. The sound echoed down the labyrinth of streets until it died away.

The woman stopped, turning, as Isaac flattened himself to the wall. "What?" she whispered.

He stared at her, confused. "You didn't hear that?" He could see by the crease on her forehead that she hadn't. But her eyes softened and she took his arm and continued to guide him north out of Prague, away from his home, away from the terrifying scream.

Isaac had to keep going. Yes. For the sake of his mother and father, and for his own dreams, too.

But if someone looked in their direction after that— someone or something like a black cat, say, or a Nazi soldier or even Isaac's own parents—they would only have seen two oddly shaped moving shadows.

Isaac had made magic happen. Isaac had made a disguise. A shift, which grew out of his startled fear and encompassed them both.

But he didn't know he'd done it.

Not yet.

As soon as Anna and Josef were inside the chamber, Anna felt a shimmer from the magic, but she also felt the strain on the old protections, on the thin places between worlds that were now stretched to the point of vanishing.

Her heart ached for Isaac, for her boy. "We gave him nothing. He knows nothing. We've failed."

Josef said, "I know. I know. I didn't realize the hunter was so close. It's the war. The world is more treacherous, the Order scattered. I would have started his lessons earlier if I'd understood . . . There's only this one magic we can try. What I began to tell you about before. I've made a study of it, these past several days." He turned to a nearby table and picked up an object, and then held out his hand, opening his fingers.

It was a watch, a pocket watch with a hinged case that opened to reveal the face, but this one was anything but ordinary. Chills ran through Anna when she saw it.

"The hunters are looking for us," Josef said. "But they don't yet know about him. The fae will sense us as we travel. They'll try to follow us, especially me. That will distract them from Isaac, and we'll have enough of a head start—I hope—to keep us safe, too. If we use this watch right, we can plant clues for him that he can follow until he understands it all. All his responsibilities. All his gifts. All the secrets he needs to keep the magic safe."

"So much for him to learn," Anna murmured. "So we travel and he follows?"

"Yes. Where we map his journey, yes."

"But, Josef, artifacts and those who seek them, for good or ill, tend to surface in times of strife and peril. With each travel wouldn't we be sending him straight into danger?"

"Yes, possibly," Josef said, rubbing his forehead. "Very likely. But Isaac needs to learn how important, how critical his role is in preventing worse things from happening. This is a harsh way to train, yes, alone as he will be." He nodded. "But it cannot be helped."

Anna gripped her husband's arm, her eyes welling.

Josef touched her hand before he went on. "We'll meet him in our last trip, and then we give him the watch. He'll put the puzzle together."

"But Moloch is so determined—"

"Isaac will put it together," Josef said, his voice firm. "Once he understands, he can . . ." Josef went silent. Then, "He's clever." Another pause. "There's only one problem."

Anna waited.

"We might be lost. Caught in the stream of time. It would be like being nowhere, or everywhere."

They were both silent, staring at the dreadful silver watch.

Anna said, "What if I stayed behind, found him and trained him . . ."

"You know full well I need you with me, Anna. I need

your skills. I need the magic you've inherited. I can't make it all happen without you." Josef stared at the powerful object on his palm. "We need each other. We have to remain together. If we do it right, he won't be caught."

"Maybe not caught in time, but caught by them," Anna said, her voice rising. "When they realize who he is, if they discover him before he knows how to protect himself. Because we won't be there to protect him."

Josef chewed his lip. "It's a risk. But it's our only choice. We have to trust in him."

Tears sprang into Anna's eyes. "Then, after that, we might never see him again?"

Josef said, "There's one other artifact I've also set aside. But, yes. That is a possibility."

After a moment Anna looked at Josef and nodded.

"We must believe that he can do this."

Anna nodded again.

Josef held out his hand. "Hold on tight," he breathed to Anna as their eyes met, and she clung to his arm.

Josef Wolf, turning the crown on the top of the watch, set the time machine in motion.

CHAPTER 4

Isaac

1942

For a full three weeks, the memory of home kept Isaac fighting to survive.

Surviving in a dark alley in Dresden where he huddled until he was fetched by yet another stranger. Surviving as he ran through rain-soaked woods, pushing to keep up with a silent smuggler. The smugglers were different with every passing day and sometimes more often than that.

Isaac wanted to go home. To Prague, his Prague, not the Nazi Prague. He wanted to be back with his friends and he wanted his friends to be back with him, safe, happy, and well, as if they'd all simply been off on a long holiday . . .

Isaac wanted to be with his mother and father.

He wanted to walk down to the river and watch the boats and throw bread for the swans and cross the Charles Bridge and stare up at the magnificent castle as it was before it had been taken by the Nazis and become home to the Reichsprotektor—as if that evil man were any kind of king. He wanted to eat the flaky jablečný závin and listen to the music of Dvořák and Strauss, the music that was everywhere when he was little. He wanted to again be allowed inside the Old-New Synagogue, as he had been with his grandfather before the occupation had closed it.

He tugged at the memories as if they were a lifeline keeping him afloat in swirling dark waters.

He remembered riding through the streets on his grandfather's shoulders. His tall, tall grandfather, who had taken him to the square with its sweets' stalls and bought him strudel and let him eat it right there so they could watch the wondrous astronomical clock and the apostles who appeared and disappeared two by two as the clock struck the hour. Isaac could see them clearly from his perch, his lips and fingers sticky with sweet pastry and apple.

The odd little apostles with their in-and-out, here-and-gone movements made him laugh.

But Isaac couldn't bear to look at one figure on the clock: that creepy skeleton called Death. He closed his eyes and clutched his grandfather tightly.

It was strange that Isaac should be so tall now and hate it. He hated being a clumsy All-Legs, Too-Tall, like a doomed fairy-tale character. No, not being tall—he hated standing out. If only he could be who he was but invisible. Could be who he was but not awkward. Standing out called attention to him. Because in his new Prague, the now Nazi Prague, standing out was dangerous.

His parents' belief in him, and his desire to believe in himself, kept him going as he left his home behind.

But in Hamburg, Isaac ran up against his worst fears.

He sat on a bench in the train station, waiting to meet his next contact, tucking his too-long legs underneath the seat. He'd learned to scan a room without seeming to, searching, this time, for a gray knit cap and blue peacoat.

So, when a man in a plaid jacket limped over and sat heavily on the bench beside him, Isaac stiffened, readying himself to move away.

Especially when the man began to talk, and much too loud.

"Have some?" the man offered in German. He leaned into Isaac, proffering a tin of mackerel and a fork.

Isaac shook his head, sliding against the armrest. Anyone could be an informant.

"Come on. You look hungry."

The man nudged Isaac so hard Isaac was afraid the oil would slop onto his pants, so he took the tin and a couple of bites, and returned the mackerel. "Thank you," he said softly, with a little smile.

"There you go." The man leaned closer and dropped his voice, though not by much. "You escaping the Hitler Youth, then? You're, what, nearly fourteen?"

"No, um, I'm only—" Isaac began, but stopped himself. His accent and awkward German might give him away.

"Ah," said the man, looking at him knowingly. "I get it." He nodded. "Escaping them, eh?"

A couple of Nazi soldiers moved in their direction, pausing before those who sat at the far end of the bench.

Isaac swallowed hard, and his heart began to pound. Where was his contact?

"Ah, don't worry. You'll be all right." The man paused. "I'm hoping my sister will take me in. They don't much like me where I'm from." He held out his leg, which was twisted in a painful way. "Doesn't hurt," he said. "Not much."

The soldiers moved closer. "Papers," one demanded of a woman.

Panic rose in Isaac. He stood abruptly, whispering, a lie, "Ah, my dad. Must go." He paused. "Best of, um, luck."

"So, I'm right." The man looked up at him. "Not German. And you're ... ah. That's the thing. And a tall one, too, aren't you." Much too loud. The soldiers were staring at the man, but he didn't seem to notice. They glanced from the man up to Isaac, and back.

Then he saw. There. On the far side of the terminal. There was a gray cap and blue peacoat. Isaac began to walk away.

Seconds later he heard a shout from behind. Isaac hunched his shoulders and shut his eyes, wishing he was invisible.

Wishing he could—would—do something for the man. But what? What could he do? This was not a moment to jump into a hero's role. Not a moment to be a wolf.

But the man. His kindness. Isaac turned. He prepared himself, even when his heart was pounding. He raised his hand, ready to intervene.

But the Nazi soldiers were already halfway across the station, dragging the limping man, whose game leg flapped helplessly as he kicked with his good one. One of the soldiers looked back and—Isaac was sure of this—looked right through him. Straight through, as if his wish had come true and he was invisible.

He was frozen with surprise as the soldiers and the man disappeared around the corner. An old woman began rifling through the man's abandoned pack.

Isaac found the blue peacoat again and he was ushered

out of the station. Confusion and then shame filled him, the shame of not having been able to act quickly enough.

The man had been taken in the same way as he'd seen Miss Rachel taken, and Isaac once again had not been able to stop it.

A few minutes later Isaac heaved mackerel and more against the outside wall of the station, tears blinding him as the cold brick pressed into his forehead. When he was finished, he straightened, shouldered his pack, and followed his guide.

He had to keep going.

The boat rocked and rolled as they approached shallower water. This was the last stage of his journey, from Norway across the North Sea to Scotland. Isaac would now be on his own, with only the paper in his pocket that he'd worn thin with folding and unfolding and the hope in his heart of seeing his parents again at last. He lifted his head above the hatch just enough to peer over the gunwales of the boat. Near to sunset.

"Down," hissed the crewman, who pressed him back into the hold, sliding the hatch shut. Isaac was sure that between the movement and the fishy smell of the bilge he would be sick. But he held his mouth tight and swallowed his bile as he tried to bend his too-long legs back into his small space among the other refugees.

They'd been pushing across the North Sea toward the Orkney Islands for what seemed like so long he'd lost track of day and night, especially since the ten passengers huddled together in the cramped hold were only allowed on deck to relieve themselves when it was dark.

Isaac had hardly spoken to anyone else. Conversation was discouraged: "Sounds travel through water. Can't risk it." He'd just met the others—men, women, no one else nearly as young as he was—as they were being smuggled aboard in the dead of night in Stavanger. Plus, his English was practiced but stiff, and that was the only common tongue among them.

But also silence, as he well knew, was best.

A smuggler pushed through the refugees, handing each of them a bit of British currency. "For here's where we leave you. Good luck." Isaac folded the unfamiliar bills into his wallet.

After maybe another hour, the hatch slid open again. "Time," came the coarse whisper, just as Isaac felt the boat's hull scrape bottom.

The refugees pushed up through the hatch into the cold

wind. Isaac tugged his coat across his chest and heaved his pack to his shoulder. The shallow beach butted against a headland. Distant fortifications loomed like hunched giants.

As the boat beached, Isaac looked up at the sky and witnessed the infinite magic of the twilight stars.

At last, he was safe, or so he thought. He leapt from the bow onto the damp sand and trailed the others toward the cliff, stumbling over jutting stones that were hard to make out in the gloom. He turned to look as the boat pushed back into the North Sea, swallowed up quickly by swell, leaving the refugees on their own. Leaving Isaac alone on a beach in a bracing wind.

He turned landward again and saw with surprise that the others had vanished like phantasms.

"Wait," he called in Czech, forgetting in his surprise to use English.

Where did they all go, and so quickly? He struggled up the cliff to the top and stopped, hearing no sound but the rustle of wind-washed bracken, seeing nothing across a wide stretch of twilit moors.

They were gone, and it was more than strange, as if he'd been spirited to this place by magic.

Isaac was alone with only his memories and his hopes.

But here he would find his parents, who had believed he could make it to Scotland. He would search for this strange symbol as his mother had told him he must.

Isaac stood on a spit of windswept barren land until the night was fully dark as the stars flitted through stringers of clouds. He gulped the unfamiliar damp, peaty air of Scotland. His cheeks began to sting, the wind bringing tears to his eyes. In the distance he thought he could see a pinprick of light.

He made for that light.

CHAPTER 5

Moloch

Thin places. Moloch knows much about thin places.

As a Seelie fae who's been banished to the grim corner of the fae world, he pays careful attention to the thin places that are the veil between the worlds, fae and human. As a fae whose heart is filled with desire, Moloch waits for human cruelty and selfishness to tear the fragile fabric of the ancient boundaries. Yet another hate-filled human war has made the boundaries, those thin places, very, very easy to cross.

Moloch stands at the top of the high tower of his isolated corner of the Realm of Faerie, twisting the object he holds in his clawlike fingers as he waits for a sluagh hunter to return with news. The object in his hand is a small cracked mirror.

Of course it's cracked. Everything Moloch has is damaged.

He stares into the mirror and wills it to open a window to the past, an act he does often in an effort to feel better.

He sees again the time when fae and humans shared space and magic. He sees himself as he was—beautiful, powerful, included in the Seelie world. Moloch's mouth twists and he clutches the edge of the mirror.

The vision changes and the ancient war between fae and humans (the war that separated the realms) rages. He sees how he stands by as humans steal the magic and lock it away. (All right, he helped them, and yes, it was a mistake, but he did it to show off his cleverness, and wouldn't anyone?) He sees how his face is sliced by a human when he tries to betray them, too.

He sees again how the Seelie fae condemn him as punishment to this dark corner of the Realm of Faerie, where he has lived in exile for miserable centuries with the sluagh host, the Unseelie fae.

Ah, thinks Moloch, *the Unseelie fae, the sluagh. They are terrifying—but feckless. A bit dim. Okay, not very bright at all.* But they admire Moloch. Moloch and the sluagh have come to a working arrangement.

Moloch believes that if he can find the Guardian, he'll have a bargaining chip to regain his old life. The sluagh search for the Guardian for Moloch, and he looks away when they harvest human souls.

The window Moloch peers through closes, and the mirror reflects him as he is. He's holding the mirror close and sees the white rib of scar that disappears beneath his black eye patch. He's tempted to smash the mirror on the stone. Instead he clutches it so tight it bites into his hand.

He wants the mirror to find what he's looking for, but the mirror, like Moloch, is flawed.

Moloch paces to the edge of his high tower and glares out over the distance to the bright, light Seelie fae world with its music and dance. He can hear laughter.

Moloch wants to be freed from the ruin of the Unseelie world and, yes, away from the loyal but rotting sluagh, and back to the bright lights and glamour. If he recovers the magic, he might be given leave to return to his former life.

He needs to find the Guardian.

Then Moloch will turn the Guardian over to the Seelie king, who will reward him. With this human war stretching the thin places between worlds to breaking—allowing his sluagh hunters to close in on the trail—Moloch feels he's finally going to get what he wants.

From where Moloch's dragon, Wyvern, is curled in the

corner of the tower, he puffs in his sleep, and smoke rises above the beast in a small cloud.

Soon, my friend, Moloch thinks, *we will fly*.

Moloch looks in the cracked mirror again, and this time as it reflects his damaged face he narrows his remaining eye, the eye that glows as red as fire. He hears in the distance the scream of a returning hunter, and one corner of his mouth lifts in a smile.

CHAPTER 6

Isaac in the Orkney Islands

CIRCA 1750

Out of the moors in the middle of the night a barn rises like a gingerbread cottage, one pinprick of light coming from a small lantern. Made of stone, the barn sports gaps the size of Isaac's fist between the boulders, gaps that let in the whistling wind. But Isaac is grateful for this bit of strange luck, finding shelter, and he tumbles almost at once into a peculiar sleep.

Peculiar because it isn't a natural sleep. It's as if he's caught in a storm at sea. As if he was knocked senseless as soon as he fell into the hay.

As if Isaac Wolf has been enchanted.

Isaac wakes stiff with cold, and for a moment he can't remember where he is. He's befuddled and not feeling rested, even though a pale afternoon light streams through the open barn door.

Then he realizes with a start what woke him and feels a surge of joy. His father—his own father—stands over him.

Isaac leaps to his feet and throws his arms around him. "Papa!" He has to squeeze his eyes tight so he won't cry.

"Isaac." His father hugs him hard and then pulls away. "We don't have much time." He turns, beckoning. "Come quickly."

Isaac hitches up his pack and follows his father out into a raw wind, making for a small hut. He remembers now that he's in Scotland, on one of the Orkney Islands. From somewhere—he can't place it, coming from under his feet maybe—he feels a low, throbbing hum.

"Where are we?" Isaac asks. "Where's Mama?" He realizes with some confusion that his parents must have arrived in Scotland before him.

"It's all right," Papa says, which only confuses him more. His father is moving fast.

"How did you get here?" When his father doesn't answer, Isaac, tripping while trying to keep stride, adds, "Papa?"

The barn and the hut stand on the edge of a moor so vast and featureless it's a wonder he stumbled upon them. Crossing the courtyard of this croft he passes a tall standing stone that wears parallel carved lines as if scratched by some great cat. The thatched hut, when they reach it, is small and tidy but spare, lit by a warming low fire. It all feels as if it belongs in another time, hundreds of years past.

But there, standing in the middle of the room, is his mother.

"Mama," Isaac says, reaching for her.

His mother hugs him tight, then pulls away. She motions for him to sit at the small table. "We have much to explain, and you must listen carefully, Isaac. They're trying to find . . ." Her eyes shift to the still-open door. "No," she whispers. "They're coming."

His father says to her, "Go. Hold them off."

She nods and begins to murmur, a low, soft sound.

Isaac demands, "Who's coming?" He rubs his eyes, trying to get them to focus. He turns to look out the door. A line of gray storm clouds has gathered on the horizon, but he doesn't see anyone outside. Aren't they safe now, away from the Nazis?

His father kneels in front of him. "You take this," he says quickly. He reaches under his collar and pulls at a chain that hangs around his neck. As he slips it off, he lets go a deep breath, as if releasing a long-held thought. He holds the chain up.

At the end of the chain hangs a pendant in the shape of the symbol on Isaac's worn-out paper. It's a looping, intertwining series of rings.

"It's called an eternity knot," says his father. "Keep looking for it. We've left it for you to find." He pauses. "Isaac, no one can take this from you by force, only if you relinquish it. Which you must not do."

"Wait," Isaac says, shaking his head. "Where am I going? Aren't you coming, too? We're all together." He reaches for his father's hand as his father presses his lips together, an expression Isaac knows means he's troubled.

"There's no time to tell you everything, Isaac. And it's safer if you learn the lessons one by one. Put them together. A puzzle you must solve."

"I can feel them," Isaac's mother says. "You must hurry, Josef."

Isaac's father slides the chain over Isaac's head and tucks it down underneath his shirt, cool against his skin. Isaac hears that sound again, that low hum, and now a soft vibration buzzes where the pendant touches him.

Isaac's father says, "Don't take it off. Ever. Not for anyone or anything. Not even for a second." His father's voice is urgent. "Promise."

Isaac nods, blinking. He can't make sense of any of this,

and he still feels disoriented, unbalanced, in a mind-fog. But he wants so badly to show his parents he's come all this way with the strength they believe he has. He wants to be the wolf.

"Say it," his father commands, pressing Isaac's hand between his own.

"I promise," Isaac says. He places his free hand on his chest, where the pendant lies, cold and throbbing, over his heart.

"Josef," Isaac's mother says. "The watch now. Quickly."

Isaac's father pushes a small casket toward Isaac. "Take this, too. There's a castle on the mainland, in Scotland, to the south. Rookskill. Village of Craig. What's inside this box will connect us. It holds answers." His father leans forward. "Another promise, Isaac. Don't open this until you're inside the castle. That's where you should be safe. If you open it before, they may sense it."

"Who are *they*?"

His mother moves toward the door, lifting her arms. "If Isaac doesn't go now, they'll find him." It sounds like she might cry, her voice breaking. She stands in the doorway, placing her hands on the doorframe as if she's a shield.

His father says, the words coming fast, "You'll return to your own time. We'll stay behind to draw them off. Be wary of the night. They come strongest with the deepest dark."

A sharp wind blows inside the hut. Isaac's skin prickles. The hum inside him grows louder, and long shadows stretch across the floor. Isaac blinks. It's now as dark as twilight.

The fire goes out with a hiss.

"No." His mother, a bare silhouette, braces and says, her voice rising, "They're here."

Isaac tries to stand.

His mother turns to Isaac, her face ashen. "Haste!"

His father shoves the casket. "Now. Take it."

The wind rises to a howl. A shadow falls across the already gloomy room, and an enormous creature appears just outside the door. The hair on the back of Isaac's neck stands straight out and his breath catches, and the pendant sends a searing charge through his heart, the hum growing in his brain to a piercing whine.

He thinks he hears a whispered word. *Guardian.*

The room is as black as pitch. His mother cries out, and the shadow-creature standing at the door screams, and his father shouts, "Isaac."

Isaac places both hands on the casket. His fingers cramp, and he can't lift his hands away. He hears a sound like a faint chime coming from inside the casket, like the ring of a small bell.

Wings unfurl behind the creature and a stench of rot fills the air and Isaac gags, then gasps. The monster turns toward him with eyes that glow as red as burning coals. Isaac is frozen, hands still on the casket, frozen by that deep hum that fills him, the hum from the cold pendant that sends another charge through his heart. As the fear inside Isaac explodes to panic, the room, the monster, and his parents glow with brilliant blue light—and he cries out, yells out loud, as, with a blinding flash, all falls to darkness.

Isaac

1942

Isaac, still yelling, eyes shut tight, hands still clutching the casket, tumbled head over heels in space, over and over until he landed on his knees on the floor of the hut. Then he opened his eyes again and pushed up from the floor, legs shaking.

His mother and father were gone and the monster was gone, too. Isaac was alone, the pendant cold against his skin, the casket clutched tight in his hands.

It was a late winter afternoon, light pouring in from above through a vast hole in the roof of the hut that was ruined—but not by a blast. It was ruined by age. Thatch littered the floor. The table and a chair were the only furnishings. The windows and doors were gaping holes. Dust filled his nose, and the wood creaked as the rotting floor bent beneath him.

The pendant pressed against his skin. What had just happened?

Isaac turned. Thank all the prophets, the monster was gone.

But so were his parents. Isaac thought his heart would break.

He sat down, his muscles turned to jelly. The casket slipped from his hands to the table. The wind stirred the thatch that drifted down from overhead. He heard the distant cry of a seabird. The smells of peat and old farm filled his nose.

He was Isaac Wolf. He took a deep breath. He had to unravel the tangle of threads he'd been handed, so he'd better get started.

Isaac swallowed hard and leaned closer to the casket.

The carvings in the wood were intricate, leaves and flowers, made by a skilled hand. The wood was rubbed glossy by handling, some of the carvings worn to mere impressions. The casket was no bigger than one of the small loaves of fresh bread his mother brought home from the neighborhood bakery.

The sun shot a sudden ray through the door of the hut. It was growing late. And Isaac suddenly realized his position.

Up until he'd stumbled onto the beach, he'd been guided.

All across Europe, through danger after danger, he'd had one adult after another looking out for him. His parents had promised to meet him and he'd found them only to lose them again. Now he was completely alone, told to keep finding the symbol of the eternity knot, having an experience that could only be described as . . . what?

Isaac clenched his fists and went through it, piece by piece.

He was in possession of this casket that his father said held answers and was a connection to his parents, a casket that he was not to open yet.

He wore a chain that held a pendant of the eternity knot that he was not to take off.

His parents had disappeared after telling him he'd *return to his own time.*

He'd seen a hideous monster he couldn't name and watched his mother performing some kind of spell against it.

They would find him.

And what was *Guardian*?

He took a deep breath.

He looked again at the casket. He was tempted to open it, for it contained answers. He reached for it, and as his fingers gripped the wood, he heard a noise again, that hum, and he snatched his hand away, surprised.

After shaking out his fingers, he carefully turned the casket so that the latch faced him. It was fixed by a lead seal that would have to be broken or cut. He leaned closer. The seal was imprinted with words.

MEMENTO MORI

His Latin was passable, and he recognized the first word. It meant "remember."

Remember that you'd better not open it yet, he thought. He wasn't supposed to open it until he reached that safe place, that castle, because they (whoever they were) might sense it (whatever that meant). Rookskill. To the south. Village called Craig.

Terrific. So helpful.

He would soon run out of daylight. This was not the time to be opening a strange box he wasn't supposed to open yet anyway, and he didn't want to meet something that *came with the deepest dark.*

Isaac stood and picked up his pack. The spine of his copy of *Frankenstein* appeared as he set the casket inside the pack and he paused. His two books, brought from home: *Frankenstein* and Grimms' *Tales.*

Monsters. Magic.

The magic he'd read about in Grimms' fairy tales and wished was real. Flying on dragons. Receiving a magical power. Wielding a weapon. Being the hero. All that he'd dreamed about happening to him if fairy tales came true.

Now magic seemed to be happening, but it had not been what he'd expected. He hadn't mastered the moment. Instead he felt what the monster in *Frankenstein* felt: awkward, fearful, and lonely.

The sun began to fade. *Be wary of the night. They come strongest with deepest dark.* That was one instruction Isaac had no trouble following. He had no more time to wait here, in this hut. He turned and made for the door.

In the courtyard outside the hut Isaac paused again at the standing stone. In the waning light it cast a long shadow across the dirt, longer even than Isaac was tall. He placed his hand on the stone, his index finger tracing one long vertical groove to other runes at the base of the mark, faint beneath lichen.

Isaac's gaze followed the stone's shadow, which stretched toward a swale in the moors. Smoke rose in the distance. Isaac stood taller. Smoke meant people. There were at least two ribbons of smoke. Which meant a village.

Maybe even a village with a sign with the eternity knot, which would be comforting, for he would know that he was on the right track.

The wind made a low moan as it rounded the crumbling barn, and the sound sent a chill up his spine. It was time to move.

Isaac Wolf made for the village as fast as his long legs could carry him.

CHAPTER 8
Isaac

1942

Having legs that were long for his age meant that Isaac was a walker. He could walk a good distance and faster than any of his friends. He was pretty sure he'd make that village before nightfall.

Even so, as night came on, so did his fear, and he sped up to a jog. Whoever *they* were, if they were anything like the monster at the hut, he didn't want to meet them.

The sun skimmed the horizon as he reached the narrow lane leading into the village that was tucked right at the edge of the moors. A dozen or so houses, a stone kirk, and a pub.

Above the pub's door a sign creaked on rusty hinges: *The Witch's Broom*. Below the name was an image of a tangle of tree branches that stuck out like spider legs in all directions.

No other symbols, as far as he could see. Although there

were plenty of knots in the branches of the witch's broom, none of them were eternity knots. But maybe someone here would have seen that symbol. Maybe someone here could point the way to Craig Village and Rookskill Castle.

He opened the door to a smoky room filled with mostly men, who stopped as one to stare as he entered.

"Ach, come on, lad, it be dreich," snapped a portly woman who, walking by, managed to yank his arm and pull him inside and shut the door behind him despite the fact that she was carrying a whiskey bottle and glasses.

Isaac swallowed. "Hello," he said, nodding to the crowd.

Silence filled the room. Many eyes on him, a stranger. Isaac felt too small inside and too tall outside. He felt different from these dour, ruddy Scotsmen, and he figured they knew he was different, too, and maybe they wouldn't like someone different. He cleared his throat, mustering his best English. "I am refugee. Escaping the Nazis."

A low murmur around the room. Some faces softened, some grew hard.

"I am looking for a, um, circle of rings," he said, not knowing how else to describe the eternity knot, so he made a gesture in the air. He'd lost the paper in the hut and didn't want to pull the pendant from underneath his shirt. And as the fire popped and the light inside glowed and the sky outside darkened, he added, "And a place to stay the night."

At that, the woman said to him, "Sit ye doon, lad. Ye can rest here, in the room above."

The rest of the company went back to their business, talking of weather and winter and war, though some cast him low, wary glances. The pub smelled of roasted vegetables and the sharp tang of alcohol, the fire crackled, and he was warmed by the closeness despite the cool looks.

Isaac found a small table and set his pack between his legs. He'd been given enough money to more than pay for his food and lodging, for at least tonight. The woman brought him a hunk of bread and a bowl of soup and he wolfed it down, starving after so many days without much to eat. Though once he was settled, his mind returned to his parents and the monster and the casket.

Just what had he stepped into when he'd stepped off that boat?

"Laddie, if ye be looking for rings, there be one na far."

The man leaned over from the adjacent table, catching Isaac's eye.

"One?" Isaac echoed, hope rising.

"Aye. A great ring of stone."

"Ah," Isaac said, disappointed, as he was sure that was

not what he sought. "Do you know of a Rookskill? A castle? A village called Craig?"

More wary glances shot his way. His accent betrayed him. It didn't matter how young he was. Boys only a couple of years older were fighting on both sides in this ugly war. And even here, he might not be accepted for who and what he was.

"Nay," said the man. "There be castles on the islands but na Rookskill. Na Craig." He turned back to his companions.

"Thank you," Isaac said. His spirits sank to a new low.

As he got up to leave his table, he felt eyes following him, and he wished he could shrink, or, like his parents had, up and disappear.

Isaac was given a small room—the only room—in the pub.

Before sleep he read a bit of *Frankenstein*, the part set in Orkney, as if that might give Isaac some clue about where he was. *Hardly more than a rock*, Isaac read, *whose high sides were continually beaten upon by the waves.* But when Victor began the *detestable occupation* of making a companion for his monster, Isaac closed the book and leaned back with a sigh into his first real bed in almost a month.

His mind drifted, and then he snapped awake.

The eternity knot.

Why hadn't he seen it? Maybe because he'd been too distracted by the coming of night.

His mind's eye went to the tall standing stone in the courtyard of the croft. He'd traced it with his finger—now he retraced it in his memory. A long, thin, incised line leading down, down, and at the bottom a depression, an etching covered by lichen, a symbol he'd seen but hadn't registered.

He concentrated, eyes closed. It wasn't exactly like the rings, but a bit more abstract like a twining vine, a winding loop that had no beginning and no end. He closed his eyes tight. There. He could picture it. It was the eternity knot. Yes!

He touched the pendant that hung around his neck, his heart pounding like a drum.

The symbol was carved into the standing stone that stood in the courtyard of the croft.

Isaac jumped out of bed, pulled the casket from his pack, and sat it on the bed. That hum he'd heard in the hut filled his head again.

The casket held answers. He wanted answers so badly. Since he'd left Prague, he hadn't known what his parents had meant by all their strange references, and now the puzzle had grown. Yes, he knew he wasn't supposed to open it.

They may sense it.

He fingered the seal. It was old and the lead seal was worn thin. He could likely break it with his fingers.

Which is what he did.

Wait. How did that happen?

Do not open it.

But he had. And now, okay, maybe, just a peek? Would just a tiny peek be a problem?

He lifted the lid half an inch, then he reached his fingers inside, touching something icy cold, a strange roundish object that popped open like a locket, his thumb slipping inside the locket and over a tiny wheel that turned, and then the object began to tick and whirr, and the locket snapped shut again as his fingers closed around it, round and solid, and what in the world?

The hum grew, became a painful throb, and then Isaac, clutching the cold orb tight in his fist, was thrust into a void.

CHAPTER 9
Isaac in the Ring of Brodgar

CIRCA 2800 BC

Isaac still clutches the orb, pulling it tight to his chest, as he tumbles and rolls. He sees pictures passing as if he's watching (no, as if he's inside) the frames of a film, images of his trip across the North Sea and then across Europe, backward in time.

Then Prague.

The arrival of the Nazis in his country.

His schoolmates, teasing him for reading so much.

The leaning houses with their red geraniums on the streets of Josefov.

His parents, reading and talking softly by the fire.

His grandfather (gone this last year), laughing, sharing a joke with him and the baker.

His grandfather next to him in the Old-New Synagogue.

His grandfather's cottage high in the cool mountains.

The old bay horse as Isaac fed it apples across the fence, a stack of books, a chessboard with his grandfather's king in check, a green-stained truck carved from wood with wheels that rolled, a blue ball, stars in the night sky.

Isaac tumbles through darkness and light, the images muddled and confused.

When he finally lands—as if he's been propelled through a long cannon—he's stumbling across a spongy-wet landscape in deepest night, the rank smell of the sea and swampy wetlands rising around him. He's suffering from some kind of delusion or trapped in a vivid nightmare.

The object he still clutches tight in his fist vibrates and hums as it digs into his palm, an orb but with sharp protrusions, and he doesn't know why but he won't open his hand and look at it.

Now in the distance are spots of fire—flames and sudden gashes of fire shooting skyward—the cries of men and women and the screams of children. It's a battle, with figures leaping and falling, shadows against the flames of burning huts. It reminds him of a cave painting, and he believes he's watching the ruin of a place that died in a war that took place thousands of years before he was born.

Then the same terrifying scream Isaac had heard in the streets of Prague and at the door of the hut. It's the scream of a monster that drops from the night sky on great wings, with eyes like burning coals.

Isaac backs away and thumps against solid rock. He's inside a ring of tall standing stones that tower above his head. He braces his hand against the stone and his fingers find carvings, and some sort of niche or recess but he doesn't reach inside. The cries and screams from the burning settlement grow, and suddenly animals—sheep, cows—stream past him, running random, wild-eyed and bawling, splashing into the muck of swamp and the night beyond.

The monsters—there are many—circle. They look like humans but fly on leathery wings. Their faces are exquisite, almost too beautiful, but also dreadful, for their teeth are sharp points and their eyes burn red. They bear down on the settlement, and it's no longer a battle of human against human as they raise their axes and pikes in defense against this terror from above. But the monsters pluck away the weapons and carry the people off into the night sky, into the stars.

Isaac clutches the icy orb in his fist, and horror fills him as he watches one after another, men, women, and children, taken away into the night. He's a witness to their end.

One of the monsters turns and looks in his direction, red eyes glaring, searching, and Isaac must close his own.

The hum begins again and a faint chime—like a bell—rings in his brain. He sinks to his knees and clutches his arms to his chest and without warning falls back into oblivion.

CHAPTER 10
Moloch's Sluagh Hunter

The standing stones of the Ring of Brodgar in the Orkney Islands are twice as tall as the tallest man. Thin and chiseled by millennia of rough weather, on a heathery piece of land surrounded by the sea, they point like accusing fingers, or the jutting teeth of a recumbent giant, to the sky. They are the remnants of worship—or perhaps they were put there to ward off evil (at which they failed)—by the ancient civilization whose homely ruins lie nearby, a complex society lost in the mists of deep time, whose collapse was sudden and complete.

Whose collapse has been witnessed by one boy in an awful time travel.

Now, in Isaac's time, eons after those people vanished from the earth, on this night when a sliver of moon illuminates the stones, a creature glides overhead on black angel-wide wings. It lands atop the tallest of the stones like a bird of prey. But it is not a bird. It has eyes that can devour a soul. Eyes as red as blood.

This is Isaac's nightmarish monster. And it is Moloch's sluagh hunter, searching for the Guardian.

It has perched on the tower of the Charles Bridge.

It has been across Europe.

It has hovered over Orkney.

It has followed the Guardian through time and space—to a stone hut and to an ancient settlement, among others—but it can't quite put its talons on what it seeks.

The sluagh turns its head this way and that, and senses . . . Ach! Some magic nearby? It can't quite grasp where or what. But it's not far away, and the sluagh will return to Moloch with even this small scrap of news.

But before it does, it will feed its own hunger for a human soul. The sluagh turns its head and opens its mouth and screams.

The Scots who live nearby shift in their beds and moan and dream of slavering wolves, of the haunted howes, of a ruined ness, of thin places. The boy who has fallen into and out of a strange, frightening time-travel vision in a small pub shudders and shakes.

The dread sluagh turns its head and its eyes burn like coals. It can't put its claws on the magic, but it will find food. It screams again, hungry, angry.

CHAPTER 11

Isaac

1942

Boom! Boom! Boom!

Isaac sat straight up, sucking in a deep breath. He was in a bed in a dark room in an inn in the Orkney Islands, gripping the coverlet tight in his fist. Next to him on the bed lay the casket. Its contents—that cold orb he'd clutched in his fist that had transported him to a terrible place in the past, or was it a nightmare?—were once more concealed inside, thank all the prophets.

Then, another loud *boom*, and "Laddie," came a voice from the other side of his door. The landlady of this hostelry. "If ye want to make the mainland, ye'd best be doon in ten minutes."

Isaac, fully awake now, scrambled out of bed. He dressed as fast as he could, pausing before he shoved the casket inside his pack, as the vision began to fade.

Isaac shouldered his pack and stumbled down the stairs.

"I am to make the mainland?" he asked the landlady.

She eyed him, sharp. "Rookskill, aye? Near to Craig? Me cousin lives in Craig. Ye take the number six bus south from Scrabster."

A farmer who spoke in an unfamiliar language—*Gaelic, maybe?* thought Isaac—stood in the shadowy pub, turning his hat in his hand. He was driving a lorry to the ferry in Stromness. The landlady had arranged for him to take Isaac to the ferry landing, and she'd packed a bit of food for Isaac's journey and would accept no payment.

Isaac was so grateful he couldn't stop thanking her, but she brushed him away.

Dawn was a thin band of orange in the east. The kindness of strangers and the morning light helped lessen the fear left from his vision. Isaac and the farmer rode in silence, the lorry bouncing down the road guided by two dim headlights.

Isaac saw, to his right, a series of mounds that he took to be ruins because they rose from the landscape in an unnatural way. Then, not much farther down the road, solid objects pushed into the sky from the flat marshes and moors, monoliths silhouetted against the growing light, sharp and tall, about a half mile off toward the sea.

Isaac's heart began to pound. The ring of stones. He pointed.

The farmer spoke rapidly, waving his hand. Isaac clutched his pack to his chest, feeling the solid casket through the canvas.

A creature was perched on the tallest stone.

Isaac leaned his face against the cold glass window. There was barely enough light to make it out. But as they passed, the creature spread great wide wings and lifted into the sky, and as it did, it turned its head.

Eyes as red as burning coals. Isaac's monster.

It swooped and turned and sped westward across the land, straight toward the moving lorry. Straight for Isaac, those eyes seeming to pierce the lorry and look right at him.

Icy terror spread through Isaac. Then a hum sang into his brain, a low and painful hum, and he threw his hands over his ears.

The monster passed overhead with a deep *whoosh*, and the farmer spoke again, craning his neck to look up through the front window of the cab.

"What is that?" Isaac whispered.

The farmer gestured, making the sign to ward off evil, and said words—repeated words over and over, his voice louder and louder—then clutched the steering wheel with white knuckles and pressed flat down on the gas, and the lorry jerked forward.

Isaac gripped the edge of his seat and tried to breathe. But that hum, that painful hum. And the nightmare—no, it was too real to be only a dream—of fire and fight he'd had as he held that cold orb clutched in his fist, the orb now inside the casket in his pack.

Just then the sun slipped above the horizon, bathing the entire landscape in rosy pink. The monster disappeared as if it couldn't abide the light, and the deep throbbing hum was replaced by silence.

When they reached the ferry landing, Isaac shook sweaty hands with the farmer, who gave him a narrow-eyed look and scuttled away.

Isaac shared the ferry across the Firth with a large number of servicemen. They lined the rails, watchful, searching the waters for U-boats.

But Isaac had his own worries, as he kept an eye on the islands growing smaller behind, searching the skies hoping not to see that flying monster chasing the waves.

Chasing him.

***

In Scrabster, Isaac found the bus to the village of Craig, a couple of hours south, paying his fare with almost his last bit of coin. Isaac sat on the jostling bus, clutching his pack, the hard lump of the casket pushing the pendant into his skin.

The bus turned into a narrow lane by a train station and Isaac craned his neck to see the sign. CRAIG STATION. Half a dozen British soldiers disembarked with him, their rowdy banter fading into the distance as they made for Craig Village, leaving Isaac on his own.

He turned in a full circle. Craig Station sat at the edge of the village. It was late, and mist hovered above the trees, and the damp air smelled earthy. There was no castle to be seen. He wondered what to do next, so he climbed the steps and went inside the empty station.

A man lifted his eyes from his paperwork and peered at Isaac through the bars of the ticket window.

"Another bairn," he said with a grim look.

"Rookskill?" Isaac asked. He didn't want to say more lest his accent betray him.

"It be hainted," the man said, his voice a rumble.

Isaac's scalp prickled. "Um, hainted?" Some of these Scottish words were a mystery, but this one he knew. *Haunted.*

The man leaned close to the bars of his window. "A place

of ancient dark secrets, that's what. And worse now than ever. Strange doings. Peculiar lights in the night. Doing work o' the de'il, says I. Says everyone. No one goes up there now. Except the strange ones." And he peered hard at Isaac. "You be strange?"

"I . . . do not think so." Isaac swallowed hard. Then he straightened. "Where?" he asked.

"Up that way. First road to the right. Then along the fence to the right and through the woods since the gate be locked." The man pulled away, muttering, shaking his head.

Isaac made for the door.

"Laddie."

Isaac turned.

"Next train for Edinburgh in two hours. And each day but Sunday. Ye keep that in mind." He paused. "And don't be caught in the forest after dark, aye? Nobody goes through that forest after dark, especially now. Nobody goes." He paused, then muttered, "'Less they be strange."

Isaac clenched his fists and nodded. The overhead bell jingled as he closed the door behind.

It was cold with a soft drizzle. Along the road that led to the castle, the trees hung low, dripping and casting gloom. Isaac took every step with increasing care.

The gate, as the stationmaster said, was locked. Black iron

with spiky points and an empty circle at the top like a round eye, the gate rose into the overhanging branches. Isaac put his hand against the gate and instantly pulled away. It felt as if it was electrified.

Probably it was the cold metal against his skin.

And then a sound, a low growl from behind him and he turned fast, and . . . nothing. His heart began to pound. He turned back to the fence and caught a glimpse of movement in the underbrush.

But, nothing. A trick of the mist.

He stood, waiting for his heart to slow to normal. The path along the fence, which he had to follow if he was to go on, led through a thicket.

Isaac took a deep breath.

Only a little farther, he reasoned. Then he'd be able to rest. If his father was right, he could open that casket in the safety of this Rookskill place. He'd find answers. Maybe he'd see his parents again. Maybe he'd understand at last.

But maybe he'd touch that orb again and fall into another awful vision.

Isaac squared his shoulders and pressed on despite the *thump, thump* of his heart.

CHAPTER 12

The Wraith

A wraith lives in the forest that surrounds Rookskill Castle.

Wards, magic invisible barriers, have been made round the castle itself to protect it, wards made by someone living inside the castle, but the forest wraith has crept as close as it can. It hides in a rough shelter barely fit for a badger. It radiates loss and menace and ancient witchery, powerful magic that it has cultivated for centuries. The wraith has journeyed through time and space—over and over again—to be close to Rookskill.

Thanks to the wraith's magic, the forest beyond the wards has grown dismal of late and good for hiding. Thorns have sprouted in the thickets. Twining brambles have grown up tree trunks. Wolves have not been seen in this part of the world for a hundred years or more, but now they howl in the glens. The wraith, a creature that was once at least part human, has drawn this malevolence.

The wraith has been reduced to its shadowy form by desire. It wants a small silvery object that rests in the pocket of a girl inside the castle.

Strange little creatures surround the wraith. They are tiny mechanicals made of bits and pieces of living beings and parts of metal and leather and wood. They skitter and scurry and squeal, eyes blink-blinking in terror. They try to hide but cannot evade their master when it reaches for them, grasping, clawing, ripping.

As it will grasp, claw, and rip any who lie in the way of what it wants, the shiny object that is the target to its poisonous arrow. Oh, such desire! Such longing! Oh, for those wards to fall!

For this small silvery object contains a soul that, to the wraith, is most dear.

CHAPTER 13

Isaac

1942

About half a mile from the main gate, Isaac found, as the stationmaster had said, a smaller unlocked gate in the fence. He went through, entering the towering thick forest that lay beyond.

It was a dank and gloomy place. It smelled of age and mushrooms. The steady *drip-drip* of water from leaves that were saturated in mist was the only sound. Every step of Isaac's tired feet went deep into squishy moss.

The trees formed a spiderweb of branches. Even though it was winter, the undergrowth pressed in and smothered the already gray light. A narrow track led from the gate and Isaac feared it was an animal trail, not a proper path. But it was the only way in.

He thought he should be dropping pebbles or bread crumbs to mark the way out. But if he turned around now, he'd never make it back to Craig Village before nightfall.

Be wary of the deepest dark.

Don't be caught in the forest after dark.

Nobody goes to Rookskill, 'less they be strange.

Isaac sped up, moving as quickly as he could, brushing branches aside with every step.

The trees closed in and he moved faster, branches thwacking him in the face, stinging his cheeks, and roots tripped him up so that he stumbled, nearly falling. The air was thick with moisture, and he shivered with damp cold. He was almost at a full-on run when movement ahead caught his eye.

A cloud seemed to be floating above the bracken, through the dim, a cloud as white as snow.

Isaac stood still, waiting, panting to catch his breath. His exhale made a faint fog in the damp air.

The cloud was iridescent in the gloom and nearly as long as he was tall. And then he realized it wasn't a cloud. He could make out a curve as of the back of an animal, and a strange thought jumped into his mind.

"A unicorn," he whispered aloud in his own language. A flurry of excitement ran through him.

He saw the crest of the neck as the animal grazed, its long, rippling mane. It moved slowly through the brown tree trunks and bare shrubs. Isaac held his breath, straining to see the unicorn's horn.

Disappointment surged through him when the animal raised its head. There was no horn. It was a horse. Just a pure white horse, grazing in the woods. It moved off and disappeared.

Isaac felt foolish. How ridiculous! A unicorn. What was he thinking? All the peculiar things that had happened to him since the day he left Prague were getting to him.

The trail led him to his left and widened, and he figured that if he'd seen a horse he probably wasn't far from the castle. Which was good because he could tell that even though the sun was hidden by low clouds, it was close to setting, the gray shadows growing deeper.

He pressed on, then stopped again.

Something else moved through the brush directly toward him, cracking twigs, crushing leaves, brushing past dry bracken.

Isaac froze and braced.

All around him, in a circle, enveloping him.

Dogs.

Isaac liked dogs, and dogs liked Isaac. When he was little and visiting the mountain cottage, his grandfather had a dog, a black-and-tan shepherd, Aldo, who climbed into Isaac's bed at night and slept curled around him. But these were strange dogs in a strange wood, surrounding a boy who was beginning to feel like he had stepped right into one of the Grimms' nastier tales, and as they surrounded him, they growled in a soft chorus of rumbles, dripping saliva.

Isaac bent, slower than slow, reaching for a stout branch that lay near his feet. At once, one of the dogs bared its teeth.

Isaac's eyes met those of a mastiff. Its head reached Isaac's waist. Its lips were curled back, exposing sharp canines. Isaac froze, his knees bent, his hand not yet on the stick, his heart in his throat.

"Canut," came a voice from down the path. "Have you found him?"

A small blond boy appeared from among the tree trunks around the bend.

"Ah," said the boy as he moved through the animals. "Jolly good. You're here."

Isaac straightened, still watching the dog, Canut, who moved to stand next to the boy but kept Isaac in a low stare.

"I'm Colin Drake," the boy said. "We were told you'd be arriving. Glad I found you before dark."

"Isaac," he introduced himself, confused but grateful. "Isaac Wolf. Are you from Rookskill?"

"Of course. Wolf," said Colin. "I like that. Ironic, considering." He grinned. "Well, come on, then. Supper's waiting."

"I am sorry?" Isaac said. "Who told you about me?" Maybe the stationmaster had telephoned.

"Leo," said Colin matter-of-factly. "He knows stuff."

"All right," Isaac said uncertainly. "Who is Leo?"

"Come on. You'll meet him," Colin said, and turned away. The animals surrounded Colin, leaving Isaac.

Almost out of earshot, Colin began to speak. "Yes, I know. He can't help it. Stop, Canut. Don't say such things. That's mean." Then a pause as Colin turned to another of his dogs. "Why, Josie, that's the first time you've spoken. How lovely. What's that? Yes, I feel it, too. Strange timing, don't you think?"

It took Isaac almost a full minute to begin walking, he was so stunned. Was Colin really talking to the dogs?

Isaac shook his head and followed them. After all, this wasn't the strangest thing that had happened lately.

A few minutes later, they emerged from the thicket of trees into a weedy meadow that surrounded a monstrous castle.

In the dusky light the castle hulked against the sky, all

spikes and points and blocky stone ramparts. It had a great square broken keep, detached from the castle but for a long parapet. The castle was three stories high, a thin tower rising above the rest, and the narrow windows glared at him like black eyes set into the stone walls.

This was Rookskill. And his parents had sent him here.

"Keep up, Isaac," Colin called from ahead. "When you reach this spot, don't be surprised. Just push through. You've been cleared."

"Cleared? What am I pushing through?" But Isaac's words didn't stop the boy and his dogs.

Colin and his pack were almost across the meadow, the dogs nearly lost in the tall grass. Isaac picked up his pace, brushing through the brittle stems that snapped and whispered as the chill wind stung his cheeks. He didn't have much time to wonder what Colin meant before he felt a soft, invisible wall of air, and he pressed on, and it popped around him like a bubble.

Isaac stopped once more and looked back. The forest remained on the other side of the invisible wall.

Isaac's childhood stood on the far side like a long-ago tale. The trees bent together and the branches interlaced. The thorny shrubs crowded together and the path was lost behind the shimmery veil.

Isaac turned back to the castle, his skin prickling. "Hello? Colin?"

"This way," Colin called. "Don't dilly-dally."

"What is dilly-dally?" Isaac called back, to no response.

The closer Isaac drew, the smaller he felt. The castle loomed, a towering shadow, leaning over him. Some of the windows were cracked, some boarded up. Heavy blocks of stone had fallen from the parapet into piles along the foot. The great front door was almost smothered in dead ivy. A damaged sign was propped against the outer wall, barely legible.

ROO KILL ASTLE REN'S ACAD The sign was broken off as if a huge bite had been taken out of the wood.

Clearly, Isaac thought, upkeep was not one of the priorities around this Rookskill.

But Isaac felt something, rising from the very ground. A hum that grew and throbbed, from his feet right up his spine. A deep heaving and sighing, like waves beating on a cliff, like a distant heartbeat. A hum that Isaac recognized now as his own reaction to magic, a reaction that defied simple explanation.

It was the same hum he'd felt when he'd arrived at the hut with his parents.

The same hum that emanated from the casket.

The same hum he'd heard in the ring of standing stones, and when he'd seen the monster with red eyes.

Yes, magic. That's what it was.

This Rookskill was rich with it. The very earth breathed magic.

"Here we are," Colin called. "Keep up, then." Colin and the dogs had reached the front door, and Isaac sprinted to catch up before the door closed in his face. The sky was nearly dark.

The door was open just wide enough for him to enter. He stepped over the threshold.

Being inside was not much better than being out. In fact, it might have been worse.

The entry hall rose up all the way to the top of the castle. It was dreary and cold, despite a pathetic fire that smoldered in the huge grate to his left. Muddled tapestries hung limply from the walls, and portraits of dim ancestors rose to the ceiling, all so buried in dust and grime that Isaac could scarcely make out the details. The wall to his right was bare stone but showed an outline of a missing painting, the stone in the blank space brighter than the rest.

When the door slammed shut behind him, Isaac nearly jumped out of his skin. He was alone, in silence, in the gloom.

Then, right before his eyes, something materialized with

a *pop*. Transparent, like gauze, and vaguely human, and, and . . .

Isaac swallowed, though his mouth was so dry there was nothing to swallow.

A blob floated three feet above the ground. Transparent, radiating cold, and making a soft *whoosh*.

And then the blob spoke, in English. "Well, we're waiting, so don't just stand there gawking."

CHAPTER 14
Isaac

1942

Isaac had to lean against the door, his pack squashed between his back and the heavy wood.

"Now, that's interesting," the blob said. "How did you do that?"

"Do what?" Isaac whispered.

The blob looked him up and down. "Huh. He doesn't know what he can do. Well, well."

"You're a . . ." Isaac began, "you're a . . . ghost?"

The blob grew in size, as if the blob's molecules were spreading apart (if the blob was made of molecules) and pulled closer—too close—to Isaac, and said (and Isaac thought that if they could spit the words, they would), "We are not a ghost."

They drew back and pulled themselves together. Or

togetherish. "We're a wight. Which is an entirely different matter."

Isaac pressed back further, reaching his hand for the doorknob. "Um, what is the difference?"

They sighed. "A ghost is a human spirit, the remnant of a human soul, stuck in this world. And generally not at all happy about it. Now, a wight," and Isaac thought they preened a little, "is supernatural. We're fearless, can see in the dark"—they widened what Isaac took for eyes—"and we collect collectibles."

"Collect . . . what?" Isaac said. His hand was on the doorknob.

The wight moved right up close, the icy cold radiating from them. "That's a very nice rucksack," the wight said in a wheedling voice. "Can we see what's inside?"

Isaac shook his head. He started to turn the knob on the door.

"We shouldn't go back out there if we were you. They say that the cu sith—dire wolves to you—have returned to the forests around Rookskill of late. You can't see them in the daylight, of course. But they roam closer at night. Hungry. Large. Big teeth. Chomp, chomp." The whole time the wight spoke they drew closer and closer to Isaac until they were right next to him. The wight grinned (or so Isaac thought), emitting a sickly cold breath of air. They reached a skinny arm toward Isaac's pack.

Isaac slid around so that he faced the wight head-on. He wasn't about to give up his pack. "Leave off," he said in a gruff way.

The wight retreated with a "humph."

"Don't let Willow bother you," came a voice from the other end of the hall. "If you tell them off, they have to obey. So, you instinctively did the right thing. But Willow's nicer to humans than most wights are. Aren't you, Willow?" A fair-haired girl wearing a tartan skirt and green cardigan, who looked to be Isaac's age, crossed the hall toward him.

Willow floated high into the air. "Thank you, Ame," the wight said in a sniffy voice.

"I think Lark needs you in the dining hall," the girl said to the wight, who popped away. The girl came up to Isaac and stuck out her hand. "I'm Amelie Bateson. We've been expecting you."

He stuck out his own hand, wiping it first on his pants, as he'd been sweating. "Isaac Wolf."

"Leo gave us a bit of a heads-up. We don't get newcomers here," she said, "at least not in a long while, and no one sent word ahead about you coming, so it's good that Leo knew. Kat has given the area right around the castle a bit of enchantment, wards, you know, to keep evil out, and they would've kept you out, too. The dire wolves aren't part of her plan, though," she said with a frown. "They came here on their own. Some other kind of magic that we haven't figured out yet. But at least they can't get past the wards."

Isaac was trying to wrap his head around it all. The wards must explain the invisible wall he'd stepped through. This Leo could predict the future. His parents had sent him here to Rookskill, a place rich with magic, populated by things like wights, he was carrying a magical object, and he could feel magic in his bones. And there were people here like this girl who were unfazed by it all.

Amelie chattered on. "Food's pretty decent, when Lark's not trying out new recipes. Unfortunately, she likes to try out new recipes." Amelie tugged Isaac's arm and began to march him across the front hall toward a dim light at the far end. "But tonight seems pretty regular."

Isaac stopped. "Wait, please. Who are you?"

She stopped and faced him. She looked confused. Or maybe concerned. "Amelie—"

"No," he interrupted. "Who are you . . . all?" And he waved his hand around to indicate the entire castle.

"Oh!" Amelie brightened. "Sorry. I guess they didn't fill you in? What, did they just send you up here with no preparation?" She paused. "That's very odd. No prep and no word to us. Rookskill was a school a couple of years ago. Well, sort of a school. Actually, a haunted castle pretending to be a school, with someone in charge who was not very nice." She paused, chewing her lip and staring away for a minute. Then, "But between the war and then Lord Craig—it's his castle—going off to America, and no money for places like this . . ." She sighed. "Anyway, now it's where the special unit of MI-Six trains those of us who have exhibited gifts."

"MI-Six?"

"You know. British foreign intelligence. They really didn't fill you in? Stranger still. Who sent you? Someone must have seen that you have a skill and sent you, otherwise you wouldn't know about this place."

Isaac said, with a sigh, "It is a long story." He didn't know where to begin.

"Well, then." Amelie led him on down the hall. "We're the MI-Six Special Alternative Intelligence Unit. SAIU. Known only to a few. We're children, but mostly because we're still unspoiled, so our gifts are fresh and we can learn to use them the right way. They kind of let us do our own thing.

Which means we don't have full approval, if you know what I'm saying. Or much support." She ran one finger along the edge of a dusty portrait. "But they leave us alone, too, except when they need information from us. Why, just the other day MacLarren gave them some information from Leo that helped them change their plans around some big operation in France next month." She turned and looked at him. "But don't tell." She smiled.

Isaac thought there was no likelihood of that. "So, you, um, have gifts?"

"Well, you do, too. It's why you're here, right? Isn't that why whoever sent you here? To help win the war by alternative means?"

"By . . ."

"Alternative means." She seemed exasperated now, stopping and putting her hands on her hips. Her blue eyes narrowed with confusion. "To help win the war by using magic, of course."

One of the passages in *Frankenstein* Isaac liked best was the moment when the monster came to full understanding. Isaac liked the quotation so much he'd written out the words and pinned them to the wall of his bedroom so he could read them over and over.

> *Of what a strange nature is knowledge! It clings to the mind, when it has once seized on it, like a lichen on the rock.*

It had not been a happy moment for the monster, learning what he truly was. Learning that he was different.

Isaac had always known he was different. He'd known it that day his grandfather had lost him, when they'd walked by the graveyard in Josefov on a dusky evening, and Isaac had been scared out of his wits, and suddenly, his grandfather was calling his name and searching the streets even though Isaac was there, right there, frozen in silence, but still there.

And that day at school when he was sitting outside reading and Carl had run past and snatched his book straight out of Isaac's hands and then ridiculed him for reading "baby stories" as Isaac yelled, "They're fairy tales." When the other boys joined in the bullying and Isaac watched his book tossed from hand to hand, and he was shoved so hard against the wall he couldn't breathe, he wished he could disappear, and then the boys stopped in confusion, staring straight through Isaac as if they couldn't see him.

And, of course, the hum. That hum he'd felt long before now.

He'd felt it in the silent pine forests above his grandfather's cottage when he was out alone one summer afternoon and was sure he saw eyes in the underbrush.

He'd felt it each time he entered the Old-New Synagogue and placed his hand on the plaster wall.

That hum, that vibration, ran right through him.

Go ahead and call it magic. Isaac Wolf now realized he was able to hear it, to feel it, and he had been able to for a long, long time. Magic was a part of who he was.

But so were *they*, if his parents were right. The monsters he'd seen in the hut and in the ring of stones. *They* would find him. *They* came with deepest dark. His parents had sent him to Rookskill with information buried in a casket that also had, at least once, opened a window to *them*.

For now, maybe he was safe here, in this castle with its wards and children who were learning to use magic—to help the Brits win the war—but he still had to understand who *they* were and what *they* wanted.

And maybe it was truly important to discover the use-fulness of his so-called gift, whatever it was, and how he could control it.

How Isaac Wolf could control magic.

CHAPTER 15
Ralph Baines

FROM 1919 TO 1942

As a boy, Ralph Baines had never thought about magic, one way or the other, until it happened.

He was out with two boys, not because he was popular but because he was not. He'd gone along with these boys because he wanted so much to be liked. He'd gone reluctantly but gone, even when they told him what they were about, even when they slipped inside the broken gate, even when his skin crawled as they stepped among the gravestones in the overgrown thicket of a graveyard in the dead of night.

"Come on," one of the boys whispered. "You go first, Ralphie."

They stood at the entry to the mausoleum, the door slightly ajar, the blackness beyond so dense it had weight. Ralph swallowed hard.

"Me mum said this was one of them thin places," the second boy whispered. "You know, between worlds."

"Thin places?" Ralph said, trying to keep his voice from squeaking.

"Right," the second boy said. "Places where our world connects with the next. You know, ours with the faerie world."

"Well, go on, Ralphie," said the first boy.

Ralph took one step forward, then another. He didn't want to enter that black place, but he wanted them to like him so much, so very much . . .

Then, "Cripes! What's that?" and a screech, and the second boy yelled, and the first yelled, and then Ralph had his back plastered to the outside wall of the mausoleum, and he was trying very hard not to see what he saw.

It was both beautiful and hideous. Its face was delicate and lovely, but it had leathery wings and hands with claw-like fingers, and its fingers held the arm of one of those boys, who hung from its grip, limp and insensible, while the other boy shouted and beat the monster with a stick.

And the eyes, oh, the eyes of that creature, red like coals, burning red, and Ralph closed his own eyes and stumbled backwards, and then heard another scream that faded into the distance.

Ralph had had enough, and he ran. He ran out of that graveyard, never looking back. He ran home and dove into his room. He ran home and vowed he didn't care about being friends with those boys.

Which was just as well, because one of them the next day rattled on and on to everyone in town that he'd fought off a monster, and he was judged to be off his rocker and taken away, especially since the second boy was found bruised and unconscious and the first boy was blamed for his injuries. Neither boy was ever the same after. Ralph never admitted to anyone that he'd been with them, never admitted to himself what he'd seen, decided once and for all that it was all some kind of hoax, that there was no such thing as monsters, no such thing as magic.

So, when Ralph, now grown and working for the SIS—the Secret Intelligence Service of MI-6—as a systems analyst, learned that an obscure branch of His Majesty's Service was looking for ways to use magic against enemies, why, Ralph (still unpopular with his peers) determined that that notion was dangerous, and that kind of madness needed to be exposed for what it was: false and ridiculous. Ralph found a way to get to Rookskill Castle, where children—children!—were learning magical skills under the auspices of the SIS, so that he could rid the world of this foolishness.

Because maybe someone would finally look at Ralph Baines with something other than disdain, and maybe, maybe, his revelations would make him a hero.

CHAPTER 16

Isaac

1942

Amelie stared at Isaac, her face showing concern. "Are you all right?"

"I think I might be hungry," Isaac said, his voice soft. He wasn't entirely lying.

"Right. We'll fix you up." She tugged him along again, saying, "I know. I talk too much. Sorry about that. My sister says I've gone chatty. I used to be really quiet but, well, I guess I've changed." Then, out of the blue, "You've got an accent."

"I am refugee. Czech." He bit his lip. Should he say more? He added, "I have spent three weeks escaping Nazis, all the way from Prague."

"Golly! How terrifying! You must have had quite a time," Amelie said. She tilted her head. "Who sent you here, then?"

Isaac hesitated again but decided he wouldn't hold back.

"My mother and father sent me to Rookskill. They said I would be safe here."

"Oh," she said. "Hmm. I wonder how they knew about us."

So did Isaac, but as he thought about it, his parents had to have magical gifts, too. They'd given him that mysterious casket and then disappeared into thin air. Maybe they'd seen Rookskill in a vision. Or maybe something else . . .

At that moment he and Amelie stepped through a partly closed door and into a dining hall lit by low lamplight.

It must have been quite a banquet room in its day, Isaac thought. Fireplaces at both ends. High clerestory windows, now blocked by blackout shades to keep the bombers from finding them. Stone walls hung with tapestries. Light from sconces that lined the walls. One long table running down the center, and a dais at the far end. The odors of musty age, of woodsmoke, of food—the last of which made Isaac's mouth water.

No one sat at the dais. And only a handful of people sat at the far end of the table. It seemed a little pathetic.

Willow hovered above the table like a floating, semi-transparent chandelier.

Amelie led Isaac down the long hall to the others.

"Everyone, this is Isaac Wolf. All the way from Prague." She paused and then added, "Sent here by his parents, but not by MI-Six, at least that he knows of, unless perhaps his parents are agents or have some other connection."

Subtle glances were exchanged among the crew.

Colin was there, surrounded by his dogs, who lay scattered across the floor watching Isaac. "'Lo, again," Colin said.

"This is my sister, Kat. Kat Bateson." Amelie pointed to an older girl with brown hair who nodded, watching Isaac carefully. "And that's Leo Falstone." Leo was also a bit older, black-haired, plump, with a slightly anxious gaze but wearing a friendly smile. He stood up to shake Isaac's hand.

"You are the Leo who knew I was coming?" Isaac asked.

Leo shrugged. "It comes and goes, my little talent. But I saw you." He smiled quickly, ducking his head. "Can't quite control it yet. Have had some lucky breaks with it, though, and Miss Gumble thinks I'll manage it before too long." Leo nodded his head in the direction of an older woman. "Then she's going to teach me how to make a doppelgänger. You know, a double of me. Which could be quite useful in a sticky spot."

Doppelgänger. Isaac raised his eyebrows.

Miss Gumble was thin, kindly looking. She gave Isaac an appraising look.

"And that's Mr. MacLarren," Amelie said of a stout, older

man. "Gumble and MacLarren are our teachers. Willow, Isaac's hungry. Can you fetch some supper?"

Willow sighed audibly, then disappeared with a *pop*, reappearing seconds later with a plate of food that they set down before Isaac.

He dropped his pack and sat on the bench, staring at the plate. Pink stuff, green stuff, blue stuff. Very, very strange-looking stuff. He took a tentative bite. It tasted far better than it looked, with a rich texture and the flavor of beef stew. He ate with gusto.

"Well, Mr. Wolf," said Miss Gumble. "Welcome to Rookskill. Can you share any clues as to why you might have been sent here?"

He swallowed a large mouthful, considering. What could he tell them? Exhaustion flooded him now that he'd had a bit to eat.

"Why don't we start with this?" Gumble said. "What is your gift?"

Isaac looked from one of them to the next. "I am not sure how to explain."

"Ye mean, laddie, ye nay ken the right words," Mr. MacLarren said.

"Oh," murmured Willow from overhead, "we've got one idea. Saw it, we did."

Isaac said, "I never thought much about it. Except that I have these feelings. And then my parents wanted me to leave Prague, leave home, but it happened very fast, and no one said anything about, about magic . . ."

"Well," said Gumble. She pulled herself upright, officiousness itself. "We'll suss it out. No one arrives at Rookskill Castle without good reason."

Isaac blurted before thinking it through, "I did not say I have no reason."

"Then you might start with that." It was Kat, Amelie's sister. She was a miniature of her teacher, Isaac thought.

Amelie, her back to Kat, rolled her eyes as if to say *bossy*, and for the first time in a long while Isaac was tempted to smile.

He said, "My parents had me smuggled out of Prague. They sent me to Orkney. When I arrived there, well, it is hard to explain." He cleared his throat. "My parents were there . . ." and here Isaac paused. How much should he say? Should he tell them about the casket or the pendant? About the feeling of being in a different time?

About the monster, and the terrifying vision of the end of days?

Leo closed his eyes and said in a strange, strangled way, "Oh, that's awful. What is that? That . . . that creature?"

Isaac said, startled, "You can see it? You can see what I saw?"

Leo nodded, his eyes wide and worried. Everyone else stirred.

Isaac shook his head. "I do not know what it was. Some kind of monster."

Leo stood, swaying a little. "Terrible." His face was drained of color, and he stared into the distance. Gumble reached over and put her hand on his arm, and he sat again, beads of sweat on his forehead.

"I think it was chasing my parents," Isaac said. "They want me to keep searching for a certain symbol. A number of circles. They called it, I think in English it means a forever knot. They told me to come here and then they vanished."

In other times and places, if he'd said his parents had vanished, Isaac was sure people would laugh. But not this crowd.

Kat said, "A forever knot? I'm guessing you must mean an eternity knot. An eternity knot is an ancient Celtic symbol. Like this, right?" She drew it with her finger on the table.

Isaac nodded. "That is the one."

Gumble said, "Not just Celtic, Miss Bateson. That symbol has been used in many cultures over time."

"Clearly," said MacLarren, "this all be a puzzle to solve."

He rubbed his hands together as if ready to go to work. "Now, laddie, have ye found that symbol anywhere?"

Isaac nodded. "Where I saw my parents it was carved into a stone." Isaac's voice dropped and he propped his head on his hand. Exhaustion flooded him through and through. He ought to tell them about the casket and the pendant. But something held him back. Possibly it was the low hum or heartbeat or ocean wash that he heard, now louder, now softer, a thrumming ache in his head. He closed his eyes, unable to keep them open.

MacLarren said, "Your parents, what else did they—"

"Angus," Gumble interrupted, "we can plainly see that the boy has suffered a long and painful journey. He's been separated from his home and his family. Fled grave danger. Let's continue this tomorrow."

At that instant, a door behind her blew open, and something came into the dining hall carrying a tray.

Some "thing," Isaac thought, because he couldn't see the whole of it, because it was only as tall as Isaac's waist and carried the tray above its head. Isaac could see its feet, which were bare and grassy green. "Not before sweets," came a lilting voice from below the tray, which it deposited on the table in front of Isaac, revealing itself.

It was a she, with green skin and curling lavender hair,

wearing an apron over a full, round, bright orange skirt. She tossed her hair and said, "I'm Lark. Did you like it?" She pointed at Isaac's clean plate.

Isaac nodded.

"Lark's a ghillie-dhu," Kat said, "in case you've never met one."

"I have not," Isaac murmured, nodding hello.

"Ghillies like to experiment with different human activities," Amelie said brightly. The way she said "experiment" gave Isaac pause. "Lark wants to learn to cook. She's still learning, aren't you, Lark?"

Lark rolled her eyes and heaved a sigh. "Have a sweet?" she said shyly, as she pushed the tray toward Isaac.

The food Isaac had finished had looked weird but tasted good. These—they seemed to be tiny cakes—looked very good indeed.

"Um," Amelie began, but stopped when Lark gave her a narrow-eyed glance.

Isaac took one of the cakes and put it in his mouth, and . . .

. . . tried not to gag.

"Good?" Lark asked in a slightly threatening way.

"Mmphf," Isaac responded. He swallowed the rest without chewing, to get that bitter taste out of his mouth.

Kat's lips were pressed together as if she was trying to stifle a laugh.

"More?" Lark asked, and Isaac shook his head and patted his stomach. He was afraid to speak until the awful taste settled, then he took several great gulps of water.

No one else took a cake, all of them looking vague or thoughtful or preoccupied.

"Come on," Amelie said. "I'll show you upstairs." She rose from the table, suppressing a smile.

Isaac raised his hand in a goodbye and grabbed his pack. Weariness overcame him. It had been a long day—a very long few weeks—punctuated by fear.

From behind him, Isaac heard Kat say, "See you in the morning."

Then they all began to murmur, and Isaac was pretty sure they were talking about him.

"You can take any room with an open door," Amelie said. "There are lots of rooms. We used to have more people here." She sounded wistful.

The castle seemed even larger on the inside than the outside. The portraits of somber figures in period dress glared down, and the eyes followed him. Either end of the long hallway disappeared in gloom.

"I think I would be lost without a guide," Isaac said.

"It's an odd place, Rookskill," Amelie answered. "Mind you, don't go wandering alone, especially at night. The hallways seem to, I don't know, bend. Rearrange themselves." She wrapped her arms around her chest. "I had a bit of a time here a couple of years ago. A bunch of us did. But that's all finished."

"I see." Isaac had the feeling that it wasn't finished at all, at least not for Amelie. He pressed his hand to his heart, feeling the pendant.

Isaac chose the first unoccupied room they came to. It was large, with an enormous four-poster bed and a cold fireplace.

Amelie chattered on. "Sorry about the dessert. Lark confuses sugar with salt. Well, maybe confuses. Maybe intentionally swaps. Ghillies are tricky. Sometimes they can be sweet as butter, but other times . . . plus, there isn't much sugar to begin with. Rationing, you know. I would've warned you—don't eat any food that looks normal, it's the not-normal-looking food that's all right—but didn't want to hurt Lark's feelings." She paused and said, "Oh."

Isaac turned. A ghost of a cat walked toward them, in the air a foot above the floor.

"Where'd you come from?" Amelie said. The cat moved between them, pausing to rub against Amelie's leg, then walked on. "I'd better find out about you."

"That is your magical gift?" Isaac guessed. "Dealing with ghosts?"

"Taking care of magical creatures of all types," she said, blushing a little. "Lark, Willow, any creature like that. Like that ghost kitty, though I've never seen her before. Right, then. Have a good rest. There are clean clothes in the dresser. You should find some trousers and shirts that fit. We'll get the rest sorted out in the morning."

Isaac nodded, closed the door, and put his pack on the nearest chair.

He rubbed his eyes. The past weeks weighed on him like a ton of stones. The hum that filled his mind now was soporific, and he fell across the bed and was asleep before he even removed his shoes.

Sometime in the night Isaac woke. He rubbed the drool from his mouth and turned over. The room was dark, but coals burned in the fireplace, shedding dim orange light.

He sat up.

Willow hovered over Isaac's pack, fingering the buckles that held it shut. Isaac's blood ran cold.

"Stop," Isaac commanded.

Willow snarled. "Light sleeper," they grumbled. "Made you a fire, we did. Think you could be grateful. Freezing in here, it was, until we fixed it."

"You are not to touch that pack," Isaac said as firmly as he could, remembering Amelie's instructions. Then he added, "But thank you. For making the fire."

Willow said snidely, "Yes, young master." They smirked (Isaac thought) and added, "Know something about you, we do." Then a *pop* and they were gone.

Just in case, Isaac shoved the pack under his bed, then undressed and crawled under the covers.

Maybe Willow knew why Isaac was here. Knew about his gift.

He'd made it to Rookskill. The castle was weird but protected. Everyone here seemed nice. There were kids his age. And they were helping in the war effort by learning how to use magic, which was both decent and pretty amazing. Maybe even fun. They were being trained. Was this what his father had been talking about?

At least some answers to Isaac's questions were tucked

inside the casket, but he wasn't about to open it again in the darkness. He didn't want to remember that cold object inside. Didn't want to revisit the dread vision. He'd open the casket again when he was ready, and in the daylight at the very least.

But before he drifted off to sleep, Isaac shuddered with the thought that those awful monsters were out there. They were out there in the deepest dark.

CHAPTER 17

Moloch and the Seelie King

Sitting in his stygian corner of the faerie realm, Moloch licks his lips and schemes.

Moloch's hunter has returned empty-handed once again. Empty-handed, but with information.

In Orkney, in one of the thinnest of thin places—a ring of ancient standing stones—Moloch's hunter smelled the scent of powerful magic.

Guardian magic.

Exactly the magic Moloch has been searching for. The hunter followed the scent to an inn where the magic appeared to have been used by a human boy, too late to find him but not too late to discover from the unfortunate landlady of that inn that the boy (she called him Isaac) was heading for a certain castle.

Rookskill.

Moloch knows this castle. Moloch has known Rookskill for a long time, but nothing truly important has stirred there lately.

Isaac, according to the miserable landlady, was looking to find a certain symbol, too.

The eternity knot.

Moloch also knows the significance of the eternity knot.

If the sluagh hunter is right, if indeed the magic is now in the hands of this Isaac, if indeed this Isaac is making his way to Rookskill, why, the hunter's information could be beyond Moloch's wildest dreams. A boy might be yet too untrained to understand the magic. Might be weak. Might even carry the key. How glorious!

Moloch closes his eyes. He imagines the look on the face of the Seelie fae king when Moloch hands him this gift. He imagines the outpouring of admiration from the Seelie fae. He sees himself restored to the bright, light world of his past, all his sins forgiven. Moloch smiles.

He stands and strides through shadowy hallways, on his way to beg an audience of the Seelie king.

***

The Seelie king remains silent while Moloch speaks. When Moloch is finished, the king rises and says, "Let me think on the best approach."

Moloch pauses, confusion clear in his remaining eye. "I'm willing to go at once."

The king turns his back on Moloch and says in a tone both short and sharp, "I need to assess."

Moloch asks, "My boon, then? Restoration?" He sounds desperate.

"If all goes well," the king answers cryptically. He doesn't want Moloch to believe he'll ever be accepted again.

Moloch disgusts the king. His courtiers hide their eyes when Moloch passes by. He's grown repulsive over time and now carries the sluagh stench of rot, and his wings—once variegated and brilliant, like colored glass—have become hard and leathery. Even his remaining eye, once the green of Seelie fae, has turned sluagh red. After centuries of exile with them, Moloch has taken on the aspects of the Unseelie. Of the sluagh, although Moloch doesn't seem to realize how unpopular he's become.

The bright Seelie fae reject him completely.

Once Moloch returns to his exile, the king calls his most trusted spy. "Find out what you can."

***

At first, Moloch doesn't want to believe it. He'd expected an immediate yes, a readmittance. "They wouldn't," he mumbles. "They couldn't."

But he saw their expressions when he approached the king. Saw their revulsion. The pain in his heart is sharp and bright, and a fresh anger rises inside him at their rejection.

Moloch uses his mirror this time not to spy on the human world but to spy on the Seelie king. His instincts, what he felt from the king and court, prove right. The Seelie fae are lazy and unwilling to do the searching Moloch has done. But they are quite willing to take the fruit of Moloch's efforts for themselves, even while they laugh at him, revile him behind his back. The superficial Seelie.

His breath comes short as he sees that the king himself intends to find the Guardian now that he has Moloch's hard-won information. The Seelie king will steal Moloch's glory. Prevent Moloch's redemption. Prohibit his return to the Seelie court.

The king and his court will leave Moloch to rot with the sluagh.

Moloch begins to shake with the realization that he's

been used and is despised. Anger floods Moloch and he lets out a sluagh-like scream.

So be it. He'll dispose of the Seelie king's spy. He's tired of waiting to be forgiven, tired of waiting to be brought back into the world he's missed. Moloch will make his own joy.

First to stop the spy. Then to find the Guardian. And at last to find all that lost magic and—why not?—keep it for himself. With that magic he could become as powerful as the Seelie king.

And then, Moloch thinks, *let's see what the selfish Seelie will do.*

CHAPTER 18
Ralph Baines

1942

In his room at the Craig Village Inn of the Green Gate, Ralph Baines carefully hung up his uniform. He brushed away a tiny piece of lint. He examined his mustache in the mirror, trimming it neatly with his scissors.

He'd sent word on ahead and was told he'd be met, so tomorrow he would make his way to that ridiculous castle and prove to himself and everyone else that he was right.

This entire magic business was a hoax.

The knock on the door was soft but intrusive. He did not want to be disturbed. He went to the door, opening it a crack.

"Yes?"

"Sir, we be shutting the kitchen for the night. I like to let guests know."

"I'm fine." He began to close the door.

"You be off in the morn?"

He paused. "Yes. First thing."

"Making for the barracks, then? The other young gents are heading in that direction and you could—"

"I'll make my own way." He paused again. "Good night." And shut the door without waiting for the reply.

Then he sighed.

Mustn't be totally rude. But no one here needed to know anything more about him, such as where he was going in the morning. Especially after what he'd heard about Rookskill Castle since arriving at this hostelry.

Magic. Tomfoolery. Sheer nonsense.

He'd been told, while eating his tasteless thin soup downstairs, that people in the village heard howls in the deepest part of the night. The man who'd told him that said gullible folk thought that wolves had returned to the glens and fens. The only wolves this man knew of were across the channel, he'd told Ralph—"The wolves of the Reich."

But then the man had leaned back in his chair and stroked his chin and added in a murmur, "But wolves or no, that place Rookskill be wicked enchanted."

Wolves. Enchantments. Ridiculous.

The forest, from the vantage of Ralph's window at

nighttime, looked like a thorny thicket. It hid Rookskill Castle in its depths.

Ralph Baines was not gullible. He was certain that he could peel away the falsehoods about this place and the children and the supposed magic they were learning and expose it all as a fraud and become the hero he wished to be.

Just as he fell asleep he had a last, somewhat comforting thought. He'd load his service revolver in case the bit about wolves was true. In case some wolves did remain in this hostile northern country.

Yes. Be practical and realistic and put this nonsense to rest. That was the ticket.

CHAPTER 19
Isaac

1942

Isaac woke to the sound of a high-pitched scream.

He couldn't remember where he was—lying in a huge bed in a gigantic room with stone walls that were barely lit by gray early morning light.

Then came another bloodcurdling scream, and Isaac shot out of bed.

By the time he'd thrown on some clothes and made it to the door, everyone was in the hallway. Amelie ran by, her thick tartan dressing gown flapping. "It's Lark," she said as she passed.

Colin stood in the doorway opposite, eyes like saucers, Canut, his fur as rigid as porcupine quills, by his side.

Isaac followed Leo to the kitchen.

The others were all there. Lark stood on top of a large worktable with Amelie sitting next to her, Lark's head buried in Amelie's shoulder as Ame crooned in a soothing voice. Kat, Leo, and Colin knelt, gathered around a tiny pile of fur on the floor, and the teachers stood off to one side, still in their dressing gowns, whispering.

But Isaac, the instant he stepped inside the kitchen, heard the hum now elevated to a screech. He backed against the wall, clapping his hands over his ears and closing his eyes.

Then slowly, slowly, the screech faded and went silent. Isaac opened his eyes and lowered his hands.

"I think it's dead," Leo said, standing, wide-eyed. He turned to Isaac. "You all right, then? You look bloody awful."

Isaac nodded. "Headache," he lied.

The ghost cat sat in the air, tail flicking, head turning from what was on the floor to Isaac and back again.

"He is dead," said Colin with a sob. "Poor little mouse. Poor mousie. Was so scared and confused and in such pain his little heart broke. He said his master would never forgive him. He didn't do what he was supposed to do. Instead he gave up when he saw the ghost cat. Who, by the way, has not a word to say about any of it." Colin buried his face in Canut's fur.

Now that the screech had stopped, Isaac wanted to see what they were talking about. He knelt next to Kat, who was poking at the tiny mouse with a wooden spoon.

"What did he say he was supposed to do, Colin?" Kat asked. "And who's his master?"

"I don't know," Colin said through his tears. "He never finished telling me."

Kat said softly, "The mouse is partly mechanical." She looked up and exchanged a wide-eyed glance with Gumble. "Reminds me of . . . you know. Her."

Gumble pinched her lips together and whispered to MacLarren.

Isaac looked more closely. Memories flooded back. Models and drawings in his grandfather's small cottage, covering every surface. "It is really clever," Isaac said. He flexed the tiny copper wing that was attached to the mouse's back. "Look how it is put together. But so sad. So cruel."

"Yes," Kat whispered. "Just like before."

Isaac went on, "My grandfather loved mechanics. He studied the astronomical clock in the Old Town Square for years. It was his dream to build a clock like it, so he made these little parts and tried to show me how they all went together."

"But not in animals," Colin said, his voice in a hitch. "Not like that."

"No," Isaac said.

"Not like that," Kat echoed, grim. She said to Gumble, "You know what this may mean."

"Is it dead?" Lark asked with a sob. "It was horrible, the way that ghost kitty chased it. It squeaked and squealed . . ." and she buried her head against Amelie again.

Colin whispered feverishly into Canut's neck, "I know. Don't worry. We have each other. I won't let it happen to you. Never."

MacLarren cleared his throat. "Mr. Falstone, ye'd best get dressed. That MI-Six chap'll be here soon. Got to get him through the wards."

"Right," Leo said, and left the kitchen.

Gumble said, "We'd best dispose of it. It is partly organic after all."

"And then find out who or what was responsible," said Kat.

"Aye," MacLarren said.

Isaac said, "I don't mind. I can take care of it." He picked up the little beast in his hands. It was soft and limp, but the mechanical parts were angular and sharp, and Isaac felt sorry for the poor mouse.

"Into the garden, perhaps," Kat said. "I'll go with you." She led Isaac out through the kitchen to the garden door.

"MI-Six chap?" Isaac asked as they went.

"We got word last week that they were sending

someone. Some kind of evaluation. We get them from time to time." Kat opened the door for Isaac and then she gasped. "Look at the forest," she whispered. "Look at the garden."

The forest was right up against the garden wall, and thorny vines crept over the wall into the garden.

"It is not always like that?" Isaac asked. He heard a low surge and wondered whether he could hear the waves that pounded the shoreline some distance away.

"No. Never. The forest should be half a mile back." Kat was rigid, staring. "This isn't right."

Isaac moved past her to a place where he could put the little creature into a deep pile of mulch. When he turned around again, Kat was holding her hand out in front of her, her eyes closed, her lips moving.

At once he heard it, painfully. A throbbing hum came from whatever she held in her hand.

"What are you doing?" he cried. "Please, stop."

She paused and opened her fist. "I'm spell-casting. Strengthening the wards."

On her palm was a small object that glinted silver. It was the source of the hum, and he could barely stand it. "Please," he begged. "Please, put it away."

She did, placing the object in her pocket, but she stared

at him, perplexed. "But I need to make sure we're protected."

"It is only," he said, "that I seem to be sensitive to magic. And that thing of yours is really powerful." He rubbed his forehead, then pressed his hand to his chest where the pendant lay cold and vibrating against his heart.

Kat put her index finger against her lips. "Interesting," she whispered. Then she said, "We should tell Gumble. She's really good at helping us refine our gifts. She'll help you with yours."

"That would be good," Isaac said with energy.

Then Kat looked past him and her eyes widened. "Well, will you look at that. My warding spell worked better than ever this time."

Isaac turned around and blinked. How had that happened so fast? The meadow stretched all around the castle, the trees had retreated to the forest, and the vines that had hung over the garden wall were gone. "Wow. That is amazing. Like *Macbeth*," Isaac said. "You know, where Birnam Wood . . ."

"Comes to Dunsinane," Kat finished. "Which was a warning that something bad was about to happen. Yes. I know quite a bit about that story. You've read it, then?"

"Of course." He added, "My parents wanted to be certain I knew English."

They stared out over the misty and silent landscape.

"That mouse," Isaac said, turning. "It reminded you of something."

"Long story," said Kat, sounding officious. "Right now I want to get properly dressed."

It was nice to be able to clean up with soap and hot water and put on the warm school-uniform clothes Isaac found in his dresser. Breakfast was another matter. It seemed to be pancakes, but with little wiggling edges.

"It is . . . moving," Isaac whispered to Amelie.

She giggled and passed him a bowl. "Porridge?"

Fortunately, it was porridge. Or it tasted like porridge. Isaac didn't want to know more.

Colin came running into the dining hall, a bit breathless, dogs on his heels. "Leo's back," he said. "With someone strange."

Isaac and Amelie exchanged a glance, and Amelie shrugged. "They're all strange," she said. "They're MI-Six. And we're kids. Doing magic. Which they like but don't really understand, even when they pretend to. But they're usually pleasant enough and let us get on about our business. Let's go see what's up."

Everyone else had already assembled in the front hallway. Leo acted deferential to the newcomer, holding his luggage and coat.

"Ralph Baines," the man said. His hands and face were scratched, and dirt spattered his pressed uniform. "Your grounds are thick with brambles. Quite a sorry mess. Almost wondered if I wouldn't get through. But I'm a persistent chap." He gave a short laugh. "Mr. Falstone, here, found me before I became too entangled."

Leo squirmed a bit. "The forest is acting odd," he said with a shrug.

"Yes, so we've noticed," murmured Kat.

Baines went for his valise and pulled out some papers, handing them to MacLarren. "Things are hectic at the home office at the moment. But this should answer your questions."

MacLarren looked up and said, "I thought this was an inspection. Not certain I understand what this means." He handed the papers to Gumble.

She glanced through them and then said, "What's this? They want us to return to London?"

"Immediately," Baines said. "On the next train."

"Impossible," said MacLarren, folding his arms across his large chest.

"I shall remain here. The children will be perfectly safe with me."

"B-but," Gumble sputtered, "we are in the midst of difficult mentoring. And we've made a number of important discoveries for the effort. Why, just a week ago a seabird brought news about an enemy landing to Mr. Drake, and that gave Miss Bateson the chance to draw down a fogging spell to thwart it. As you must know."

Baines lifted one eyebrow. "Fog on the coast. Pretty regular, I imagine. Yes, I'm sure you're onto something," he said, not sounding sure at all. "The home office needs to update you two on some of the latest intelligence, so they require you there for at least a week." He checked his pocket watch. "I believe the next train leaves in an hour." He glanced between the two teachers. "Well?"

MacLarren's mouth dropped open, and Gumble's eyes narrowed to slits.

"Now, see here—" Kat began, her hands on her hips.

"I am in charge, missy, and I caution you against any childish interruptions," Baines said to her. He turned to Leo. "Please show me to a place where I might wash up. That forest, you know."

Leo raised his eyebrows at the others as he led Baines away.

Kat followed Gumble up to her rooms, the two whispering as they left. Ame, Isaac, and Colin waited in the hall and exchanged confused looks and awkward comments. "Goodness." "I can't imagine." "Has this happened before?" "Nothing like." "What do we do?"

Ten minutes later, Baines and the five children stood in the hallway of Rookskill Castle as their teachers, small suitcases in hand, bid reluctant goodbyes.

Gumble turned to Kat. "You'll know what to do, Miss Bateson. We can make our own way through the, well, the protections. The castle will be in your capable hands." She glared at Baines. Then she and MacLarren stepped out into the cold, damp mist, which seemed to have grown mistier, damper, and a little darker, and Baines slammed the great door in their wake.

He turned and surveyed the children with a stern expression. "A terribly small group of children. Not much of a school, is it? Costly endeavor. Well. Why don't we start by having each of you demonstrate your, *ahem*, magic?"

As the children exchanged glances, Baines's expression changed and he launched into a barking laugh.

His laughter echoed through the castle, up and down and around. The echo went on for so long that it was as if the castle had joined right in.

CHAPTER 20

Isaac

1942

The children exchanged glances again. Amelie said under her breath, "I think he's daft."

Baines broke off abruptly and glared at each of them in turn. "Well?"

"You want us to demonstrate our . . . magic?" Kat asked. She sounded as if she could hardly wait to get started.

Baines tugged at his cuffs. "Let's get this nonsense over with."

Colin whispered to Canut. The dog lowered his head and bared his teeth at Baines, a rumble in his throat.

Baines took a step back. "Remove this menacing creature at once! Outside. All these animals outside, now."

Colin's dogs encircled him protectively. Several began to whine. Canut growled. "What?" Colin said. "No. They stay with me."

"Out," Baines cried, brandishing a short crop he yanked from his belt. Isaac remembered with a sick feeling the crops wielded by Nazi soldiers in Prague, and he shrank away.

Colin whistled, turned, and ran for the stairs, all the dogs following at his heels.

"I'll find you later," Baines called, flicking the crop, and Isaac flinched.

Amelie muttered under her breath. Willow appeared with a *pop*, directly in front of Baines. They began to make rude noises at the man, and Isaac suppressed a snort. But Baines glared after Colin and the dogs, looking straight through the wight.

"He doesn't see Willow," Amelie whispered. "He doesn't even see them there, right before him."

Willow hung upside down, bobbing like a cork, but Baines registered no notice at all. Willow made a loud *pfft*, and lifted up to the ceiling, muttering.

"How disturbing," murmured Kat.

Leo cleared his throat. "I can predict the future, and I have visions of what's happening in other places."

Baines stared at him. "What are you talking about?"

"It's my gift," Leo said. He closed his eyes, his face scrunching in concentration. "A great storm is coming," he whispered. "A storm to end all storms."

Isaac shivered. A storm to end all storms?

Baines snorted. "I should think that's an easy prediction to make. A storm in these northern climes in winter?"

Leo opened his eyes wide. "No. This storm is different."

"Really. You should try some other act," Baines said.

"It's coming," Leo said, plaintive. Isaac exchanged a supportive glance with Leo, who gave him a little awkward smile back.

"What about you?" Baines said, pointing his crop at Isaac. "You don't have anything to say?"

Isaac shrank away, shaking his head. The pendant against his chest began to vibrate with a low hum. He pressed his hand to it, trying to quiet it. "I do not . . ." he began.

At that moment Kat, her hand in her pocket, her voice low and commanding, said out of the blue, "Haud yer wheesht!"

Baines's eyes went blank. Then he stuck out his tongue and reached up and took it between his thumb and forefinger.

Amelie and Willow both burst out laughing. Leo said, "Golly!"

Isaac turned to Kat, the hum still filling his head, not sure whether to laugh or be shocked. "What did you do?" he asked.

Kat made a face. "He's bloody ridiculous, so I just wanted to see him that way." Then she said soberly, "All right. That's enough of that."

Baines blinked and dropped his hand. "Where was I?" His eyes narrowed, and he went on. "Right. It's quite clear that this is all a great hoax. Waste of resources. There's no such nonsense as magic. I'll recommend commandeering this castle for our forces. We need another military outpost in Scotland. You children will be sent home and back to regular school at once, as soon as I've completed my paperwork." He pointed at the small parlor that stood off the front hall. "I shall set myself up in there. Mr. Falstone, you will assist me. Falstone." He paused. "Is your father perhaps Bernard Falstone, with the home office?"

Leo nodded miserably.

"Well, well." Baines smiled at Leo, suddenly warm, all teeth. "Terribly sorry about the comment about your . . . prediction. A storm could very well be on its way. I'm certain your father will be happy to see you home and away from this nonsense."

Leo smiled faintly, clearly not happy about the prospect of returning home himself.

Baines moved away, Leo trailing. Kat turned to Amelie

and Isaac and said, "He doesn't believe in magic? What is going on at MI-Six?" She grimaced. "If only Papa wasn't away on one of his missions." She looked at Isaac. "Our father is with MI-Six, and he understands what we're doing here. He'd take care of this." She went on, "This silly Baines could seriously damage our mission, and we can't let him."

"What do we do?" Amelie asked.

"I'm going to check on Colin," Kat said. "And then we can decide our next move. Meet me in the small library in ten minutes."

The hum in Isaac's head faded as Amelie led the way down the hall. If only he understood and could use his gift, whatever it really was . . .

Willow popped into view overhead. "That was insulting." They floated alongside Amelie and Isaac. "Even though it happens all the time."

"What do you mean?" Isaac asked.

"When people don't believe, they don't see. The truth can be square in front of their eyes, but they simply don't see."

Amelie said, "I was hoping you'd scare the living daylights out of him."

Isaac said, "What was it that Kat said, you know, when she made Baines . . ."

Amelie giggled. "She said, 'Hold your tongue.' Clever, that spell, don't you think? Double meaning. She's getting better and better at spell-casting."

When Amelie opened the door to the small library, Isaac had to stop to take it all in. It was like his own personal dream come true.

The room, not very large, was filled with books. Floor-to-ceiling bookshelves stuffed with books. Books on tables, in stacks, books on the floor, piled almost as high as Isaac was tall, books open on stands. Isaac moved slowly, letting his hand stray over the leather covers, turning the spines so he could read the titles.

"I know. I love it here, too, although it would take me a thousand years to read them all," Amelie said, standing next to him, her head tilted as she surveyed the room. "Do you have any favorites?"

He nodded. "*Frankenstein*. By Mary Shelley. Do you know it? It has helped me with my English, but I like it for more than that."

She shook her head. "Heard of it but haven't read it yet."

Isaac, relishing telling about his favorite book, said, "Victor Frankenstein, who wishes to be a scientist, plays with the idea of creating life. Of course, that is treading in something dangerous—how do you say it—sacrilegious, and he ends up making a monster, who haunts his every step and destroys everything and everyone Victor loves."

"How sad," Amelie said. She was silent for a moment. "Then you understand about monsters."

"Only in books," Isaac said.

Willow dropped down and floated right in front of Isaac, so close to his face that Isaac had to take a step back. "We may all be monsters under the skin," Willow said, their voice a slimy whisper.

Isaac swallowed. "What?" he whispered back.

Willow floated away. "It's a saying we particularly like. Speaking of books." They paused. "We, for one, don't have any skin."

Amelie said, "Kat saved everyone in Rookskill from a monster who was using a magical artifact."

"What does this mean, a magical artifact?" Isaac asked.

"An artifact is an old object, of any kind," Amelie said. "Jewelry. A sword. A mirror. A potion. But a magical artifact is infused with power. Some of the stuff of legends, like, you know, Excalibur. Or Aladdin's lamp with the genie inside or the Chinese emperor's nightingale. Other objects may have magic but no stories about them. Yet." She paused. "A magical artifact can be just about anything."

"Wait," Isaac said. His mind was spinning. The casket and its contents. "Anything?"

Amelie nodded. "In the case of Kat, her artifact is a piece of jewelry called a chatelaine. The monster she used it on wanted to enchant all of us who were here then." She stared away, at the gray mist outside. Then she said, "Kat didn't believe in magic back then, at first, but thank goodness she found her gift before it was too late. It was a scary time," Amelie ended in a whisper.

Isaac said, "That object she carries in her pocket, yes?" That powerful silvery object Kat carried that made Isaac's head hum. "What happened to you?"

"It's hard to explain," Amelie said slowly. "The monster tried to enchant us children. There were a bunch of us here then, and it wanted to . . . It tried to steal our souls."

"What!" Isaac couldn't believe it.

Ame nodded. "It was such an awful feeling. Like being ripped into shreds. I was awake, but I wasn't. It hurt horribly but it was also so, so sad. If it hadn't been for Kat . . ." Ame set her lips in a thin line and shook her head.

Willow floated down in front of Amelie. "Want us to make some goofy faces to cheer you up?"

"What happened to the monster?" Isaac asked.

"Mostly it's at the bottom of the well," she said. "In bits and pieces. Good and gone."

Mostly, Isaac thought.

"That's right," said Willow, and they contorted into the shape of a puffy cloud before making a distinctive noise that made Isaac want to hold his nose. "Good. And. Gone. In pieces."

Isaac, gazing up at the wight, found his eye straying to the library's ceiling that was decorated with designs. Colorful and intricate, they reminded him a little of the cathedral windows at home. Except that these were more elaborate natural images of trailing vines and peculiar fruits.

Isaac squinted and stood to see better.

The jumble of vines converged at four points, and at each convergence was a particular design. One that Isaac knew. He pressed his hand against his chest, the pendant cold against his skin, and that distant throb rose again in his brain, like the sea pounding the cliffs or a low, slow heartbeat.

"That," he said, pointing.

"Oh!" Amelie turned and stared. "Why, isn't that what

you were telling us about last night? The eternity knot?"

He nodded. Monsters. Artifacts. The eternity knot.

It was time to open the casket. To find the next piece of his puzzle.

"I will be right back," he said, making for the door.

CHAPTER 21

Isaac

1942

Isaac closed the door to his room and pulled his pack from under his bed, sitting cross-legged on the floor with the pack before him. He pulled out the casket, pushed the pack aside, and took a deep breath. At once the throbbing hum flooded his brain.

Slowly, carefully, he opened the casket, its hinges squeaking a little, and he squinted at it with one eye shut, as if that would help.

A moan fled from inside.

The hum grew louder, and the cold press of the pendant burned against his skin, and a moldy smell like age filled the room. Isaac shivered.

The casket was lined with fabric, satiny and faded to pink from what must have been a deep blood-red, and it was falling to dusty bits. He leaned over. There it was, the object nestled inside, the orb he'd held in his fist when he'd had that nightmare. It glinted silver and his breath caught.

It was a small skull, about the size of an apple, polished and decorated.

The image of the Old Town Square's astronomical clock and its skeleton of Death rose in his memory. When the skeleton of Death chimed the hour and the grinning skull stared down at him, his grandfather said, "Kostlivec is nothing to fear, Isaac."

Nothing? The skull inside the casket grinned up at him, the empty eye sockets staring.

Miss Rachel was the sister of his schoolmaster. She had come sometimes to bring a food basket to her brother. She was quiet, one dark curl escaping her scarf, and Isaac had a crush on her.

But on the last day she didn't bring lunch. She came to say her brother was not coming to school any longer and they had to leave, leave at once, go straight home, do not stop for any reason.

A van had pulled into the schoolyard as the boys were leaving. But Isaac paused at the gate, sliding to one side, his hand on the wall as soldiers ushered Miss Rachel toward the van. Isaac's heart slowed to a crawl and his feet were encased in lead.

Jan, behind him, whispered, "They're monsters."

Don't stand out. Isaac hunched his shoulders, trying to make himself small.

"We must do something," Jan whispered.

"What can we do?" Isaac whispered back. "They'll only take us, too."

The soldiers pushed Miss Rachel into the van.

Jan shouted from behind Isaac, "Stop! Let her go."

The SS officer turned. He pointed his crop at Isaac. Isaac was the tall one. Isaac stood out. "You!" Isaac's eyes fixed on the badge on the officer's collar. The Totenkopf. The laughing skull.

"No," Miss Rachel cried. "He's just a child."

The SS officer turned back to her, and Isaac ran.

He didn't wait for Jan. He didn't stop, even when he heard the shouts. He ran and ran and ran.

A Totenkopf. Isaac's shame from the memory of running away.

This skull in the casket. *Memento mori.* Isaac remembered the full Latin translation. *Remember that you will die.*

There must have been a reason his parents gave him this object, and Isaac was certain it wasn't to scare him. Steeling himself, sweating a little, he reached inside and lifted the skull out of the casket.

It was as icy cold as he remembered. As he lifted it out, the skull moved as if alive and he dropped it back into the satiny fabric out of shock. Then he leaned over again.

The skull was hinged at the jaw, and the jaw had fallen open.

Isaac leaned closer. Ornate and tiny but detailed carvings covered the skull. Flowers and birds. A man and woman in a garden. An image of Death with a sickle, standing before a hut to its right and a castle to its left.

If it hadn't been carved on a skull, Isaac would have thought it beautiful.

With one finger he pried the jaw all the way open, and inside, enclosed within the skull, was a watch.

The clockface was fixed on the jaw's underside with the movement beneath, all the tiny gears just visible. The hands, shining gold, were set at eleven o'clock. The crown at the top of the watch was filigreed. Isaac leaned closer still. The crown was in the shape of the eternity knot. Carefully, he lifted the skull with the watch out of the casket and set it on the floor, the jaw open.

Then he saw that a piece of parchment lay at the bottom of the casket.

A note?

It crinkled in his fingers. *Dear Isaac.*

The handwriting—there was no mistaking it—was his father's. Isaac took a breath and rubbed his eyes hard.

> I cannot put this gently. You must not delay. You are, as we were in our last days in Prague, being hunted. By something that has been searching for us for a very long time. And I do not mean the Nazis.

Isaac glanced at the window, at the swirling mist outside, the gray light.

> We must give you these lessons from afar because that will help throw off your pursuers for a little while. This watch is a time-travel device.

A what?

> Wind the crown to set it in motion. We've set the first four travels for you. In each time

and place, you must seek the next piece of information. Find the object or clue we have left for you. Be absolutely certain you hold the watch firmly in your hand when it chimes at the end of each travel.

Your mother and I can't help except in this way. We are now—in all probability—locked in a time-stream.

A what? Isaac wanted to shout. His parents were locked in a what?

It's too dangerous to give you every clue at once. Protect the information. Discovery would be disaster, for you, and for everyone.

Perhaps we shall see you again.
Your loving father.

P.S. Do not delay. Set the watch in motion as soon as you have read this.

P.P.S. Do not give the watch away during your travels.

*P.P.P.S. Do not, for any reason, interact with
the past.*

Isaac read and reread the letter to try to make sense of it.

His mind flew to dinner table discussions. He'd often rolled his eyes at yet another of his father's windy lectures on the benefits of Latin or the deeper principles of Greek democracy. He could see his father tamping his pipe before launching into another explanation of Aristotle's discourses.

Now Isaac would give anything to be lectured to boredom by his father.

He stared at the skull that held the watch.

Time travel.

He'd like to travel, in fact, to another time and place, when he thought about it. It might really be fun. To see ancient Rome or Greece—maybe even sit and listen to Aristotle in the flesh. See woolly mammoths roaming across North America. Witness the building of the Great Wall of China, the Hagia Sophia in Constantinople, or Machu Picchu in the Andes. Why, he could think of a million places he would go with a time-travel device.

Could he even stop the Nazis, make the whole ugly war go away? Be back at home again, with his parents, in Prague, tell them how much he missed them? See his grandfather once more and say goodbye properly?

Except for that admonition from his father: *Do not interact with the past.*

But then again, all his time travels might be like that nightmare in Orkney and the ring of stones, which he was now certain must have been the first of the four set by his parents. And what should he have found there? What object or clue had he missed, in his ignorance, when he'd foolishly set the watch into motion by accidentally winding the crown?

So, he'd already made one terrible mistake.

Do not delay.

Right, then. No more mistakes. He had to answer this call. For his parents. For himself.

Isaac picked up the watch and turned the crown, setting the timepiece to ticking, closed the face, gripped it tight in his fist so the cold skull dug into his palm, and fell into a whirlwind.

CHAPTER 22

Isaac in the Library of Alexandria

CIRCA AD 415

It's like plunging into the back end of a kaleidoscope, stripping away reality. As before, Isaac passes through moments in his own life, further and further back, and then before his life and still further back, with flashes of places he sort of recognizes and many he doesn't. He lurches, his stomach trying to catch up with his mind and his eyes.

Isaac stumbles and falls to his knees against cold stone, his free hand gripping a wall as he tries to steady himself. Colors and lights spin to a slow, slow stop. His head aches and he closes his eyes, then opens them again, hoping to quiet his pounding heart.

Isaac is outdoors and it's warm. He's in a colonnaded court, thick marble columns rising to three times his height on his left, and an open doorway set in a pale beige blocky stone wall on his right. Above him, the sky is cerulean blue.

He's bathed by a soft breeze that carries the salty, fishy smell of the sea. From a distance come the creaks and rumbles of wheels on stone, voices calling out and intermingling, bells and gongs, mules braying and dogs barking, and bird calls. Gulls.

He rises to his feet. His fist encloses the skull watch that ticks against his palm. The sun is low over his shoulder, slanting on the wall and floor in such a way that he thinks it must be near sunset.

Rustling noises come from behind him, and Isaac turns swiftly and braces.

A girl a bit older than he is with dark skin and eyes and curling black hair, dressed in a simple white garment and carrying a small satchel over one shoulder, runs toward him, her face tight, feet in sandals slapping the stone.

Isaac raises a hand, and says in English, "Hello, I wonder whether you can . . ."

But she looks right through him.

She can't see me, Isaac thinks. *I'm like a ghost.* Then he thinks with relief, *So maybe I can't interact anyway.*

She runs past him and bolts through the doorway. Because he doesn't know what else to do, Isaac follows the girl.

She runs ahead of him down the enclosed corridor—all

gray-white stone—toward another open wood door, and then through that, and Isaac follows her into an enormous room that is filled, floor to ceiling, wall to wall, with shelves and cubbies crammed with paper.

In the center of the room, standing at a great table and leaning over a stack of documents, is a woman. She, too, is dressed in a simple white garment, and she also has very dark skin and eyes, and hair streaked with gray. The paper on the shelves and in the cubbies is stacked neatly and bound as books or rolled into scrolls and tied. The shelves are organized and labeled with stamped clay but he can't read the letters. But he knows the lettering, thanks to his father, and he thinks, *That is Greek.*

The girl begins to talk to the woman, her voice pitched high, in a language Isaac doesn't know. She pulls a codex book from her satchel and hands it to the woman, who places it on the table and braces her hands to read it. When she finishes and looks up again, her face is drawn.

Isaac thinks her beautiful even in age, with her thin face and lively eyes and curling hair pulled into a winding crown. But her expression makes his heart hurt.

She speaks to the girl, retrieves a stack of papers and sets it aside, then reaches into the depths of the shelf for something hidden at the back. From deep in the shadows she pulls out a large box, and after setting the box on the table she opens it and lifts out an object that she has to hold in two hands. An instrument made of brass.

It's about the size of a dinner plate. Layers and parts all made of tooled brass, stacked together with gears and cogs. She turns the instrument and shows the girl what it does, explaining in rapid speech, and as she moves it, the plates twist and wind and the hands on a clockface rotate.

Isaac is reminded suddenly, sharply, of the great astronomical clock in the Old Town Square, with its complex gears and movements.

"Our clock in the square is an astrolabe, Isaac," his grandfather had said. He was working on one of his own mechanical devices, standing over his messy kitchen table showing Isaac how he put his pieces together. "It not only tells the time but also the positions of the stars in the zodiac, of the sun and moon, and it's a calendar, with months and years. And, imagine! It's almost six hundred years old."

And his grandfather added, "Long before that, the Greeks knew about astrolabes. The Antikythera mechanism that was found at the bottom of the Mediterranean Sea not so long ago is one such device." He shook his head. "Such wonders in the ancient world."

The Antikythera mechanism, Isaac thinks. *The ancient world. This may be ancient Greece, then. That makes sense.*

The woman is still explaining the workings of the mechanism to the girl. She's talking fast, as if she's in a great hurry.

Then she takes the instrument and moves to the far wall, the girl following, and stands before a blank space in the wall. She places her hand on the stone, leaning a little against it, her free hand on her chest.

Isaac's eyes widen.

A carved wood door appears, as if out of a mist, forming itself right within the stone. The door opens, and the woman and girl go through it, and before Isaac can fumble his way across the room they disappear and the door disappears and Isaac is left standing facing a solid blank stone wall.

Except . . .

As Isaac stares at the wall, he sees a carving in the stone. He lifts one finger and traces it, looping and winding.

The eternity knot.

He blinks and tries to breathe. What kind of magic is this? Is this what he needs to find here?

The watch in his fist tick-tick-ticks. Panic tightens his lungs. He's afraid he'll run out of time before he understands his purpose here.

He turns back to the table and the documents scattered there and leans over them.

Mathematics. Lots of complicated equations. Diagrams, measurements, calculations. Geometry. This is very sophisticated stuff, all written out in a fine neat hand. The woman had been working these equations.

The book brought by the girl still lies on the table. Isaac sets down the watch, opening the skull so that he can see the watch face, and reaches for the book.

He can touch it, feel it, pick it up. Aha.

Isaac makes a connection. He must be a ghost only when he holds the watch, for as long as he holds the watch. When he doesn't have hold of it, when he isn't touching it, he becomes visible. He can interact with the past.

Well, he's alone, so what harm can he do?

The paper of the book is thick and rough with long embedded fibers. There are words, and Isaac recognizes Latin. He can read at least some of the words.

Closed. Expelled, he reads. And *Iudaeum*, which means "Jew."

Isaac's stomach drops as he realizes. Expelled from this place in ancient Greece. Just like he was, from Prague. Just like his friends were. He takes a step back and has to pull himself together. Try to focus.

If only he'd paid a little more attention when his father rattled on about ancient history, he'd understand where he was and what to look for.

He moves away from the table, wondering what to do next. He glances at the watch that he left lying open on the table—if he reads it right, he has about twenty minutes left before the hand reaches the top of the hour.

The sun is just at the brink of setting, the last rays piercing a low window, and Isaac has to shield his eyes and turn away. The sun's rays strike a cubby on the far wall.

Unlike any others in this room, this cubby has a pattern inscribed in the wood around it. He stares. The sun illuminates the cubby like an electric torch. Like a beacon. So that Isaac can't miss it. It's right there, the eternity knot carved into the wood, tracing the entire outline of the cubby, a sign.

He runs across the room—the sun is dipping quickly below the window—and stares at the cubby with its pile of bound books and scrolls. One of them must be for him, he's sure of it. He'll have to look through them all, though his time is running short. He jerks them out of the cubby and lays them on the table. One by one he opens or unrolls them. Sweat beads on his forehead, as he stares at the jumble of what he now knows must be Greek. *No, no, no*, he thinks, as he sets them aside one by one, hearing from across the room the *tick-tick-tick* of the watch.

He reaches the second-to-last scroll, despair filling him. As he unrolls this one, though, right away he sees that it's different. For one thing, the paper is not the same, but it's also not in Greek.

It's not even in Czech.

The words on this paper are English.

The scroll is some kind of architectural drawing or map or both. Symbols and lines form a pattern, and words are scattered throughout, but they make no sense on a quick scan. It has to be a kind of puzzle that will take time for him to decipher. But when Isaac sees again the eternity knot, drawn in the upper corner, he's sure this scroll is meant for him.

He rolls it up and slides it inside his shirt and buttons his shirt over it.

At that moment a creaking noise fills the room, and he turns. The carved wood door re-forms in the stone wall, and the woman and girl walk through the door, which disappears behind them.

As does the sun, disappearing below the horizon, leaving a purple sky rimmed in orange, soft light in this room behind the woman and girl.

Isaac stares at them, and they stare back, mouths open in surprise.

They are empty-handed, and he thinks they must have left the astrolabe behind, wherever they were. On the table between him and them is the watch, tick-tick-ticking. The woman looks at him, looks at the watch, looks back at him. He has to fetch it. He must not interact. Has he already made a mistake, just by being seen by these two?

A sudden noise grows from outside the room. Isaac begins to move toward the watch. Why did he leave it so far away on the table? The noise outside increases, then voices, urgent and angry, swell, and they, whoever they are, are in the corridor just outside this room. Someone yells and pounds on the actual door of this room, and then, just then . . .

The watch begins to chime the hour. *One, two . . .*

Be absolutely certain you hold the watch when it chimes at the end of each travel.

. . . *five, six.* Isaac throws himself across the table to grab the watch but can't quite reach it. Needles of panic sweep over his skin.

The woman exchanges an anxious look with the girl, then reaches to her throat. She yanks a chain from around her neck and hangs it around the girl's and speaks to the girl in hushed tones. The girl protests, but as the noises grow, she hugs the woman and then dives for the wall and vanishes once again through that magical door, leaving the woman behind.

The woman picks up the watch as the sweet, soft chime strikes, *nine, ten, eleven,* and then she moves swiftly toward Isaac as he makes for it, too, and they just meet so that she can drop the watch onto Isaac's open palm, her expression broken and sad. Isaac closes his fist around the orb.

"Thank you," Isaac says, as the door behind the woman opens with a crash and men bearing flaming torches and drawn swords and angry faces step into the room and the watch chimes, *twelve,* and . . .

. . . the room around Isaac faded into a swirl of fire and bright swords and shouts and despair. Then another kaleidoscope of color and movement, and he folded his arms over his chest, gripping the watch tight, as he whirled back through space and time until he landed with a thud and a gasp on the floor of his room in Rookskill Castle on the coast of the North Sea in Scotland.

He pitched forward onto his knees, his head spinning

and stomach lurching, and he clutched at his shirt to feel the scroll still safely tucked inside. The skull spilled from his hand and rolled across the floor, coming to rest barely out of sight underneath his bed.

CHAPTER 23

Moloch and His Fae Hunter

Moloch bends over the Seelie king's spy. He's never killed one of his own kin before. Once he might have retched at the thought. Now his anger makes it easy to set his qualms aside. He'll dispose of this body and then set out to find the Guardian.

He has a little time before the stupid king starts thinking that something has gone wrong.

Moloch clutches the mirror in his hand and rotates it until it becomes a window again and he can make out the image on the other side more clearly.

"What's this?" he mutters. "Ah!"

The object that glints from the shadows in a room in Rookskill Castle is an object he's seen before. The beautiful silver skull of the Witch's Watch. Moloch remembers the last time it was used. Poor unfortunate Queen Mary of

Scotland. Her interference with time may have doomed her.

It's a magical artifact that Moloch is quite certain has not been used in the human world since then, which means it must be in the hands of . . .

Moloch smiles.

He twists the mirror, trying to see more of the room, but the crack distorts the image. He sees what might be a human moving or might not, and the window closes to become just a mirror. Moloch tosses the mirror aside and summons one of his sluagh hunters.

"Rookskill," he tells the hunter. "Quickly. Tell me what you find. I must make ready."

The hunter bows its head. The sluagh have lately begun to treat him as more than just a leader—they're treating him as their king.

The hunter flies through the thin place between worlds and lands atop a swaying pine tree deep in the forest that surrounds the hulking castle. Thick, swirling Scottish mist fills the air and hides the fae from anyone who might look in its direction. It lifts its head and sniffs.

And is confused.

There are strange enchantments within the forest.

Ancient magic that is not faerie magic. Magic that has been invoked from a primal past. Dire wolves slink through the underbrush. Skeletal shadow-banshees lurk, and pixies and powries wait. Even for this Unseelie fae hunter, the evil magic in Rookskill's forest reeks of fear.

And other magic—wards—protects the castle itself like invisible walls, wards that come from somewhere within the castle, wards that are for the moment strong enough to fend off the dark magic. But for how long?

The fae hunter spreads its great leathery wings and swirls back through the thin place to return to Moloch with the news that the castle is both protected and under threat.

Moloch listens carefully.

The smile spreads slowly. So perfect. Great magic both good and bad is awake again at Rookskill and that can mean only one thing.

"Ready my dragon, Wyvern," Moloch demands of his sluagh. He'll wait until the Seelie fae are drunk or sleeping, the silly Seelie. Moloch will be ready to pass through a thin place when the moment comes.

And he will fly Wyvern because a dragon spreads terror

to humans. Breathing fire, screeching . . . such a lovely thing, a dragon.

Moloch strokes his scar with one clawlike finger (when did his fingers begin to look like claws?). Maybe he's been wrong all this time. Maybe he's happier exactly where he is. With the stupid sluagh in the dark corner of the fae realm.

He'll certainly be happy when he's found the Guardian.

Moloch strips off the patch that covers his missing eye. The exposed eye socket, the puckered scar—he might as well own them. He might as well stop trying to be loved by the Seelie fae. Yes. He's done with trying to get back into the good graces of his treacherous kin. With the magic that is controlled by the Guardian, Moloch could take the entire fae realm for his own and turn the bright Seelie place to ash. Make them all look just like him. Make them all stink of rot. Make them all feel the pain of loss, rejection, and loneliness.

When he has this magic he's been searching for, he'll get rid of the king and any others who refuse to worship—yes, worship!—his scarred Unseelie face.

CHAPTER 24
Isaac

1942

Nausea roiled through Isaac and he tried to steady himself. His head swam, and the hum that followed him everywhere rose and fell, rose and fell, until it finally began to subside. He pulled the scroll from inside his shirt and grabbed the watch from underneath the bed. He was still recovering from his near miss, from almost not having the watch in hand when it finished chiming. If the woman hadn't been there to help him, why . . . He took a sharp breath.

He couldn't make that mistake again. He was certain that he'd doomed her, that she might have escaped those men and their swords, escaped with the girl through that magical door if it hadn't been for him. If it hadn't been for her helping him reach the watch in time. He clenched his fists, angry with himself and miserable for the woman. He didn't know what had happened to her, but it didn't look good.

Then he sat back, leaned back against the bed frame, settled himself, and thought.

He needed to understand what his parents were trying to tell him by sending him to that time and place, to where he'd just been.

He'd been in ancient Greece, he was pretty certain. He'd seen a woman mathematician there use magic and create a door where there was none. He'd witnessed her sending a girl into a magical place, handling a possibly magical object, and being threatened. Somehow his parents had planted the scroll and left the eternity knot for him to find.

Was his only purpose there to find the scroll and bring it back? And what had he missed when he traveled to the circle of standing stones and watched those monsters carry people off into the night sky?

First things first, he thought, and Isaac leaned forward onto his knees and unrolled the scroll.

It was a plan, for certain, but strange and complicated. It appeared to depict a three-dimensional building, in great architectural detail, but the building (if that's what it was) was only shown as an interior and appeared to be floating on the paper. Moving. Changing before Isaac's eyes.

He blinked. The image did change. He picked up the scroll and held it by one side.

Yes, exactly. A wall—if it was a wall—shifted here. A corridor moved there. Each move, each change was slight and slow but steady. The image was not fixed on the paper. It moved by some strange magic. The low hum whispered in his brain.

And the words were threaded in and around the diagram, strung through the structure like a poem, weaving in and out of the moving parts like seaweed in a shallow ocean or a vine waving in a breeze.

The words made no sense whatsoever. He turned the paper this way and that but couldn't make it out at all.

He needed help. And he'd come to the right place to find it, hadn't he? His parents had sent him to Rookskill, where magic wasn't just present, it was taught and studied by people who knew what they were about. Magic was being used by kids his own age.

Well, he thought, with a wry twist of his lips, *don't tell that to Ralph Baines, who doesn't believe in magic.*

And then Isaac wished, with a sharp pang, that he could thank his parents. *Thank you for sending me where I can find answers. Thank you for believing in me.*

Plus, he thought, *time travel is pretty amazing.*

Yes, he'd made the mistake of using the watch once when he didn't understand it. And he'd made the mistake of interacting with the past. But he had to keep trying. He took a deep breath.

Right.

Isaac tucked everything—scroll and casket with the watch back inside—into his pack, hoisted the pack over his shoulder, and made his way downstairs to the small library.

Amelie was right where he'd left her and it occurred to him that, maybe, for her, he'd only been gone a short time, while for him it had been more than an hour. She'd barely moved, the light in the room was just as when he'd left, and the clock on the mantel confirmed this idea. Even Willow was still hovering up near the ceiling. *Interesting*, Isaac thought.

"I need your help," Isaac began.

She looked at him with raised eyebrows. "Of course. What is it?"

He began to tick off his thoughts on his fingers. "My parents sent me here because I have some kind of magical gift but I don't know what it is, so that makes one. Two, they have given me a time machine—"

"A what?" Ame interrupted, her eyes wide.

"Ooh," Willow said. "What fun!"

"I will come back to that. Third, they are leaving hints

each time I time travel that I need to puzzle out and put together. And last, my parents said I am being hunted. And it is pretty sure I am being hunted by some magical monster, and though I have only seen it a couple of times, it is terrifying." He paused for breath. "What do you think?"

"Wow," Amelie said. "That's quite a lot." She stood up and paced across the room and back, her hands on her hips. "Well, Kat is brilliant at puzzles. When she comes back, we need to fill her in. And Leo is cleverer than he acts. He's just got no self-confidence. He wants to impress his dad, who I gather is a bit of a tosser."

"A . . . what?" Isaac interrupted.

"Stuffy," Ame said. "Not very nice. But Leo reads a bunch, and he loves history, and he can see the future. And Colin"— she paused and smiled—"Colin's sensitive. Plus he can speak to animals, which is more useful than it might seem." Her smile faded. "The only thing is, Colin went through that time when I did a couple of years ago, maybe even worse because he was under the spell of our monster for even longer. So, he's a wee bit fragile." She paused again. "Sorry. I chatter out loud while I think."

Isaac nodded, waiting.

She stopped pacing and looked up at the bookshelves. "Since my specialty is magical creatures, why don't we start with them? Maybe we can figure out what it is that's hunting you, as you called it. Can you describe it?"

He nodded. "It is big, as big as a very tall man. Black wings. And red eyes that are . . . how do you say? . . . creepy. One of the times I saw it was in Orkney when I was on my way to catch the ferry, just at dawn. The farmer who drove the lorry repeated words over and over, and he seemed afraid. But I could not understand his words."

"Huh." She moved across the library and pointed to a high shelf. "See that book with the red binding? Can you fetch it down?"

Isaac pulled the ladder along the wall and climbed up and ran his hands over the old volumes. He tugged out the book and brought it down, placing it on a table, next to several other books Amelie had stacked there.

She picked up Isaac's book, and he read the title on the spine: *Folklore and Legends of Scotland with Particular Attention to Magical Monsters.* Isaac shivered as Amelie opened to the index. The pages were thick vellum, crinkled with age and illustrated with images that reminded Isaac of gargoyles—leering faces, animals with fangs and claws, slithering dragonish creatures.

"From your description, I suspect this one," she said, pointing to the listing for "Faeries, Unseelie." She turned to the entry, and goose bumps rose on Isaac's skin.

Amelie read out loud, "'Fae who inhabit the Realm of Faerie. See also: Unseelie Court; Host; Sl—' Oh!" Amelie clapped her hand over her mouth. "I shouldn't read that one out loud. That would be asking for trouble."

Willow, hovering overhead, made a whimpering noise.

Isaac leaned over and read the word she wouldn't say: *sluagh*. "What do you mean, trouble?"

"That word is dangerous when said aloud," Amelie answered. "Look here." She pointed to an illustration.

It was a great tall man-like creature dressed in a cloak and wearing a necklace of small bones. It had large leathery wings folded partly back against its shoulders. Its hands were long, its fingers like claws. Its face was almost too perfect, too beautiful, but its eyes were red coals, staring out of the book like it saw Isaac with those burning eyes. Isaac's insides twisted.

"That," he said. "That is what I saw. A sl—"

"Stop," Willow commanded. They lurched away, flattening themselves against the ceiling. "Never say that name out loud. Thankfully, it's daylight, but even so . . ." Willow shot looks into the shadowy corners. "Read what it says and you'll see. Read it."

Amelie read out loud: "'The shadow fae of the Unseelie Court are the most evil of faeries, living in a dark corner of the Faerie Realm. Malevolent, they appear most often in times of strife and in the twilight hours or the borderlands between day and night, fall and winter, and life and death. Flying as a host, they seek to harvest the souls of mortals. To speak their formal name, the I-won't-say-it, is to invoke them to you. Never utter that name out loud, especially in darkness, or you may be taken, for they are devilish hunters.'" Amelie leaned away. "And that's what you saw? Goodness."

Isaac moved to sit in the nearest chair. He remembered the people he'd seen near the ring of stones who were taken into the night sky. "One was there, with my parents. And then in my first time travel and again when I was in that lorry. My parents said something was hunting me. That must be it."

"But," Amelie said, "why?"

He shook his head, his eyes meeting hers. "I do not know."

The door to the library flew open.

"You need to come look," Kat said. Her face was white. Colin was right behind her, his hand on Canut's back. "Come look outside."

The four children and one dog stood at the open front door, staring into the woods.

The forest was pushed right up to the edge of the drive.

"Just like earlier," Kat said. "The forest is trying to break the wards."

The air was cold and damp and smelled moldy. Isaac was reminded of the cemetery in Josefov, the crush of tombstones leaning like bad teeth, the shadowed, dank oldness of it.

This forest was now so thick they couldn't see beyond the first trees.

"There's some dreadful magic at play," Kat said. "Those brambles are shoving right up against my warding spells. If only Gumble was still here."

Isaac heard a noise and looked up.

"Rooks," Kat said. "They're always here. But that seems like a lot more than usual. Colin?"

"They aren't our rooks," Colin said. "They won't tell me where they're from." He paused. "They're laughing at us."

To Isaac, they sounded like ordinary birdcalls, which made him wonder about all the other animal sounds he'd ever heard.

"What's going on?" Leo emerged from the parlor where Baines had stationed himself.

Kat pointed outside.

Leo stood silent for a moment, then said, "I can feel it.

It wants in." The trees were moving even though there was no wind.

"What about him?" Kat pointed at the door to the parlor. "Baines?"

"Don't know yet," Leo said. "He went on and on about my father. It was awful. And magic. He seems to think I'm on his side, that I couldn't possibly believe in what he called nonsense."

"Maybe that'll come in handy," Kat said, as she turned and closed—and locked—the great door.

Amelie said, "Isaac needs our help. This may be more complicated than we think. More than just about the wards and the forest. It may be that everything since he arrived is connected. Maybe even bigger than last time, with, you know."

Colin made a small noise.

The five children exchanged looks, and then Kat, putting her hands on her hips, said, "Well then, let's get started."

CHAPTER 25

The Wraith

A gift has been given to the forest wraith.

A boy entered the forest and with him came a magic so strong it still shivers through the trees and whispers through the shadows. The vines snake toward the warding boundaries searching for the boy. The trees stretch their branches nearer the castle. The wolves prowl closer, sniffing for his scent. The boy's very presence strengthens the ancient magic the wraith has brought to the forest. Soon, the wraith thinks, the wards will fall.

A man entered the forest, too, but he was as blank as bones, as dry as dust. Useless.

But then came the gift, the true gift.

Two quite useful humans left the castle, and now they are unconscious, wrapped up like spider-catch and twisted in the branches of the largest tree in the middle of the dis-mal glade that forms the center of the wraith's tiny world. The humans' heads loll and their eyes stare blankly through the Scottish mist that settles, thick and thicker.

The wraith lurks beneath them, gazing up in glee. Its little mechanicals stir, their strange eyes wide and staring. The wraith was able to send one of its mechanicals through the wards and inside Rookskill, but the pathetic mousie was too vulnerable.

So, the wraith thinks, rubbing what is left of skeletal fingers, grinning to expose what is left of sharply pointed teeth. The wraith will use one of those humans, oh, yes, to find what it most wants.

It begins to lay out what it will need, while the mist grows thicker. It pulls out the knives and saws and tweaking tools and lays them on the ground beneath the tree.

All the little mechanicals in the glade begin to chirp and twitter with anxiety, for they sense that sinister magic is about to be made by their master.

Ah! But the wraith may have looked away from its vic-tims too soon.

For one of the humans has come unspelled. One of the humans rolls eyes in the wraith's direction and knows she must make magic if she can, and quickly. One of the humans struggles in her spider-silk cage, careful, quiet.

The mist is a gift, too, but a gift for the human and not for the wraith.

1942

The children gathered in the small library. Kat, closing the door softly, said, "Let's agree we're not saying a single word about this to the nincompoop in the parlor." Then she said to Isaac, "All right. What do you have so far?"

Isaac put his pack on the table. "This is probably the most important." He took out the skull, placing it in the palm of his hand, the hum in his brain growing again. He opened the jaw to reveal the watch face, and the skull caught the light in a sinister way. "A time machine," he said.

The air in the room was electric as the children leaned over the watch.

"I know what that is," said Kat. "I know lots about watches." She paused. "That's a Death's Head watch."

"Death's Head," Isaac breathed. He saw Death, standing

next to the great astronomical clock, hammering down the hours.

"They're some of the earliest watches," Kat went on. "Made to remind the owner that time is fleeting and life is short. *Memento mori.* Remember that you will die. Mary Queen of Scots had a Death's Head watch," Kat said. "Legend has it that hers was cursed. That the watch itself played a part in her downfall and execution. It disappeared after she died, though some say that she gave it to her favorite lady-in-waiting when she went to the block."

"You don't think this could be the very same watch, do you?" Amelie asked.

"Impossible to say, but interesting that this one is here in Scotland," Kat said.

"Because if so," Amelie said, "then this watch could be cursed."

Leo whistled. Colin threw his arms around Canut's neck.

The hum in Isaac's brain grew again, and this time he concentrated on breathing, in, out. In, out, and the hum subsided.

"And how did you come by this?" Kat asked.

Isaac told them the story, then, from his departure from Prague to his landing in Orkney, to seeing his parents and receiving the watch. He read them his father's letter. And he told them what happened when he mistakenly set the watch in motion at the inn and saw the destruction of an ancient civilization.

"Or that is what it seemed to be," he said. "When those monsters carried off the people who lived there."

"And those monsters," Leo began, "they're . . . what?"

"They're Unseelie fae," said Amelie. She fetched the book and opened it to the page with the illustration.

The room was silent for a minute.

"You think they're hunting you," said Leo to Isaac. "Those monsters." He pointed, his finger trembling a little. "The same monsters I saw in my vision of your nightmare."

Isaac nodded.

"You think," Leo said, then cleared his throat, "they're going to try and find you, so they might have followed you here to Rookskill."

Isaac blinked. "I had not thought about it that way."

"He didn't mean to bring them here," Amelie said, sounding defensive.

Leo said, "I know." He rubbed his hand over his head. "I thought we were here to learn how to win the war by using magic. I guess we're also going to have to learn how to fight these . . . Well, the Nazis are monsters. And so are these." Leo pointed at the picture.

Isaac looked up at Leo in surprise. "You are not angry at me?"

Leo gave a fleeting smile. "Why should I be angry? I am a little scared, I'll admit. But we're all in this together, right? I mean, I'm not keen on waging war with them," and he again pointed at the picture. "But we can't just sit here and let them do . . . whatever they're going to do. That wouldn't be right, would it? You're part of the team now, Isaac."

"I am?" Isaac paused. "Thank you, Leo," he said. He smiled back, grateful.

"So," said Kat. "Is that everything?"

Isaac had to suppress a grin then at Kat's businesslike question. "Not quite." He recounted his time travel to what he thought was ancient Greece, and he pulled out the scroll.

Once again that hum began to sing in his brain. Once again he was able to tune it out, and this brought a bit of a surprise realization. He thought he might be getting better at controlling his reaction to magic.

Isaac unrolled the scroll on the floor and the others crowded around. "It seems to be some kind of map, but I have not yet figured it out."

Leo fingered the scroll and said, "This isn't paper or parchment. It's papyrus. That might mean you were in Greece, or Rome, or Egypt."

"Well," said Kat brightly. "This place you saw. Can you describe it again?"

Isaac did, adding as many details as he could.

"I think I know where you might have been," Kat said, "and maybe who she was. She's one of my personal heroes. I'm thinking you were in the great Library of Alexandria."

"The Library of Alexandria!" exclaimed Leo. "What I'd give to see that."

"In fact," Kat continued, "you might have been in the last bit of the Library, most of which was destroyed. And the woman, if I'm right, would have been Hypatia, because she was a famous mathematician who lived in Alexandria around AD 400."

"Golly," whispered Colin.

"Hypatia's father was one of the last members of the library. She was far ahead of her time. The patriarch of Alexandria decided to exile the Jews who lived there and confiscate their property. Hypatia was friendly with the Roman prefect who supported the Jewish people, and that made her the patriarch's enemy. So, it's believed that he had her murdered. Some legends say she was murdered in broad daylight, on the street, by an angry mob." She paused, and then said, "History repeats itself. I'm so sorry, Isaac."

Isaac swallowed the lump in his throat. It felt like there

was no place safe for people like him, not even in past history. And he grieved again the loss of Hypatia. Even though it sounded like he wasn't responsible for her death, maybe if she'd been able to escape through that magical door rather than help him retrieve the watch . . .

"The astrolabe fits, too. Hypatia was known to have used them."

"What's an astrolabe?" Colin asked.

"It's an astronomical orrery. It shows the positions of the stars and planets. Hypatia was brilliant, really," Kat finished, and sighed.

"Did you see that?" Leo asked. He'd been studying the scroll. "Did you see what it just did?"

The others leaned over again.

"It moves," Colin said. "The images move."

"I saw that, too," said Isaac. "It makes it hard to read the words because they are always changing."

"Interesting," Kat murmured.

"I can't make it out," Colin said.

"Well," said Kat, "I think it's time to make a list of what we know and what we don't." She went to the desk to fetch a paper and pencil. Amelie nudged Isaac and he met her eyes and then Leo's and Colin's and everyone smiled.

Kat's orderly manner, Isaac realized, could be annoying,

but in this moment of confusion it was also most welcome.

Kat sat down again and looked around at the others. "What?" she said.

"We're just admiring how you think," Amelie said sincerely.

"Oh." Kat shifted. "Well. Thanks. Now." She began writing. "Anything else?"

"I missed whatever clue or whatever I should have found in the ring of stones. My mistake." Isaac's cheeks grew hot.

"Can't be helped," Kat said.

"And there's this," Isaac said, and pulled the pendant out from under his shirt.

Everyone leaned forward. "It's the eternity knot," Amelie said. "Where did you get that?"

"My father gave it to me." Isaac put it back under his shirt, where it once again lay cold against his skin. "I don't know what it's for, but Hypatia had a pendant that she gave the girl before she disappeared."

Kat tilted her head. "Curious."

Colin lay on his stomach staring at the scroll. "The words. They flow like water. Or, like a snake. See? That almost looks like the head of a snake. In fact"—Colin pushed up to hands and knees—"that may be where the words begin. Right there with 'Dear Isaac.'"

"Good one, Colin," Amelie said. "Look there. It seems to be followed by 'Well done.'"

"Could this be a plan of the library, Isaac?" Kat asked. "Did it look like that?"

Isaac shook his head. "What I saw was only one story high and simple, just a room full of scrolls and books and papers. This looks like a really complicated building with stairs and corridors."

Amelie gasped. "Look! Look! It's a plan of Rookskill. It's Rookskill Castle."

CHAPTER 27

Isaac

1942

Once Amelie said it out loud, it was obvious.

"Brilliant," Kat said. "Exactly so, Ame. It's a three-dimensional plan of Rookskill."

"And it's a living plan," said Leo. "I think that's us, right there. Look, there's Baines in the parlor. And that's Lark, in the kitchen." He pointed. "And I'll bet that's Willow."

Willow dove down to hover over the scroll. "Doesn't look anything like us," they huffed.

"No," said Leo, "it's a symbol. You're represented by a blob."

"A blob?" Willow zipped to the ceiling. The blob moved, too, Isaac noted. "We're . . . we're . . . mortified. A blob!" They asked, "What's Lark?"

"A flower," Leo said.

"We're a blob and the ghillie is a flower? Not fair." Willow moved to the corner of the room, muttering.

"No wonder it looks like the walls and corridors are moving on the scroll because that's exactly what they feel like here in Rookskill," said Kat.

"So then, we need to try and follow the words," said Colin. He jumped up and added, "Canut says he's ready."

"The blob is staying right here," Willow said, huffy.

Amelie said in a soothing voice, "Maybe you could keep an eye on Baines for us, Willow? I don't think you're a blob."

Willow sniffed. "Thank you, Amelie." They popped away.

The five children and one dog went into the front hall, moving quietly so as to not alert Baines. Colin led the way, and Amelie kept track, while Kat took notes on what they could follow and read.

"Look," said Isaac when they reached the second floor near their rooms, where Colin thought the words began. "Can you see that?" It looked as if the drawing came to life, shimmering in the air around them, moving from the scroll to the walls themselves.

"Wow," whispered Leo.

"This way," said Colin, following the coiling form of the words that were revealed in order with every step they took. He read the words aloud and Kat transcribed.

Dear Isaac, Well done.

You've got the watch, the map, and the knife . . .

"Wait," Isaac said, halting. "I don't have a knife."

"Maybe that's what you were supposed to find in the ring of stones," said Amelie. "I seem to remember reading about an iron knife that could render the Unseelie fae a mortal blow. I'll have to look that up."

"Assuming you can get close enough to an Unseelie," Leo observed. "Which you might not want."

"Then I'm missing a possibly important weapon," Isaac said. He remembered then that his fingers had felt a niche in the stone where he stood inside the ring. He wondered whether that niche held the knife he should have found. He shook his head. He should have been more careful. Next time, he promised himself, he would be. Except, that was twice now. The knife, and Hypatia. He bit his lip as Colin continued reading.

What we do is guard magical artifacts that could be used for good or ill. The hunters seek what we hide.

They were walking along a windowless corridor, and Colin led them through a door, and down a narrow flight of stairs, a twisting, winding staircase. The blue-white shimmering in the walls that corresponded to their path on the scroll was the only light.

This map will take you to something that's been hidden for centuries. Something you can use to help you uncover the next clue. Remember that if any of these artifacts land in the enemy's hands . . .

"Wait," Isaac said, stopping again. Now they were deep inside the castle, on the landing of the stone staircase. It was gloomy and cold. "Artifacts. That is the clue." Colin took a few more steps.

. . . it will be dangerous for all humans.

"Whoa," said Leo. "That sounds pretty bad."

"Um," said Colin, "it looks like the words end here." He opened a door into a long wood-paneled room that was barely lit by windows at one end. "I think we have to look for whatever will help uncover that next clue in this room."

The children and dog stepped inside. It was filled with stuff—heavy, upholstered wood furniture, flowers in glass domes, sculptures on shelving, magnifying glasses on tables. Thick Turkish carpets covered the floor. Portraits hung to the high ceiling. The room was so large that Isaac thought it might have been the size of a football pitch.

As they stood there, Colin holding open the scroll, the walls of the room began to shine with that unearthly blue light. Canut whined.

"Like electrification," Leo said quietly, "but without the wires."

"Wicked," Colin whispered.

"Let's spread out," said Amelie. "Look for the eternity knot."

Each of them took a different part of the room. The carpet muffled the sounds of their movements. Isaac stood staring at his corner. It was a dusty, cluttered collection of stuff. Any single object here could be an artifact.

Why, that petrified rock looked strange. And the stuffed raccoon, teeth bared, ugh. And what about the wad of fuzz inside the glass ball that reminded Isaac of dust under the bed? He moved around his corner, taking it all in. The walls still glowed with wavy blue lines.

"Oh!" The gasp came from Amelie. They all turned.

Ame's arm was glowing, too, but with gold. A gold rope was wrapped around her bare forearm from wrist to elbow. But the rope moved.

Amelie looked horrified, frozen with terror.

Isaac ran to her.

"Stop," she whispered as he skidded to a halt. A snake wrapped her arm, a snake all of gold, shining. Its tongue, near her wrist, flicked in and out. "I'm afraid it will bite."

The others were there, too, and it was Colin who stepped forward. "It won't," he said. "I promise it won't bite." He reached out his hand toward Amelie. The golden snake slithered from her arm and onto Colin's hand, and then coiled—and froze solid, its head vertical, tongue out.

Amelie staggered back, leaning against an overstuffed chair.

"Look at the pattern of its skin. It's the eternity knot," Kat said. "And it's a bracelet. An actual bracelet."

"I know. I picked it up and it came alive and crawled up my arm," Amelie said, sounding strained. "I hate snakes."

"It's also a snake, a real one," Colin said. "It told me that it's looking for home. And that Isaac could take it there. It says that when you find its home, you'll find the next bit of answers."

"Wonderful." Isaac asked, "Where's home?"

Colin looked up at Isaac, holding the snake-bracelet out toward him. "The snake told me it's your next time travel."

Isaac put the snake-bracelet in his pack. "Will it stay like this?" he asked Colin as they made their way back up the winding stairway to their rooms. "It will not uncoil and slither away, or, or . . . ?"

"Only if you ask. Then it comes alive. But if you ask it, it'll do stuff. Like spy under doorways. Lead you somewhere."

"But how do I ask it, Colin?" Isaac stopped in his tracks. "I don't talk to animals."

"It'll listen. Trust me."

Isaac exchanged a look with a wide-eyed Amelie.

"Just don't bring it into my room," she said. "I only picked it up to bring it to you because I saw the pattern." She shuddered. "I really hate snakes."

"Do not worry," Isaac said. "I'll put the pack in my room."

"It's almost time for supper," Colin said. "I'm famished. How about you, Canut?"

The dog gave a happy grumble and they moved off together.

"And we'd better find out what Baines has been up to in our absence," Kat said with a sigh. "Leo, do you mind?"

Leo shrugged and gave a little smile. "I'll go check."

"Kat," Isaac said. "What more can you tell me about time travel?" Ame paused and turned to listen.

"Time travel," Kat echoed. "Well. Scientifically speaking, time travel disrupts the space-time continuum."

"The what?" Isaac asked.

"Space-time continuum. Albert Einstein has written about it. How space and time are related, how they work together. It's physics." She paused, tapping her lips with her index finger. "I'll read up on it some more."

"All right," he said, still pondering. "So, is time travel science? Or is it magic?"

"Great question." Kat looked away into the distance. "Until something can be explained logically by science, maybe we call it magic. I think magic has substance. I think it sticks, rather like lint. But it's invisible. If we could see it, we'd probably give it a different name, like science. I think magic has stuck to Rookskill Castle for thousands and thousands of years, for as long as people have been in this place."

Isaac wondered whether magic was sticking to him. Magic from his parents. Maybe that explained his so-called gift. "My parents said they are locked in a time stream. What is that?"

Kat shook her head. "Not sure. But I can find out. I'm guessing they aren't in any specific time or place. But how they got there, I don't know. Sorry." She paused. "You do know about the law of unintended consequences, right?"

"Um . . ."

"If you change something in the past, you can change the future. You could change everything. Like a little ripple effect that can grow."

"I know about that." Isaac bit his lip, thinking about Hypatia, and his father's admonition to *not, for any reason, interact with the past.*

Kat nodded. "Good. Next, we need to figure out your magical gift, Isaac."

"Right," he said.

Kat moved off and Isaac turned to Amelie. He asked her, "How would you like to time travel with me?"

CHAPTER 28

Ralph Baines

1942

Ralph Baines sat behind his newly constituted desk in the repurposed front parlor of Rookskill, his eyes glued on Leo. Leo was the only one of the children he could trust, not the least because Leo's father was very high up. Someone who was important to know.

"I know you've said you don't believe in magic," Leo said, "but it's quite possible."

Baines shifted and took a sip of his strong tea. "Magic is possible," he echoed, not believing a word of it. But he didn't want to contradict the boy. He smiled, trying to encourage him. Must make Leo trust him.

"I've seen it myself," Leo said. "Kat works spells, like the warding spells. Amelie can speak to spirits, and Colin can speak to animals. And Isaac has a time machine, and he's carrying a map he picked up in ancient Egypt, a magical map of the castle. And that helped us find a really strange, well, bracelet. And the time machine is in the shape of a skull. Rather creepy, if you ask me."

Baines wondered whether the boy had suffered a head injury. "A time machine?"

"Kat said it was called a Death's Head watch and that Mary Queen of Scots had one like it," Leo went on. "So, anyway, magic really does exist and we're all learning to use it. I thought you should know so you won't send us away from Rookskill."

Completely barmy. Baines looked into his teacup, wondering whether there was something in the water here or whatever the children ate. He was pleased he'd brought a few days of rations along, which would do for the moment. He wasn't at all certain how the children were getting their meals since no other adults were present in this crumbling ruin of a castle.

Leo said, "I'm hoping that you'll put in a good word with my father."

"Aha." Just what Baines was hoping for from Leo.

"My father doesn't understand all this," Leo said, gesturing. "Magic and such. He's never understood really what I can offer king and country. Even when I was invited here to join this special unit because of my abilities, my father was disappointed that I chose to come to Rookskill."

Leo was definitely soft in the head. Baines began to wonder how he'd approach the boy's father unless he reported to Falstone Senior that he would help stop the boy from making any further mistakes.

"So, I'm hoping you'll keep an open mind," Leo finished. "About me. About us, here."

Baines nodded. "Always. Open." Right. Bonkers. "Can you tell me, please, why the telephone is not working?"

"Oh," said Leo. "It's been down for a while. We really don't need it."

"I see. Then how do I contact my superiors?" Baines looked the boy in the eye.

Leo said, "We do have a wireless. Kat can show you."

"Please let her know that I require it. As soon as possible."

Leo nodded. "Dinner is in a few minutes," Leo said. "I'd advise eating the food that looks inedible and avoiding what looks like normal food."

He'd been right about the food, then. "I'll be taking dinner in my room tonight." Baines stood and gestured at his nearly empty desktop. "Now, if you don't mind . . ."

"Of course," Leo said. He left, closing the door softly.

Baines sat down. They were all insane here. Time travel? Talking to ghosts and animals? MI-6 had been duped.

He turned and looked out the window. Ralph Baines had always liked being out of doors. Liked tending his tiny pocket garden at home. But this place . . . The forest loomed not far off, a mass of thorns and vines and scratchy bare branches. It was pernicious and nasty. Perhaps a little tree pruning, put these children to manual work outdoors.

Gardening was healthy for the mentally weak.

Yes, that was the ticket. Tomorrow morning straight-away he'd get these children outside for a little hard work. Exercise and discipline. Outdoors in the fresh air, while he collected enough information about what was really going on here before he contacted the home office through that wireless.

Ralph Baines rubbed his hands together. He loved a good plan. Especially if it was his.

CHAPTER 29

Isaac

1942

"Can we go anywhere in time?" Amelie asked.

"Right now we have to go where it's been set to take me, so I can collect the clues. But after that, why . . ." Isaac realized that Amelie was right. Maybe once he'd made these necessary trips, they could travel to really interesting times. Just as long as they didn't interfere. And if he could figure out how to make it work. "Tomorrow, straight after breakfast?"

She nodded, her eyes bright.

Dinner that night was pretty regular, if you didn't mind that it tried to skitter off the plate under your fork. Isaac gave up on that one but some of the side dishes were decent. And he knew enough not to eat that six-layer confection that was covered with what looked like sugar flowers and leaned like it might slide down the table.

He finally managed a good sleep after so many exhausting days and nights.

Straight after breakfast Isaac stood alone in the small library, waiting for Amelie and staring out the window. "Birnam Wood comes to Dunsinane," he murmured. Trees should not be doing what these were doing, but they were, for the second time. They were definitely closer, denser, nastier.

It was a grim morning all around, with low clouds and sleet. The deep hollows beyond the trees were inky black.

"Right," came Baines's voice. Isaac turned. The other children trailed in behind Baines. "I've called you here for a purpose. It's high time you were exposed to some healthy physical activity. The woods around this castle are badly in need of grooming. Miss Bateson?" Baines said, looking at Kat.

She glared back at him.

"Where are tools and such?"

"I'm sorry?" Kat said.

"Garden tools," Baines said slowly, as if speaking to someone who couldn't understand English.

Kat answered equally slowly. "In the garden tool shed, I expect."

"Jolly good. You shall all put on weatherproof clothing and shoes and make ready for outdoor activity."

"Um," said Colin, "it's frightfully cold and wet today."

Baines sighed. "And what of it? You are English, are you not?"

"We're here to learn our magic," Kat said tartly, "and we were about to start lessons."

"That can wait," Baines said, with a smirk. "The woods are a fright."

"We can't go past the boundary," Amelie said.

"Boundary?" Baines echoed. "The only boundary is a mile off." He clapped his hands together. "Coats and galoshes and back here in five minutes."

They looked at one another in astonishment until he clapped his hands again. "Chop-chop."

As they marched upstairs, Isaac whispered to Kat, "What about spelling him again?"

"Oh, I shall," she answered darkly. "I'm looking for the right time and trying to come up with the perfect spell. And I don't want to make a mistake. Much as that might be interesting," she added with a snort.

"Telling him to take a leap might turn him into a frog," Amelie added with a giggle.

"Or hop to it," said Colin. "Or jump through hoops."

Five minutes later the five children and Baines trooped in boots and mackintoshes through the hallways of the castle toward the kitchen. As they passed through to the back door, Baines stopped in his tracks.

"And who are you?" he asked.

Lark made a deep curtsy. "Lark, chief cook and bottle washer," she answered. Today she was wearing a green skirt and jumper that matched her skin and her hair was flaming red. Above her, Willow hovered, rolling, as near as Isaac could tell, their eyes.

"A flower," Willow said with a snicker.

Baines drew up. "Now, see here. How can a child of your age . . ."

"I'm one hundred and thirty-seven, if you don't mind," Lark answered, drawing herself up to her full three feet. "I haven't been a child for eleven years. Officially."

Isaac was gobsmacked but he wouldn't show it. Willow made a rude noise.

Baines's mouth dropped open and then he shut it quick. He muttered, "All. All completely daft." He cleared his throat and said, "We're going out for some exercise, which is good for body and mind. Get your gear."

Lark narrowed her eyes at him. "I shan't."

"Hah," said Willow. "Now, that's the ticket."

The two faced off for what felt like several minutes, Lark clutching a long wooden spoon, her arms folded across her chest.

"Fine," Baines said at last. "We'll finish this later. The rest of you, out."

It was nasty weather and Isaac pulled the collar of his coat tight around his neck. A dense fog hung over the landscape and the ground was squishy wet. Isaac was especially grateful for the uniform's trousers woven of thick, warm Scottish wool. Kat led the way to a garden shed that sat next to an old barn. Plenty of tools—pruners, saws, and axes—hung on the walls in neat order.

"I miss Hugo." Amelie sighed. She glanced at Isaac. "He took care of everything here at Rookskill, for Lord Craig, but now he's joined the local regiment. Look how nicely the tools have been left."

"Let's get to work," Baines said, leaving the shed and heading for a place where the trees pushed right up to the edge of the castle. Isaac thought that the trees had again crossed Kat's warding boundary, and he exchanged a glance with her that confirmed he must be right. She had wide, worried eyes. The thorns on the vines were huge and sharp, and the vines themselves were fat and knotty as if hundreds of years old.

Baines raised pruners and began to clip ferociously at the thorny branches.

The five children watched, mesmerized, as the branches fought back.

"What the devil?" Baines exclaimed, backing away as thorns reached for his arms and head, and vines grabbed at hunks of his hair and mustache. "Give me a hand!"

Leo was frozen with horror. Colin laughed so hard he was doubled over. Kat and Amelie bent together and whispered, so Isaac moved to extract Baines.

That was when it happened.

CHAPTER 30

Isaac

1942

The instant Isaac reached for a branch, trying to dislodge a thorn from Baines's coat, he heard that hum—so loud his head ached and he had to take a step back.

As he did, the trees followed him. The vines, the thorns, let off attacking Baines and went for Isaac.

But they didn't attack Isaac—they reached for him. Tried to enfold him. Cradle him. Absorb him. He couldn't get away. He was a fly in a spider's web, a fish in a net. When he moved, the trees moved with him, grasping as if they might tear him apart out of need and want. The entire forest hummed, singing in a low vibration so intense that Isaac clapped his hands over his ears and shut his eyes.

From a distance Kat was chanting. "'Who can impress the forest, bid the tree unfix his earthbound root?'"

The next thing Isaac knew he was lying on his back on

the soggy ground, the other children peering down at him. Baines exclaimed from behind them about "those dratted thorns."

"What happened?" Isaac began.

"I get it," Kat whispered urgently. "I understand. Your magic. Wow."

"I have the kind of magic that makes trees attack me?" Isaac sat up and began to pull the dead leaves from his hair.

"No, no," Kat said. "Look." She pointed. "Listen."

The entire forest stirred, moving restlessly. From deep in the woods came wolf howls that made Isaac's skin crawl.

"I think," Kat said breathlessly, "you're like a wireless."

"A wireless?" Isaac echoed. "I don't understand." He struggled to his feet.

"I do," said Amelie. "That's it. That's why magic responds so well when you're around, Isaac. You're an amplifier."

"An . . . ?"

"An amplifier. Like, you make things clearer. More distinct. Remember the ghost cat? I'd never seen it before. You channeled it to appear."

"Right," said Colin, excited. "The first time I ever heard Josie's voice was when you arrived."

Kat added, "I had the feeling that not only was my warding spell stronger yesterday when you were there, but I think you're making the magic that's moving the forest through the wards stronger. Which is weird because you've got the trees breaking through the wards, but also helping me keep them out." She folded her arms over her chest. "You're an amplifier for magic, Isaac. Whatever magic. Good or not."

Isaac looked from one to the other. "An amplifier," he echoed. *Whatever magic—good or not?*

Baines called out, "Mr. Drake, call off your dogs."

"Dogs?" Colin said. Then, quietly, "Oh, dear."

From the depths of the forest, they could all see the eyes. Pairs of eyes staring out from the shadows, shining.

"Dire wolves," said Colin.

"Baines thinks they're dogs," Kat whispered.

"Mr. Baines?" Leo said urgently. "We need to get back inside."

"I don't see why—" Baines's words were interrupted by a howl. Very close.

The hum inside Isaac had become a steady, pulsing beat, louder and louder. "They are coming," Isaac said.

"Don't run," said Colin as the children began to move toward the castle. "I don't think they can cross Kat's boundary, but we still shouldn't run."

One of the wolves stepped out of the woods, and Isaac realized just how monstrously huge they were.

"Isaac. You can amplify not only good magic. You can amplify all magic. Bad magic, too." Kat reached into her pocket and muttered under her breath.

He could feel it then.

A war raged inside him, a painful clash between the magic from the forest, grim, evil, and the magic that Kat clutched in her fist, shiny, sharp, bright.

He threw his hands to his head. He stumbled, and Amelie turned.

"No." She grabbed him by the shoulders. "Try to control it." She shook him, and he stared into her serious, wide blue eyes. "Try to focus."

Isaac took a deep breath. He focused on the magic in Kat's hand. He felt a sharp pain, and then a shift, and then, yes, energy zinged through him, from his head to his feet and back again. He closed his eyes and concentrated.

The pain was terrible, as if he was being torn to shreds, his skin bleeding from a thousand paper cuts, his veins on fire. But he refused to give in to it.

He refused to give up.

He thought about his parents, somewhere in time.

About how they'd given him a responsibility to discover who and what he was and what he could do, and he decided—right then—that no matter how it hurt, he would never give up.

Never.

Little by little he could sense the magic. The two opposite magics, light and dark, good and evil. Little by little he could isolate them as if magic was a thread that ran from his brain to his hands. He took hold of that thread and pulled and then . . .

. . . and then he had control. He could choose the good magic if he wanted.

It was almost too much. It zapped and zinged, but he was also strong, and he pulled himself straight to his full height. He concentrated on the good, bright magic, fighting the other, which surged against him like a wave pounding a cliff.

"Ah!" Kat cried. He opened his eyes. Her face was contorted by pain. She held out her fist, glowing with a blue flame. "I can't let go!"

Leo pulled at Baines.

"Really, now. Stop this nonsense," Baines said. Colin, staring at the wolves, muttered under his breath. Amelie tugged at both Kat and Isaac.

They reached the castle wall.

Isaac turned and tripped and stumbled, and lost concentration, and then, lost control.

The pain in his head became unbearable again. He froze, flattening his back against the hard, cold stone wall, pressing against it as if he could push himself through.

Ahead of him, Baines, Leo, Colin, and Amelie tumbled inside the castle door.

"Kat," Isaac cried. The wolves all began to howl at once. Terror filled him. Blind terror. He had to disappear.

She turned. "Isaac, where are you?" She looked right through him. As if he was invisible.

He reached out his hand. "I'm here."

She squinted, searching.

He closed his eyes and concentrated again. *It must be the fear*, he thought. *I wanted to disappear, and I did.*

When he opened his eyes, Kat's eyes widened. "Wow. For a moment there, you vanished."

They both heard the movement of the wolves, making through the brush straight for them.

Kat reached for him. "Run!" she cried, and jerked his arm. He turned, slipped, stumbled again, nearly falling before he could get his gangly legs under him. Then he ran.

Kat led him, yanking his arm, and he could almost feel

the hot breath of a wolf, until suddenly they were inside the castle, shoving the door closed behind.

Kat and Isaac leaned against the door, panting. Wolves thudded at the door with a shuddering jolt and then scratched at the wood. Kat threw a bolt, and when their eyes met, hers were wide with shock.

CHAPTER 31

The Wraith

The wraith is rapturous. The wards around the castle are breaking. The ancient magic the wraith has called to the forest has become stronger. The dire wolves beat against the castle doors, the trees have moved right up against the aging stone walls, and the snaking vines are climbing, climbing the crumbling towers and seeking entry through the mullioned windows.

The wraith looks up from what it is doing—a task so disturbing that all the little mechanicals have gone into hiding—and thinks, *Hurry. Hurry. Now is the time. Now we will have what we've longed for. Now we can find what we've sought.*

Back before, two years ago (what feels like thousands of years ago) the wraith had found her. It loved her before she ever knew it did. Before the wraith itself knew. The wraith longed for her, and gave her what she wished for—all those mechanical replacements that gave her power—and then it realized. The wraith re-created her (yes, as a monster) but also loved her.

It gave the Lady what she desired, but lost her in the end. Lost her and realized—too late! Oh, agony, too late!—that it loved her.

But now . . . it will bring her back. It can do that. It has many of her parts. All it needs is what is locked inside Kat's chatelaine.

It will bring her back to life.

The wraith bends to its current task, to the human captive that lies prone and helpless, the human captive that will steal the chatelaine, and the little mechanicals dare not peek.

CHAPTER 32

Moloch

Moloch lifts his head and sniffs the air.

When Isaac opens his heart and mind to his magical gift, and the wolves throw themselves against the doors, and the forest presses on the stones of Rookskill Castle, a shudder passes from the human world right through the thin places to the Realm of Faerie. Right through to Moloch.

He stands. "It's ready," he whispers. He tilts his head, listening, feeling. He's sure that he's right, that his hunter is right. He's found the Guardian at last.

And at Rookskill. Perfect.

Before the fae king discovers that his spy is gone, Moloch must seize this moment. With the Guardian and the magic, Moloch will make his own kingdom. He'll become master of the sluagh. The Seelie fae will be forced to grovel at his feet. They'll be forced to look at his scar, at his empty eye socket, at his leathery wings, at his red eye. Moloch will have the joy he's wanted for too, too long.

Wyvern beats his wings and Moloch turns to face the dragon. He places his hand on the scaly green snout, and the dragon snorts. Moloch whispers, "It's time, at last. You will take me to Rookskill."

CHAPTER 33

Isaac

1942

Leo shepherded Baines away as the other four children remained just inside the door, leaning on the walls and stairs.

Willow popped in overhead. "Heard a noise, we did. Sounded grim outside."

Isaac rubbed his forehead as the painful hum subsided. For a moment, when he was in control, it had felt wonderful. But when he stumbled . . .

"You vanished," Kat said, staring at him. "You completely vanished. What was that?"

Willow snorted. "We tried to tell you. Saw it when you arrived."

Isaac shook his head. "I thought you said I am an . . . what did you call it? Amplifier."

"I think you are. I think that's one of your magical

gifts. But only one because you seem to have other skills, too, like disappearing on the spot." She folded her arms. "Not to mention you have a time-travel machine and you've seen monsters. You're obviously quite magical. You've never known?"

Isaac shook his head, then looked away, thinking for a minute, and said, "Well, that's not really true. I have always known I was—different from anyone else. And, when I think about it, I've had the feeling before of being—I do not know—not-seen. Like when I get really scared. When I wish to disappear."

Willow said, "Ha! And there you go. Saw it when we met. Disappears like . . ." And Willow seemed to snap their fingers.

Colin, Amelie, and Kat watched Isaac in silence.

"But I have no idea how to control any of it. Like I have no idea how to control that amplifier stuff." Isaac looked from one to the other. "I can scarcely control what happens in the time travel and that has all been set for me." He paused. "But I want to learn. I need to."

"We can help," said Amelie. "We can help you manage your magic. You can do amazing things, Isaac."

He smiled at Amelie. He could do amazing things. Well, he could also do terrible things, as the scratching on the door made clear.

Anyone powerful enough to do great good can also do great evil. Like Victor Frankenstein.

We may all be monsters under the skin.

"Come on," said Kat. "It seems you've amplified the dark magic that's working against my wards. We need to sort this out."

As they made their way through the castle, Isaac saw that vines and branches trembling in the wind pressed against the windows of the castle, blocking the light. Dire wolves howled all around the outside.

Kat led them into the small library.

"I'm going to go check on the dogs," Colin said.

"Look in on Leo and Baines, too, would you?" Kat asked. "Make sure Baines hasn't done anything else foolish?"

Colin nodded.

Willow said with a snicker, "Baines, foolish?"

"Right. Let's get started," Kat said.

She and Amelie took turns. Kat would make a spell or Amelie would conjure the ghost cat out of thin air, and Isaac would respond and try to control the magic. After a short time, he found that if he pressed his hand to his chest, pressing the pendant against his skin, he had a stronger response.

It was a bit like trying to control lightning. Electric shocks zoomed from his feet to his head and back. But, little by little, he could grab it more easily, direct it, focus it.

He was able to make the ghost cat flicker or look more solid or freeze in place. He was able to undo one of Kat's spells, when she made a book float and he made it crash to the floor.

"Does the kitty feel like a good ghost or a bad ghost?" Kat asked. "I'm trying to see how you can affect one or the other. Good or bad."

"Neither," Isaac said. "It feels like a kitty."

Kat put her hands on her hips. "So, what does a kitty feel like?"

Isaac tried to remember the cat his neighbor had in Prague. The tabby would move along the window balconies until she came to sit at his window, taking in the sun. When she turned her green eyes on Isaac, he always felt she was watching him narrowly, with disapproval. "Like a kitty," he said.

Amelie laughed and Kat gave her a scowl, and Isaac pointed at her expression and said, "Just like that." Which made Amelie laugh harder.

Kat rolled her eyes and said, "Let's try this." She stuck

her hand into her pocket and pulled out the odd silvery object.

Isaac felt the power from it at once. But this time he could focus his response and turn the pain aside. "What do you call that again?"

"A chatelaine," Kat said. She opened her palm. Chains holding three small silver objects—a pen, a thimble, and a pair of scissors—shone in the dim light.

Isaac gritted his teeth. The chatelaine began to glow a brilliant blue, and Amelie gasped. Kat froze.

He felt the shift as he absorbed its power. The thimble. There was an aura about that thimble.

His mother had a thimble in her sewing box. But this was different. Dangerous. It held something. Something . . . sad. He concentrated all his energy there. Something lost. Something unfinished. It throbbed like the heartbeat of the castle itself. It throbbed with an ancient longing.

The thimble became a ball of light, brilliant, painful. And needy, desperate, grasping, and then the wolves were howling, howling, and the trees banged as if in a high wind against the windows and doors of the castle, and Isaac knew he'd shifted from channeling good magic to bad. Evil magic was flowing from inside the thimble to Isaac.

He pushed back and sent the evil magic reeling. The wolves and trees slowly went silent. The darkness lifted a little. Isaac's head ached.

Kat, trembling, pocketed the chatelaine. "Well," she said, and leaned against a table. "Goodness."

"That . . . whatever it is," Isaac said. "Whatever's inside." He rubbed his temples, trying to calm the ache. "Now, that's definitely bad magic."

"It's the soul of a witch," Kat said, sounding exhausted.

"The soul of a what?" Isaac said, shocked.

"Remember what I said about what happened here a couple of years ago?" Amelie said. "About the monster who tried to steal our souls?"

Isaac nodded.

"That's the monster. She was the Lady Eleanor. Kat was able to capture her soul instead, inside the thimble."

Isaac gave a low whistle. "No wonder it sends out so much . . . anger."

"She only wanted one thing, really. But she didn't know how to get it without hurting others." Kat took a deep breath. "I think we're done for now."

He nodded. "I agree." Then, "Kat?"

"Yes?"

"Thank you. I mean it." He rubbed his sweaty hands on his pants. "I still don't know exactly why my parents sent me to Rookskill, but I am glad they did. Really glad. Glad to know all of you. Glad you're here and willing to help me. Glad you're my friends." He paused. "So, um, thanks to you. Again."

Kat smiled, for the first time in Isaac's memory. "You're welcome." She pushed away and walked unsteadily out of the library.

Isaac turned to Amelie. "What do you think?"

"I think you have quite a gift."

He shook his head. "I wish I knew more about this. About myself. About where this gift came from. And why."

"I don't know about the why. But maybe you inherited it?"

In his mind's eye, Isaac pictured his mother standing protectively in the doorway of the hut, whispering.

"Maybe," he said, pacing away, staring out the vine-covered window at the gloomy forest beyond.

His mother had been casting spells. She was magical. And his father—his father had given him a pendant that was also (Isaac was sure) magical. Isaac had inherited a magical gift from his mother. And been given a magical gift by his father. Which made the initial conclusion pretty clear, even if the why was still elusive.

Not only did Isaac Wolf have magic, he had it from both his parents. They'd given him magic and he had a whole ton of it.

Now he had to find out why.

CHAPTER 34
Ralph Baines

1942

Ralph Baines was thoroughly confused. Why were vines covering the windows? Why were trees pressing up against the walls of the castle? Why had he become so entangled with grasping thorns and sticky brambles? His fingers found rips in his jacket and he pursed his lips.

This was his best jacket, a personal purchase, acquired at great expense.

He paced across his commandeered bivouac, rubbing his forehead. He was never fooled for long. There was always a logical explanation.

The forest, when he'd arrived yesterday, had been a mass of thorns and brambles, but this overnight growth was ridiculous. He hadn't been able to make a dent with the tools before that pack of wild dogs taken in by the youngest boy was at their heels. Well. It was obvious, wasn't it? The groundskeeper had been negligent for so long that the ivy was running amok and that small rain shower had given a boost to new growth. As for the dogs—they would be dealt with.

Ralph Baines did not like dogs.

He didn't like children either.

And this lot had been able to pull the wool over some eyes, but they weren't fooling Ralph Baines.

He would recommend taking this castle, tearing it down, and putting up a practical fortification in its place. A modern facility with guns and barracks. Concrete. Ready to defend the coast against a Nazi incursion. Not a bit of it to do with magic.

He marched to the door to make his way to the kitchen. He was hungry after dealing with all this nonsense, too hungry to rely on his rations alone. He'd have to chance the food of Rookskill. Leo had told him not to eat the bangers and mash. Some nonsense about it not being bangers and mash but slugs and glowworms in some kind of magical disguise. And that addlepated child who claimed to be the cook was no doubt being coached by an adult he hadn't yet seen.

Ralph Baines liked bangers and mash. He would eat them with gusto.

CHAPTER 35

Isaac

1942

"Are you ready?' Isaac asked.

The watch sat open on the floor between him and Amelie. He was wearing the snake-bracelet—Amelie refused to touch it—around his right wrist.

The skull grinned its hollow, chilling grin. The hands of the watch were fixed at eleven o'clock.

Amelie asked, "Will it hurt?"

He shook his head. "It feels a bit like being bounced around on a rough road, that's all."

"And they won't see us or hear us?"

"As long as I am holding the watch," Isaac said, uncomfortable as he thought about Hypatia. "We had better hold on to each other, too. You may need to be touching me to stay invisible. Remember the law of unintended consequences. We do not want to change anything in the past."

She nodded. "Do you know where and when we're going?"

"No. But I trust my parents. So, are you ready?" Isaac asked again.

She nodded again and smiled. "It might be fun. Maybe we'll see an amazing place and time."

Maybe they would. In fact, Isaac thought, they almost certainly would, no matter where they went. After all, how many people were lucky enough to travel through time and space and come home again?

He smiled back. "We just have to remember what we need to do. Find that next clue."

"Right."

"All right, then. Hold on tight."

Isaac wound the watch.

CHAPTER 36

Isaac and Amelie

PUMAPUNKU, TIWANAKU VALLEY
CIRCA 1000

As the kaleidoscopic whirl begins, Isaac can feel Amelie's tight grip on his left arm. He clutches the watch in his right fist with the snake-bracelet wrapping his arm just above, and they tumble backward through space and time—the space-time continuum, Kat had called it—and Isaac is seeing places and events from his own life that he'd seen before.

Then they're high above a treeless, rocky plain, one side edged by snow-capped mountains, a long flat lake dotted with islands on another, and the far-off sea sparkling in the sunlight opposite the mountains. The plain and the lake draw closer and closer as if Isaac and Amelie are falling out of the sky, and he hears a small cry from Amelie as they plunge toward the earth, toward a green field in the middle of the plain, a field that is laced with narrow ribbons of water and they fall down, down, down.

Isaac shuts his eyes, sure this is the last thing he'll ever see.

And then, a soft thump.

Isaac is lying on his back. Amelie is lying by his side, still clutching his arm. He's not sore, not even winded. When he opens his eyes, the sky above is deep blue. The air is cold and the earth beneath his back is soft and wet. He smells fish and rotting vegetation, and when he sits up, his head swims.

"Isaac?" comes Amelie's small voice, as she sits up. "Where are we?"

The mountains, bright with snow, form a long line in the distance to his right, a spiky high ridge. He turns and they both stand. Isaac shivers. The plain around them, a field of crops that's rocky where it's uncultivated, stretches away as far as he can see.

"I'm dizzy," he says.

"Me too."

Long moats of water enclose raised terraces of some kind of plant. Then he hears a girl singing, and he and Amelie turn.

The girl is bent over, picking beans and filling a reed basket. A long black braid snakes down her back and her skin is light brown, and she wears a flat hat and a long shawl over a full skirt. When she straightens, she lifts the basket to her shoulders and grunts. Her shawl and skirt are woven in elaborate geometric patterns in brilliant colors—red, turquoise, orange, and blue.

Isaac points. Amelie's mouth makes a round O.

Winding, interlocking rings—the familiar eternity knot—are woven throughout the girl's shawl in a bronze thread that shines.

She walks along the strip of earth, still singing, and they follow as she marches up a low hill. When they reach the top, Isaac pauses and points again.

About half a mile away a small city spreads across the plain. Or rather, a great stone temple (that's what Isaac thinks it looks like) squats in the middle of a vast ring of buildings made of stone and clay with thatched reed roofs. It's a riot of color, people dressed in brilliant clothes moving through the winding streets, the stones, too, painted and decorated. Smoke rises in spirals, people crowd the streets, chickens and dogs mill in the crowds. The girl makes for that city.

The temple at its center is long and rectangular and resting on a low terrace surrounded on all sides by broad steps. Men work on one section of the wall with hand tools. They hammer at the pale stones that are shaped and tightly fit. At the center of the complex is a blocky building with receding doors to a shadowed interior. It's huge and, Isaac thinks, extraordinary, the complex geometric shapes of the doors and windows framing the inside. The walls are decorated with colorful frescoes.

A road leads away from the city to a stone quarry, and carts and people move back and forth on that road, which also winds away toward the lake in the distance.

The sun beats down, but the air is cold.

"Where do you think we are?" Amelie asks.

"I've never seen a place like this before," Isaac answers.

They walk down the hill toward the city, following the girl at a distance.

Framing the entrance to the city is an enormous carved gate in a surrounding wall, and on either side of the gate are free-standing rock pillars—stone giants of men holding up the lintel.

"Wow," Isaac says. "That is amazing. It is huge."

"And snakes," Amelie says, pointing at the carvings of what appear to be cobras that twine up and around the legs of the stone giants.

"Ah. Speaking of snakes," Isaac says. He slips the bracelet from his arm and holds it on his free palm. "What do you suppose I say to it?"

"Didn't Colin say that it wanted to go home?"

"Yes, right." Isaac clears his throat. "Snake, go home."

As soon as Isaac says the word *home*, the snake comes alive. Amelie jumps behind Isaac, still clutching his arm, but the snake lowers itself to the ground and moves away fast, following the girl. She's already at the square arch of the gate and walking into the city.

"I guess we had better follow," Isaac says.

When they reach the gate, the snake slides along the walls, making for the temple complex, while the girl moves off through the crowds in the streets.

"Which way?" Isaac asks.

"The snake," Amelie answers. "We need to follow the magic." Then, "Look! Those are llamas."

"Llamas live in South America," Isaac says. "I guess, then, that these mountains are the Andes." He tries to remember his geography. "Maybe that big lake is Titicaca?"

"That would explain why we're dizzy. We're at a high altitude," Amelie says. "Somewhere in the Andes, and some-where in the distant past. Wasn't the Inca culture in the Andes near Lake Titicaca?"

"I do not know for certain."

Ahead of them the snake passes through the streets as they follow. It is climbing the stone steps to the terrace when Amelie pulls at Isaac's arm.

A man steps out of the crowd and makes his way toward the terrace ahead of them. He wears a type of loincloth and a brilliant cape and a pendant around his neck, hanging from a thick leather strap.

The pendant is the eternity knot.

Isaac's pendant.

Isaac and Amelie exchange a glance. His heart begins to pound.

A procession approaches. Men in elaborate woven robes in scarlet, blue, and yellow, with high feathered headdresses, march past and climb the steps of the terrace toward the temple. The man with the pendant falls into step at the tail end of the procession. The snake, now on the top step, coils and turns, as if it's waiting for Isaac and Amelie, so they follow.

Three sides of the terrace are bordered by walls inset with stones bearing carved faces. Just faces. No two faces are alike, and their highly realistic expressions of pain, of terror, of anger make Isaac shudder. The snake slithers straight across the terrace, weaving among the men in the procession, making for the center of the temple with its smooth-fitted stone walls.

Then something happens, and for a moment Isaac is confused. He and Amelie pause.

The earth has—for an instant—shuddered beneath their feet.

Everything stops. Time, the sun, the procession, sounds from the surrounding city, the wind, even the snake. The world freezes.

Then, dogs in the city begin barking.

A flock of roosting birds bursts into the air.

A deep rumble like thunder rolls through the earth and a heavy gray cloud billows from somewhere outside the walls of the temple complex, expanding up and up, blotting out the sun.

"Come on," Isaac cries, and he and Amelie hurry up the last of the stone steps. Isaac's legs are wobbly, and he falls and smacks his knee on the second-to-last step, and then he realizes that the ground is moving in all directions at once.

"Earthquake," Amelie shouts—shouts because it's unbearably noisy. Walls begin to collapse, blocks of stone crash to earth, people scream and shout, animals bray and bellow and bark, and still the earth rocks and rolls, up and down and back and forth. Isaac and Amelie try to run for the center of the terrace but are tripped by blocks of stone that heave out of the ground that boils as if it is water.

It grows darker by the minute.

The man wearing the pendant is trying to run toward

the blank wall near the center of the complex. The snake, too, makes for the wall, so Isaac pulls Amelie to her feet and yells, "Run," and they stumble onward as the earth continues to heave.

The man makes straight for the wall and then Isaac sees it. The eternity knot is carved into the stone in the center of the wall.

"There," Isaac shouts. "But . . ."

The man reaches the wall, only a few tens of yards ahead of them, but he might as well be on the other side of the ocean. The snake is close behind the man, sliding up and over the heaving and rolling earth.

Isaac and Amelie run and trip, continuing to follow.

In the middle of the confusion and fear and noise, with people falling to their knees and reaching hands heavenward, the man stops and places one hand on the wall. A door materializes there out of the stone—a great carved wooden door—and it's open.

The man turns and sees the snake. He makes a sound, and the snake slides up the man's leg and then his arm and freezes, a bracelet again. The man does not seem surprised, which surprises Isaac.

Isaac feels the *tick-tick-tick* of the watch against his palm, but he knows he must follow that man and snake.

He yanks Amelie's hand as the man steps through the door and vanishes, and the door begins to fade.

"Hurry," Amelie cries, and they both stumble for the fading door, reaching it just as it's almost gone. Isaac pushes against the wall and clutches the watch to his chest. He feels the pendant press deep and cold into his skin, so cold it burns.

Isaac wishes for that door to stay open, and then yells out loud, "Please, door, appear and open." Without any warning, it stops fading and re-forms in the wall, shimmery at first, and then real and made of wood, and it's just barely open.

Isaac summons whatever strength he has. Magic zings through him, sharp and bright. Isaac and Amelie fall through the door into utter black, and the door disappears, leaving the heaving city on the other side.

They stand in an echoing, pitch-dark space. The ground beneath their feet is solid and firm, and Isaac takes a deep breath. Amelie's hand is warm in his.

"Where are we?" she whispers.

"I don't know," Isaac says, and as he speaks, a dim yellow light, from no clear source, grows around them as if sensing their presence.

"Do you think your parents meant us to feel that earth-quake?" she asks.

He thinks about this. "I am not sure," he says. "They said my travels would be dangerous. But it seems I am to experience a number of dangers." Isaac wonders why his parents would do such a thing. Then he remembers his father's word: "training."

Maybe this is his fate. Isaac must learn to face this kind of danger. But, why?

The door behind them has vanished, the wall a smooth gray plaster. The man has disappeared. Isaac runs his hand down the silky-smooth wall where there had been a door. He turns.

They are in a long, windowless room, or series of rooms, the far wall disappearing into shadow. The walls on either side are lined with shelves, and a long table runs down the center.

On the shelves are myriad odd and wondrous objects.

"Look," Amelie says. She moves away from him now that they are alone and goes to the table. There, perched on it, frozen into its coiled bracelet self, is the snake. "Do you think this is its home?" Amelie says.

"It led us here," he says. "To this place. To that man who wore the pendant and seemed to know about the snake."

Isaac's grateful to be away from the terror of the earthquake, and grateful for the hushed safety of this place. Whatever this place is.

The shelves are crowded with objects of all shapes, sizes, colors, types. They're labeled by hand in an array of languages.

"Wow," Isaac says.

"You said it."

"It is like a museum," Isaac says. Amelie begins to walk down the room examining the objects on the shelves. "My grandfather would have loved this."

On the table next to the snake-bracelet is an open ledger. Isaac bends over it and can see entries and lists, also in a number of languages.

Amelie says, "Look at this." She's pulled out a sword, its hilt encrusted with rubies and emeralds. "And that," she says, and points.

There's a strange cap, embroidered with stars and moons. Next to it, a staff entwined with a pair of snakes wrought of gold. A pair of sandals with wings that flutter as if in a light breeze. A small carpet that floats above the shelf. A primitive burnished wood figurine with bright, white pebble eyes. A vial that gives off sparks of light as if the liquid inside is in constant motion. A snow globe with a perfect tiny house next to a perfect pond set in a perfect winter wood.

Everywhere are marvelous objects, no two alike.

"Oh, my," Isaac whispers.

He walks down the length of shelves, running his fingers along the shelf edge. The objects are labeled with a system of letters and numbers, some in ancient and some in modern alphabets, which he thinks must be recorded in the ledger. He stops before one of the items, so very familiar.

It's the—what did Kat call it?—the astrolabe that Isaac had seen in the Library of Alexandria. The astrolabe that Hypatia and the girl took through a mysterious door much like the one he and Amelie just tumbled through.

Isaac has the sudden realization that Hypatia and the girl left this astrolabe in this very place many centuries earlier.

But . . . they had been in ancient Egypt. Not South America.

Isaac steps away as the watch tick-tick-ticks against his palm.

"I know what these are," Amelie says. "These are magical artifacts. Like the snake. Oh, look at this one. I think I know what it is." She picks up a ring of mottled stone that's large enough to fit over her wrist like a cuff.

Isaac takes it back to the ledger and finds the corresponding letter and number and reads in English: "'Adder Stone. A faerie stone capable of rendering one invisible when worn, but only for a short period of time.'" He hands the cuff back to Amelie.

"Very strange," he says, awed. He reads a couple of the ledger entries. "Here's another. 'The Elixir of Life can heal a fatal wound. Or, given the right conditions, bring someone back from the dead,'" he says, and glances at Amelie.

"Ew," she says, wrinkling her nose. "That could be really icky, if someone's been dead awhile."

He looks back through the ledger again, turning the pages one by one, and then he sees that the last entry is not quite like the ones above.

Instead, he realizes, he's reading a letter. A letter from his father, addressed to him.

> Isaac, if you have arrived here, you have
> already made great progress. This is the
> Vault, which holds magical artifacts. You've
> been led here by one of those artifacts, and
> they are both useful and dangerous. They
> must be guarded at all times, for there are
> some who would use them for terrible

*purposes, to win wars or even destroy the
human race.*

*Your mother and I wish we could have trained
you properly, but it was not to be. You must
continue to piece this puzzle together.*

You, Isaac, now hold the only key to the Vault.

Isaac pulls away. *I hold the* only *key? To a Vault that holds
magical artifacts? But—*

"What is it?" Amelie says, interrupting his thoughts.
"Have you found the clue? We probably should hurry,"
she says. She moves down the room, searching the shelves.
"What do you think it could be this time?"

Isaac shakes his head and leans over again and reads,

*Now that you are in Rookskill Castle, you
should know that your next set of clues can be
found in the . . .*

Isaac has to turn the page.

But before he can, he feels the movement inside the

watch that's clutched in his right hand as it begins to stir.

Time's up. *One, two, three . . .*

Amelie is far away, down the room.

"Amelie," he shouts. "Come back at once. Now!"

She turns, her eyes wide with panic.

Isaac runs toward her as she runs toward him, the watch's quick, sweet bell echoing through the room.

. . . nine, ten, eleven, and Amelie dives for Isaac's free hand just as it rings for the twelfth time. Isaac whirls through time and space, and he has her hand in his as all goes dark.

CHAPTER 37

Moloch

Moloch waits until the Seelie have exhausted themselves with food and drink and dance, and it is deepest night in the Realm of Faerie.

Wyvern snorts, riffling his green scales as if they are feathers. Moloch knows he is impatient to lift into the sky. So is Moloch.

But now it's time. He mounts and flies Wyvern to the thin place between worlds, where they slip through. Wyvern is sleek and fast.

At last.

Moloch breathes deeply of the human air, the shadows of storms and smokes of war. Ah, misery. It hasn't smelled so good in the human world in a while.

Wyvern settles on a tall tree in the middle of the enchanted forest that surrounds Rookskill Castle. Moloch will take his own sweet time to find what he's been search-ing for, which must be hiding within the castle walls.

Not too much time, though. Moloch is salivating. When he's found the Guardian, he'll be the most powerful fae in Faerie.

No. He'll be the most powerful being in both the worlds.

CHAPTER 38

Isaac

1942

Through the tumble and whirlwind of their journey back, Isaac held on tight to Amelie so as not to lose her. He'd almost lost her in that last second.

They landed back in Isaac's room as if they'd been dumped out of a bag. It took Isaac a full minute to realize they were back, the world was spinning so furiously.

Amelie shook herself and then put her trembling hands over her eyes.

"It's all right," Isaac said to her. "It's okay. We made it." He put his hand on her shoulder. "You know I would never leave you behind. Never. I'd rather stay behind with you than leave you there alone."

She dropped her hands and looked at him with wide blue eyes. Then, slowly, she smiled and said softly, "It was kind of neat, that place. The whole experience. Except for that last bit, almost getting lost. But I'm okay."

He smiled back. Then he stood and walked to the window. "Wasn't it daylight when we left? I think the last time when I traveled I was only gone a few minutes in Rookskill time, but . . ."

Amelie stood and turned to the window. "Oh! It's grown so dark so fast."

"It looks like a storm is coming."

"It looks like a storm is already here." Amelie was at his side. "The sky. Look at the sky."

The clouds, black and purple, boiled, covering the sky and hiding the sun so that it was as dark as twilight. A fierce wind shuddered the window glass. The ground was covered in icy spittle. The forest, now right up against the castle, was thornier and taller than the castle's highest tower. The branches writhed and tossed in the wind, and the stones cracked and groaned.

"I'm thinking about Leo's prediction," Isaac said, as he exchanged a glance with Amelie. "Remember?"

She nodded. "That a storm was coming. A storm to end all storms." She hugged herself, then winced and reached into her pocket. "Oh, I meant to put this back." She held up the Adder Stone cuff. "You should take it."

Isaac raised his hands. "But I . . ." and then he remembered his father's words. *They must be guarded at all times.* He took the cuff and twisted it in his hand, examining it—the smooth variegated stone—then slipped it into his pocket with the watch. Was this his clue? Or was his clue still in the ledger—which he didn't finish reading? He'd gotten as far as reading something about Rookskill, but what? "Amelie, I need help finding some information."

Amelie waited, watching him.

"Rookskill holds answers. That is what I read in the ledger right before time was up. I need to find at least some of the remaining answers here. Maybe by finding another artifact like the snake or this cuff. Or maybe in a book." He paused. "You seem to know the library, so I'm wondering if there's a book—"

"No, I don't know the whole library, not really," she interrupted. "I know about magical creatures. If you want to know what's in the library—in fact, if you want to know anything about Rookskill, you need Leo."

"Leo?"

She nodded. "I know he seems a little strange. But Leo's spent hours in that library. Hours learning about Rookskill."

"Right, then. Let's go find Leo."

Isaac glanced out the window once more, and then paused and leaned against the glass. Was that . . . ? It looked like . . . No, it couldn't be. Isaac blinked. And when he looked again, it was gone.

"What?" Amelie asked.

"Nothing," Isaac said. "For a second, I thought I saw, well. Just my imagination, for certain." He laughed. "At the top of one of those trees, I thought I saw a dragon."

Amelie and Isaac found Leo in the library, reading.

"Brilliant," Amelie said. "Where's everyone else?"

Leo shook his head. "Dunno."

"Leo, I need help," Isaac said.

Leo gave an embarrassed half smile. "I'm not much of an adventurer."

Isaac said, "I need help finding something that may be in the library or somewhere else in the castle."

"Oh!" Leo brightened. "In that case . . ."

"What do you know about a Vault that holds magical artifacts?"

"Vault?" Leo echoed. He stared up at the ceiling. "Artifacts. Right." He stood and walked to the other side of the library, mumbling to himself. He pulled the ladder along the wall until it came to rest in the far corner, and climbed it to the topmost shelves. "Here we are. Come. I'll hand these down."

Amelie stood on a lower rung of the ladder, passing books from Leo to Isaac. Isaac took the first one and turned it in his hands.

The title glittered gold. *Secrets of the Vault: The Revised Oxford Translation.*

While Leo was handing down books, Isaac told him about the time travel he took with Amelie.

At one point, Leo paused and said, "So there was another door that appeared and disappeared, like the one you saw in Alexandria? And you think the astrolabe was left in this Vault place by Hypatia way in the past? Interesting."

Soon there was a stack of books on the table, and Amelie and Leo joined Isaac to read the first one he opened.

The title page read, *The Artifact Hunters' Diaries, Years 1753–1785. As Noted by Guardian Q.* And below that, the symbol of the eternity knot.

Isaac looked up and met the others' eyes. "This is it," he said. "Very nice, Leo."

Leo's cheeks grew red, and he mumbled, "Oh, it's nothing special. I've explored the books here pretty thoroughly, that's all. The word *Vault* rang a bell."

Isaac turned the page and began to read, and as he did, he felt that familiar hum again.

Foreword

This set of diaries spans a fraught time in human history. The magical artifacts that have been gathered in the Vault in those years are particularly dangerous, as war enhances the power of such items. In addition, those who wish to win wars will stop at nothing to use magical artifacts for evil purposes . . .

"This is amazing," Isaac said. He leafed through the book. It was filled with images and references to magical artifacts, and notes about where they were found and by whom. "Listen to this. 'The best teams are those whose members—also known as the Order—are strongly connected. Hunting for artifacts is a group endeavor. Although it is always the Guardian who carries the key, the entire cohort of AH is crucial to success.'" He looked up at the others again. "AH?"

"I'm going to guess that stands for Artifact Hunters," Leo said with a shrug.

Isaac, lost in thought, stared at the swaying tree branches outside the library window.

Vault. Guardian. Artifact Hunters.

Isaac held the key. He pressed his hand to his chest, and the hum grew. The pendant. The eternity knot. He had been holding the pendant when he thought the door in the temple wall was closing, and he begged it to open.

And the door had reappeared, opened, and dumped them into the Vault.

"The key," he said out loud. "I think my pendant is the key. But . . . where is the Vault? It seems to be everywhere."

"Or maybe it's anywhere," said Leo casually. "Anywhere you want it to be. Maybe it comes when whoever has the key calls it. I mean, we are talking about magic, aren't we?"

Amelie and Isaac both stared at Leo.

"That's good," Isaac said.

Leo turned bright red.

"Leo," Amelie said, "I know you can see the future. But have you ever thought about why?"

"Um, no, not really."

"Well, I'm wondering whether you can see the future because you know so much about the past. Because you read so much. Study so much."

Leo's eyes widened. "I like reading."

"Yes." Isaac said, "Maybe, Leo, that is your magical power. You know things. You read, you study, and that makes you really, really smart."

Leo's cheeks couldn't get any redder. He said, "Well, maybe, but . . ."

The door blew open and Kat raced into the room. "We've got a new problem," she said.

CHAPTER 39

Isaac

1942

Kat led the others to the library window. The thorns press-ing against the glass scratched at it with an agitating noise. Thick bruised clouds blanketed the sky. A low throb from the forest pushed against the castle.

"The only reason she can't get inside is because I'm still able to hold the wards within the walls themselves. But I don't know how much longer they'll work," Kat said, her voice shaky. "And I don't know if they'll work if a door is open."

"Wait," Amelie said. "She who?"

Kat pointed.

Amelie cried out, "We've got to go get her." She began to run for the door when Kat grabbed her arm.

"No," Kat said. "Look at her. Look carefully!"

Isaac pressed his face to the glass. Through the thorns

and vines and shadows he saw a figure about fifty feet away, standing still, staring at the castle. Though she looked hazy through the glass and windblown brambles, Isaac knew her at once.

"Miss Gumble," he said. "What is she doing?"

"She's been spelled," Amelie said with a sob.

"Or worse," Kat said in a low voice. "Look at her eyes. Look at her hands."

Isaac framed his face to see better. *Unnatural* was the word that came into his mind when he looked at her eyes. But her hands . . . He gasped.

They were no longer human hands. They looked mechanical. He was reminded of the mouse, the poor little mouse from the kitchen.

Amelie pulled away and began to weep. "She reminds me of her," Amelie said. "She reminds me of the witch. Like she's not Miss Gumble any longer. Poor, poor Miss Gumble."

"Yes," said Kat, her voice flat. "We'd better keep every door to the castle closed tight. Another reason not to go for her."

The library door burst open again and Baines strode into the room. "There you are. Mr. Falstone, I need you to go to the village at once. Mail this for me while I finish my paperwork."

Leo shook his head, eyes wide. "I can't."

"Sorry?" Baines said. "You what?"

"It's too dangerous now. The wards and all . . ."

"What? It's just a little rain outside. You children act like you've never seen rain before. Miss Bateson?"

Kat and Amelie looked at each other.

"Fine," Baines said. "Then I shall go myself. I'm a busy man but work must be done." He grumbled and turned away.

"You've got to stop him," Amelie said, grabbing Kat's arm. "He might completely break the wards. Or get into serious trouble."

"Right," said Kat. "Isaac, I may need your help enhancing this one."

Isaac nodded.

Kat began to whisper, "Silence is golden. Silence is golden."

Isaac felt the hum again that emanated from Kat, and he concentrated, sending the spell toward Baines, the electric vibration humming through him, an invisible bolt between Kat and Baines.

Ralph Baines opened his mouth to speak, but no sound came out.

He was wrapped in a pale golden light, frozen, a still, golden statue, completely solid, openmouthed and staring.

Leo went to Baines and tapped his arm. "He clinks," Leo whispered. "Like metal. I think he's solid gold."

"Don't worry, Leo," Kat said. "I can break the spell later." She paused and added in a low voice, "I hope."

"What can we do about Miss Gumble?" Amelie said. "Is there a spell you can use to help her?"

Kat shook her head. "I don't think so," she said. "I think she's too far gone."

"Where's Colin?" Leo said. "Has anyone seen Colin?"

"Not for a while," Kat said. "Under the circumstances, between this storm and the wards and the changed Gumble, we all ought to stick together."

"Willow?" Amelie called.

Willow appeared with a *pop*.

"Can you find Colin?" Amelie paused. "And maybe check in with Lark?"

Willow snorted. "She's a flower. We're a blob."

"But you're a lovely blob," Amelie said. "Please?"

Willow sighed and said, "Only for you, Amelie," and popped away.

Isaac returned to *Secrets of the Vault*, turning the pages, and then paused as he looked across the library at the other three, who were conferring about poor Miss Gumble.

Miss Gumble, who'd been transformed into a monster.

Isaac's grandfather had talked about the making of monsters on one warm summer afternoon after the Nazis had arrived. The two of them sat on a bench in the tiny park before the Old-New Synagogue, shooing summer bugs and watching birds flit from tree to tree.

"You remember the story, Isaac, about the golem?" his grandfather had asked, staring into the distance with rheumy eyes.

Isaac nodded.

Isaac's grandfather pointed to the topmost part of the Old-New Synagogue where the golem was rumored to be, albeit in pieces.

"The good Rabbi Loew who made his creature out of clay, eh? Would that Rabbi Loew were here today. With his creature, his golem alive, yes?" Isaac's grandfather shook his head. "That would take care of them, those Nazis."

"But wasn't the golem a monster?" Isaac asked. "A creature without a soul?"

"Of course. But the rabbi kept it from becoming wicked because he created it to protect the people of our ghetto. Such a thing we surely need today." Isaac's grandfather sighed, then stood and rubbed his hands together.

"But, how did Rabbi Loew stop it from becoming wicked?"

"Ah. Interesting question, Isaac. Very thoughtful." His grandfather scratched his chin. "I think the rabbi might have had to make a choice at some point, yes? To keep the monster at bay by breaking it was right in the end, even if that was hard. Because the right thing is not always the easiest." His grandfather stretched. "But it's time to find something to eat." He took Isaac's hand and leaned close. "I think a strudel."

A few days later, alone in his rooms, while Isaac was at school, Isaac's grandfather died suddenly and without a goodbye.

Monsters. *Frankenstein.* The monsters chasing Isaac. And how he'd always felt about himself.

Amelie came to where Isaac stared absently out the window, and she looked past him. "What is that?" she whispered, pointing upward. "What is that?" She turned to Isaac. "Didn't you say upstairs that you thought you saw a dragon?"

CHAPTER 40
Moloch

Moloch sits astride Wyvern as the dragon moves from tree-top to treetop in this forest, his dragon wings stretched wide for balance. The trees sway with the storm that Moloch knows is not a natural storm but born out of primitive magic that resides inside the forest.

Primitive magic. Moloch knows—all fae know—there are older and more mysterious magics than even the fae. Magics that come out of the earth, from the burns and rills, from the stones and sea, from lichen and moss, magics that are older than anything that breathes. These magics were born when the universe was nothing but fiery-hot gas spinning in the void. These ancient magics are greater than any magic he or any other fae can perform—with or without artifacts—and Moloch bows to their power.

But he can use them, he thinks, and smiles his broken smile. He just has to find the right way.

Wyvern spits fire into the sleet that pelts him as Moloch takes a survey of the crumbling castle.

He feels the wards in the walls, but he's sensing weakness in them. That primitive magic has breached the wards.

Moloch leaves Wyvern and circles the castle, searching. He pushes through the thorny brambles and clinging vines until he finds what he's looking for.

There.

A small door lies ajar. It creaks, and Moloch steps into a tight hallway.

He waits for his eye to adjust to the darkness.

For a human, it would be a ghastly sight. For Moloch of the Unseelie fae, it is of interest. A horrific mechanical creature that might have once been human has cornered a small, cowering boy and a dog that barks and bares its teeth. The creature turns her peculiar head to stare at Moloch. She's soaked from being outside in the storm, and her hands are fearsome pincers. She's accompanied by a dire wolf.

She stretches the pincers toward Moloch, but with a simple wave of his hand, he freezes the creature and her dire wolf. The boy cries and calls out a name. *Mumble*. Or *Crumble*.

The boy sees Moloch then and his eyes go wide and even more fearful, and he starts to back away. Moloch freezes him and his dog as well.

Moloch can sense that neither this small boy nor this mechanical creature is the Guardian.

What Moloch does next involves the simplest of the fae skills. Any faerie child could perform this trick. It is not entirely without risks, and it saps magic, making other ordinary tricks impossible. Still. Moloch can use this trick to spy.

He unfreezes the dire wolf and calls it to come to his side—which it does without hesitation—then makes the transformation work for them both.

Moloch and the dire wolf, now in disguise as boy and dog, find their way deeper inside Rookskill Castle, searching. Moloch has no doubt that he'll find his ages-long quarry.

CHAPTER 41

Isaac

1942

Kat, Amelie, Isaac, and Leo stood together at the window. It was very clear that a dragon was moving from one tree to the next. An occasional spit of flame lit up the storm, and its wide red wings were etched against the clouds as it balanced, its long neck and tail flexing.

"We need Colin," Kat said. "We need to figure out where the dragon came from."

"Do you think Colin can talk to dragons?" Amelie asked.

"I hope so," Kat replied.

"It's pretty amazing," murmured Leo. "Big, scary, but amazing."

Kat said, "I'm going to revisit the wards. Make them stronger. Isaac, can you help me with that?"

"Of course." Isaac was glad he could help protect the castle.

But he wasn't sure how he'd finish his own mission. If the clue he was to find in his last time travel was in the ledger, then he'd missed it. If it was any of the artifacts, he couldn't figure out which. Maybe he'd failed with this last time travel, as he had with the first, and even, if you counted his mistake with Hypatia, the second.

Isaac swallowed hard. He still had one more time travel to make, one more chance to understand what he had to do with the Vault, its key, and the artifacts.

One more important puzzle piece to find. But how could he deal with that, when there was a castle to protect?

Kat closed her eyes, and Isaac took the jolt of magical energy from her and harnessed it, sending it through the walls in wave upon wave.

Isaac said, "I sense that a door is open."

Kat opened her eyes. "I felt it, too."

Willow popped into view. "Can't find Colin anywhere."

"Anywhere?" Amelie asked.

"Well, we can't scour the entire castle," Willow sniped. "We're a wight, not a gruagach."

"We need to find Colin and then stay together in a safe place," Amelie said.

"What's safe?" muttered Leo.

"This is my fault," Isaac said, sinking against the wall.

"This is all because of the monster that's been hunting me. I brought these problems here."

They were all silent for a moment. Then Leo offered, with a slightly shaky voice, "I said before, and I really mean it, that even though I'm scared out of my wits, I'm with you." Leo squared his shoulders and forced a smile.

"Me too," said Amelie.

"And me," said Kat. And she added in a low voice, "Though I've got no idea how we're going to conquer the problems."

"Salt and iron," Willow sang. "Salt and iron."

"What's that?" Isaac asked.

"Yes! That's great, Willow," Leo said, brightening. "Both salt and iron repel evil spirits. Both would repel a dark fae. We need to surround ourselves with salt and iron."

"The kitchen. That's where we'll find both," Kat breathed. Then she straightened, becoming her officious self again. "Right. We'll fortify ourselves in the kitchen. We'll be safe there until we can figure out our strategy. But we have to find Colin. Leo. You go to the top two floors. I'll take the middle two. Isaac, you take the ground floor. Amelie, you and Willow go to the kitchen and help Lark in gathering salt and iron. We'll rendezvous in the kitchen in thirty minutes."

"Do we just leave him here?" Leo asked, pointing at Baines.

Kat tapped Baines with her finger. *Ping, ping.* "He won't be going anywhere, and since he's made of gold, he'll be impervious to almost anything."

"Wish I could say the same about us," Leo said, and Isaac silently agreed.

Rookskill had a mind of its own. Isaac even wondered whether it conspired to trick. He remembered what Kat had said about Rookskill and magic. That it was filled with old magic. That magic stuck to places, like lint.

Well, then. Magic—the confusing kind—was clinging to these walls, because Isaac was well and thoroughly lost in no time.

He twisted and turned down one strange corridor after another, up one set of stairs and then down another, getting more and more lost. The ancient men and women in the portraits glowered and then sneered and then seemed to be openly laughing.

He broke into a trot, turning this way and that, and then he stopped to catch his breath.

"Colin?"

Nothing. Not even an echo.

He turned and trotted back and was surprised when the

corridor dead-ended. On his left was a door, with a narrow, twisting, winding flight of stairs behind it.

These stairs led him up to a part of the castle he hadn't yet seen, and he entered a long, almost empty room with rough stone walls and no portraits, just a few tattered tapestries. The only light came from the far end, filtering down through a high opening. Isaac stood for a moment.

And then his head filled with an aching hum. A familiar hum, but painful, as someone stepped out of the shadows.

"Colin, thank goodness," Isaac said, relieved. "You must come with me. We must stick together and protect the castle, and there's a dragon you need to speak to . . ." Then he paused. "Um, Colin? What in heaven . . ."

Isaac took a step backward.

Colin stood at the far end of the room with a dog. Or a something. Because this was not Canut. This dog that looked a bit like Canut bristled with fur, and its eyes shone with a bluish spark. It had a sharp-toothed grin and its feet were the size of one of Lark's platters.

Isaac's head throbbed.

"That is not Canut."

"No." Colin smiled. "This is Daemon." He put his hand on the beast's back. "He's a dire wolf."

"A . . ."

"I heard him scratching at the door and it's so nasty outside, don't you think?" Then Colin grinned, and a chill ran down Isaac's spine. It was only for an instant. Just a flash. A shift in Colin's face. A spark of red in one of his eyes.

"We have been looking for you," Isaac said uncertainly.

"Oh, and I've been looking for you, too, for ever so long. And here you are." Colin took a step toward Isaac.

Isaac took a step back.

"What's wrong, Isaac?"

Isaac stepped back again, placing his hand on the wall, trying to find the door. This was not Colin. This was awful. An enormous threat emanated from this small boy and his giant dire wolf. Isaac groped for a way to escape.

Colin lifted his face and he sniffed the air, and Isaac shuddered as Colin's voice dropped an octave. "I've been looking a long, long time for you."

Isaac's fumbling fingers found a door handle.

Daemon growled. Colin frowned.

Isaac twisted the knob and pushed, and fell into the dark space, slamming the door and throwing the iron bolt that was on the other side, just as the wolf threw its body against the door with a thud.

Isaac leaned against the door, which was thick and old.

He could hear the wolf as it scrabbled and the curses as Colin-not-Colin tried to open the door.

As Isaac's eyes adjusted, he saw that he was in the stairwell again, and he moved fast, running, turning downward in a tight spiral. The stairs were no wider than his shoulders, and the stairwell and steps were stone. Down and down and down and at least he could breathe again as the noises behind him faded, and he wondered what had happened to Colin.

He was certainly spelled. But by what? And how?

Isaac lost count of the steps.

He needed to get to the others. He wanted to find out if Kat knew some spell that would free Colin. Isaac hoped he was heading in the direction of the kitchen but this castle was so mysterious . . .

The stonework became solid rock. The stairwell was carved into the bedrock itself. Isaac was deep inside the earth beneath the castle and nowhere near the kitchen.

Isaac stopped and leaned against the rock wall, breathing hard. What was happening in Rookskill, he was sure, was his fault.

But what, if anything, could Isaac Wolf do about it all?

Something had taken over Colin.

That storm outside wasn't natural.

A dragon perched in the trees.

Whatever happened to poor Miss Gumble was magic, of the bad kind.

If Isaac was an amplifier, if he could make magic stronger—good and bad magic—he needed to control it at all costs. Because he was sure that not only had evil followed him to Rookskill, he could make—why, he might already have made—the evil worse.

Isaac pushed away from the wall and went down the steps, faster this time. Down and down until abruptly he reached the bottom, facing a great wood door with iron strap hinges and a ring latch. He pulled and the door groaned. He had to tug hard several times to open it wide enough for him to pass through.

The castle—for good or for ill—had led him here. He was meant to be here. Yes, there it was, that hum again, his signal that magic was near. Of the good kind, he hoped.

He squeezed through into pitch-darkness.

It was cold, so cold that he wrapped his arms over his chest. It smelled musty, metallic, and old.

His feet clapped against a stone floor. As he stepped inside, a pale light grew, reminding him of the light that grew inside the Vault, although this light was blue and luminescent. He took another step and gasped.

The room was long and narrow, and the ceiling disappeared into shadow. Lining the walls of the room were figures facing the center, two rows of suits of armor, glinting faintly from their pedestals. The walls behind them were covered with armaments of war—pikes and staffs, shields and banners, axes and blades.

"An armory," Isaac said into the space. It was cold enough for him to see his breath.

Each of the knights was a little different. They stood straight, staring through helmet eye-slits. Isaac admired the workmanship, the intricate joints, the way the metal was bent to deflect a strike, the tight piecing at shoulders and hips. He walked slowly down the rows.

Then came a noise from behind him, and he turned, fast, fearing Colin-not-Colin and that wolf.

But, no.

One of the knights was no longer standing on his pedestal. One of the knights was now standing in the middle of the room.

Facing Isaac.

With a raised sword.

CHAPTER 42

Isaac

1942

Isaac braced, staring straight into the knight's empty visor. His hand went to his pocket. There was the watch, and the Adder Stone cuff. Then he pressed his hand to the pendant, cold and hard against his skin. He had magic. "So. What will it be?" he asked the knight.

The knight remained silent. It stood completely still, a ghost knight in heavy armor raising a great sword.

For an instant Isaac wondered whether he should go for one of the pikes fastened to the wall. But that was not his skill. He didn't know how to fight hand to hand. His skill was . . .

He pressed the pendant again and this time took the hum and amplified it the way he had with Kat and Amelie.

The blue light in the room began to grow. The knight began to move, taking a step toward Isaac.

"That is not what I had in mind," Isaac muttered. But he stood his ground. Squared his shoulders. He did not try to disappear or shrink away, but instead stiffened and braced and clenched his fists. The magical power that he could amplify—he could feel it, bright and good, so he knew it was not evil—zinged through him, and he even imagined he might be glowing. "But this is," he said out loud.

The knight paused and turned the sword in his gloved hands until he held the blade so that the hilt faced Isaac. Then he went down on one knee, slower than slow, with a clinking and creaking, until his knee clattered on the stone floor. The knight inclined his head.

Isaac had seen plenty of pictures. Medieval history was his favorite. This was the image of a knight swearing fealty. Surprise and pleasure flooded Isaac.

Isaac took a step toward the knight, and that's when he saw it. The sigil that the knight wore, embroidered on the tattered tunic that hung over his armor, was the eternity knot.

"Ha!" The small laugh escaped Isaac, because he could also see that the eternity knot was carved into the bronze hilt of the sword, the hilt that was within Isaac's reach. He wrapped his hand around it, the eternity knot imprinting on his palm.

The knight released the sword, and Isaac Wolf stood in the middle of the armory facing a ghost knight performing an homage on bended knee, and Isaac held a (very heavy) sword in his right hand.

He grasped the sword in both hands so as not to drop it, and even more energy surged through him, as if the sword itself fed him with a powerful force.

The knight straightened and stood and waited. The entire space around Isaac waited as the magic hummed through him until his arms began to shake with the strain and he lowered the sword until the point touched the floor and he could hold it with his left hand on the hilt. He took a deep breath.

When Isaac heard the pop in the air behind him, he didn't jump.

"What is it, Willow?" Isaac asked without turning.

"Ah," the wight said. "You knew it was us. Splendid. We've come to fill you in." Willow flitted around until they hung in the air above the knight's shoulder. "We've been around here for a long time. Maybe even since the very, very beginning. Since before the beginning." Willow paused. "We're fond of Rookskill."

Isaac waited. "So?"

"So . . . even though Rookskill is in trouble, it's time for you to use that watch in your pocket again."

"But isn't there something I should do here? What happened to Colin? Is he going to be all right?"

"Ugh," Willow said. "We saw Colin skulking through the hallways. What's happened to him is unpleasant."

"Yes," Isaac said, impatient, "but you have not answered me."

"He'll survive. They all will. We think."

Isaac's skin crawled. "You think?"

"A fae has taken Colin's form. One of the things fae can do is shapeshift." Willow paused. "As you should know."

"Me?"

"It was one of the first things we noticed about you, remember? You can shapeshift or disappear when you're scared."

Isaac was taken aback. "Wait. That's what I did when I disappeared?" He pressed his free hand on the pendant.

"You haven't figured it out yet, have you?" Willow came down right in front of Isaac's face. "It's time. Time for you to go and find the last bit of instruction. Before it's too late. Before they . . ." Willow gurgled.

"They are here, then. The hunters. The sluagh," Isaac ended with a whisper.

"Ssh! Don't use that word. Even in the armory." Willow shifted and, if they could, would have looked miserable.

"We're magical, yes. We owe loyalty to magical beings. But those evil fae? We don't go around trying to get rid of humans. What would be the fun in that? Whom would we tease? What could we steal if there were no humans left to steal from? Wights love being nasty. But we are not . . . them." Willow paused.

The wight continued. "Listen carefully. Not all the evil magic surrounding Rookskill has been made by the Unseelie fae. Some of the magic—the storm, the wolves, the trees that walk—has been brought here by a much older creature, sad and desperate." Willow sighed. "A wraith has brought primal magic to Rookskill. Magic that has little to do with you, Isaac Wolf, though it's been made stronger by your amplifying presence."

"Another magic? Primal magic?" Isaac put his hand to his forehead. He wanted to shrink away. "Willow, what if my gifts are not enough?" Isaac closed his eyes. He asked, "What will happen to the others, to Leo, Kat, and Ame? Will Colin be all right? What has happened to Miss Gumble? What about MacLarren? This is my fault."

"Ach! If you sit here moaning and groaning instead of getting on with your mission, you won't find out what you need to know. And what you find out might help."

The silence in the armory had weight. It weighed on Isaac

until he straightened, standing as tall as he could. He opened his eyes and looked into the empty visor of the knight, and then up at the evanescent wight hovering in the air.

A wolf should be a hero in a grand tale.

It was time.

"Okay, then." Isaac nodded. "You are right. You are absolutely right. I must get the last bit. I must find the last puzzle piece." And he thought, *And maybe it's the only puzzle piece I will find now, since I've missed two of the others.*

Would it be enough?

He squared his shoulders, because he had to try. He moved toward the knight, who slowly stretched out his arm and accepted the sword back from Isaac.

Willow flittered back to the shoulder of the knight, sat down, and crossed their legs. "We hope you have a pleasant journey."

"Thank you, Willow." Isaac dug into his pocket and pulled out the watch, flipping open that hideous skull and turning the crown to set the Death's Head time-travel device in motion.

CHAPTER 43

Isaac in Camelot

CIRCA 1300

Isaac knows what to expect from time travel now. The tumbling turbulence feels, this time, like flying, and when he thinks about it that way, he can control it. In fact, he can move like a bird. He rights himself and soars.

He flies through the past, through scene after scene, through day and night and winter and summer, each flashing by so quickly that the seasons are impossible to count, until he comes to a place of rolling hills and green forests. Then he flies—it's exhilarating—to a very green hill at the top of which stands a narrow castle surrounded by battlements. He circles high, high above and then down and down to the castle, the freedom of flight running through every muscle.

It's a spring day, the new leaves on the trees an iridescent green and flowers blooming white and gold in the meadows.

The air is fresh, with a snapping breeze. Isaac lands on his feet, gently and easily at the top of the tallest tower of the castle. From within the castle below come the comforting sounds of a household at work.

Isaac peers over the wall. The hill on which the castle stands is surrounded by a broad moat, and a bridge is lowered, leading to a road that runs away from the castle toward a town in the distance. People cross the bridge on horseback and on foot, in and out, and he can see from the way they are dressed that he must be in some medieval time.

There's no sign of the eternity knot. He's on a flat terrace with a crenellated edge and a single stairway leading down.

Then he hears voices, as someone is climbing the stair to where Isaac stands.

Knowing that he's invisible doesn't stop Isaac from shrinking back against the wall as two men—two knights, in partial armor—step onto the top of the tower.

". . . Majesty has hidden himself. I share your concern," says the first knight. "Something is threatening us all."

"Coming from within," says the second.

"Aye," says the first. They move to the edge of the tower, gazing out over the wall toward the town.

Isaac notes two things. First that the two speak English. Then that the second wears a familiar tunic—the same tunic (only much brighter and newer) as the knight's in the armory at Rookskill—emblazoned with the sigil of the eternity knot.

This knight is Isaac's own ghost knight, and he feels an instant kinship with this long-dead man. He's broad-shouldered with a craggy face, a trace of beard, and piercing blue eyes. He says, "There is evil sorcery at work. Last night I heard a rending cry from the forest, and at dawn heard that the old hermit living out by the stile claims to have seen wolves in the shadows. Great beasts with fierce eyes."

"Dire wolves?" asks the first, dropping his voice. "They've not been seen for generations."

"They are not, I think, of this world."

Some moments of silence pass before the first knight speaks again. "'Tis my thinking that great evil has been lured here by the bewitcher. It has an uncanny hold over His Majesty. All from a stone that has no human soul." He adds in a low voice, "I've never liked the thing."

Isaac's knight nods agreement. "All matters have become worse since the queen's banishment."

"Aye. Our king has fallen prey. The bewitcher should be locked away for the sake of the realm and His Majesty." He pauses. "And the other—Caledfwlch—as well. It is too potent. Dangerous. An object not to be left in the hands of a brooding king who has fallen prey to a fae invention."

"Agreed," Isaac's knight says. "I can count on you, then?"

"Aye. And you'll find others in our camp."

The two stare out in silence. Isaac's knight says, "We must be careful in our approach. It could be seen as treason. Our only hope lies with Mistress Vivienne."

The first knight nods. "You have my word."

They stand a moment longer, then move to leave.

Isaac, stepping behind them into the narrow stairwell, follows the knights as two words—*bewitcher* and *Caledfwlch*—turn in his mind.

The noises of the busy place grow as they descend. Smells of cooking meat and smoke, and laughter and loud talk, fill the air.

They step out into an arcade that leads into the heart of the castle and then to a great door that opens into a central room. In that tapestry-draped room the castle noises are muffled, and a dozen or so men—and women, Isaac notes, women in armor—are gathered around a great table. They're in the midst of what seems to be a heated argument.

"Where is His Majesty?" asks Isaac's knight.

"Sir Bedwyr," answers a woman knight, "he will not

listen to us any longer." She gestures toward a closed door.

Bedwyr moves toward the door.

"You enter at your peril," the woman says.

He pauses. "We're all in peril so long as the bewitcher holds him in thrall." He moves on and Isaac follows close behind, entering a chamber lit only by a low fire. Bedwyr closes the door softly.

Slumped in a chair before the fire is a man wearing a crown and a filthy cloak that drags on the floor. The room smells of smoke and sweat and grime, and even with the fire the air is chill.

"Your Grace," Bedwyr begins.

The king (as Isaac supposes) waves his hand. "No," he says, his voice a rasp. "Go away."

After a moment's silence, Bedwyr says, "Your Grace, it is time for you to remove that which troubles you."

The king stirs. "And how do you judge that which troubles me, Sir Bedwyr?"

"I would judge it to be in part the Myrddin, Your Grace."

Myrddin. Isaac wracks his memory, for he's heard that word before.

The king stands, swaying a little. "What if I judge you to be wrong, Bedwyr?" He looks up, his eyes sharp. "What if I judge you to be the source of my troubles?"

Isaac's knight, Bedwyr, drops to one knee. "You may have my head, if it please you."

Isaac sucks in his breath.

The king paces. "The Myrddin gives me advice. The Myrddin is all I have left." The king's voice cracks. "Treachery is all around me."

"The Myrddin is possessed, some would say, by an evil magic. They call it 'bewitcher,'" says Bedwyr quietly. "It tells you what you want to hear, not what you should."

"And why is that wrong?" the king asks, petulant. "Do you call it bewitcher? Do you betray me, too?" He moves suddenly toward Bedwyr, drawing his sword.

Isaac pushes backward, tripping over his own feet, pressing his back against the wall.

Bedwyr does not move but bends his head, waiting.

The king raises the sword in one swift swipe, and Isaac throws his hand over his mouth to stifle a cry.

But just as the sword reaches the top of its arc, the king pauses. "Bedwyr," he cries, choking back a sob. He lowers his arms and lets the sword fall to the floor with a ringing clatter. The king follows, bending until he kneels, facing Bedwyr, who puts out his arms to steady the king.

"I am lost," the king whispers. "You're my oldest friend. What do I do?"

"Your Grace. I would remove this burden," says Bedwyr in a soft voice. "The stone whispers lies."

They remain still for a few minutes, then the king nods.

Bedwyr rises and moves to a corner of the room. Isaac follows, sliding along the wall, as the watch ticks in his hand. Bedwyr lifts a box that holds an orb the size of a football. The orb appears to be made of glass, and it begins to glow with a white fire.

The hum fills Isaac's brain and he knows it at once. Dark magic lies within the orb. Dark magic that immediately tries to use Isaac and his skill.

The white glow is replaced by two red eyes and a grinning mouth, and the eyes are fixed on Isaac, who presses his free hand to the pendant and pushes back against the evil magic, refusing to amplify it, refusing to accept it, and then . . .

Bedwyr snaps a cloth over the orb, hiding the eyes, and the hum fades to a low hiss.

The bewitcher. The Myrddin. Isaac remembers now. He's read so many of these tales. Myrddin is another name for Merlin, an ancient Welsh name for Merlin the wizard who was mentor to Arthurian knights and to Arthur himself.

Isaac is in Camelot, near its end.

But this Myrddin is not a benign teacher. This Myrddin

is a dark fae using the orb as a spyglass, watching, waiting, searching, and turning what was good toward evil.

Bedwyr returns to the king, who has retrieved his sword and moved back to the chair by the fire. "Sire, it's time to put this into the hands of Mistress Vivienne."

The king nods.

Bedwyr says, his voice careful as he picks the words, "And Caledfwlch, as well. The sword was always meant to be returned. That was the promise made at the beginning. The Vault is waiting."

The Vault!

The king mumbles, looking up at Bedwyr with narrowed eyes. Isaac moves closer to the two of them.

Bedwyr goes on, "The orb and the sword will be safe in this lifetime. Mistress Vivienne will see to it."

"And the next?" asks the king, standing again, the sword dangling from his hand. "What of the next? Is my perfect kingdom to turn to dust and vague memory?"

Bedwyr lowers his head. "All things turn to dust, my friend. But the Guardians keep these artifacts locked in the Vault. That is their duty."

Guardians. The Vault. Isaac feels a chill. This is why he's here. This is what he needs to learn—how the Vault and the Guardian fully connect to him.

Behind him the door opens abruptly.

An old woman crosses the room, holding a heavy cane that taps the floor, echoing. Stooped, her white hair falling in countless braids that hang to her waist, her eyes blue-white, she pauses halfway across the room. "I heard my name."

"He wants to take them," the king says, petulant. "He wants to take what little magic I have left. I'm only trying to keep the kingdom alive."

Tap, tap. She moves to confront the king where he stands. "You've grown up. I may be blind, but you are not and your eyes are too far above my own," she says.

The king turns and drops slowly to one knee so that their eyes are level, but it still takes him a minute to look at her straight.

"I've known you since you were born, have I not?"

The king nods. "Yes."

"And cared for you. But I've let you rule as you would. Sometimes, mistakes have been made."

The king shifts, mumbling, but then goes quiet.

She says, her voice gentle, "All things change. All things end. These objects do not give you power. You have that all to yourself. But they must not be left loose to be used by those who would do evil." She leans closer to the king, and Isaac moves behind him so that he can overhear her whisper.

"We do not live forever. We are not masters of time. Only of what we leave behind, for good or ill. Even if it is lost in the mist of memory." She straightens and looks directly at Isaac.

He startles. He grips the watch to be sure he still has hold, but he's certain that she can see him with those white-blind eyes.

She looks back at the king. "Let go. You'll feel better for it, even as ill winds blow. You'll have the strength to keep them at bay for a while."

Bedwyr, still carrying the orb in one hand, comes to stand next to Vivienne.

The king slumps, then straightens and sighs. He stands as if weary and places the sword in Bedwyr's free hand.

Caledfwlch, Isaac realizes, must be Excalibur.

"Mistress," says the king, "I hope this is not the end of all I tried to make good."

"All things change," she repeats, touching his cheek. "What you've done here is diminish the bad that may follow." She turns and the knight follows her, and Isaac does, too.

Mistress Vivienne tap-taps her way out of the room. She and Bedwyr and Isaac pass through the gathering of astonished knights and then out into the arcade. She leads them down a long hallway draped in tapestries, away from the castle bustle and noise, then turns into another empty and silent hallway with bare stone walls, and stops.

"Here we are," she says, and leans her cane against the nearest wall. She pulls at her high collar and tugs at a chain that hangs around her neck. When it falls free, Isaac knows. It's his pendant. The eternity knot.

The eternity knot has also been scratched into this stone wall.

She looks straight at Isaac. "This is how it is done," she says.

"Mistress?" says Bedwyr.

"Not for your ears, knight, though you will play a part yet to come." She holds up the pendant. "The key opens the Vault, which appears at a place the Guardian chooses and marks with the symbol."

Vivienne holds the pendant tight in one fist, places her other hand on the wall, and says, "The Guardian requires you, door, here and now."

The wall shimmers like water. A door forms, a door Isaac recognizes, and it opens to darkness.

"Do you understand?" she asks Isaac. "The words that work make a request for the door to appear."

Leo was right, Isaac thinks.

Though he wonders how she can see him, Isaac nods, and she nods back.

"Give me the Myrddin and Caledfwlch, knight," she says. She takes the orb and the sword from the knight. "I will not return. It's time for another, who is waiting for me even now. Bedwyr, see your king to the end." The knight bows and backs away.

Vivienne turns back to Isaac. "That watch you have. It carries a witch's curse and a witch's promise. Your parents made a choice to give the watch to you, and their choice saved everything, except them. Everything else you need to know you'll find in your own time."

Isaac's heart aches for his parents, for the choice they made that has trapped them in time.

"Isaac Wolf," Vivienne says, "you are already a master of your magic. You already know what to do. Be true to your heart and believe in yourself and in the power of your friends."

Mistress Vivienne steps in through the door and before Isaac can move, the door vanishes. He's left standing before the stone wall with Sir Bedwyr.

"I cannot see you," the knight says aloud. "But I've pledged myself to the Guardian." A smile creeps across his rough face. "I think you shall see me again, though I may not be as I am today." He walks away just as the watch in Isaac's fist begins to chime the hour, its sweet bell echoing through the stone hallways of Camelot.

CHAPTER 44
The Wraith

The wraith has been watching. Has been trembling with excitement. Its newest mechanical creation lurched inside the castle through an opening in the wards. Then a fae came from nowhere to land a dragon in the topmost tree near the castle, and the fae followed its mechanical creature and her dire wolf inside.

The clouds lower as the wraith pulls ancient magic on the wings of storm. As the winds pick up, branches break and giant pines twist out of the ground. The dire wolves howl and close in tight, and the fae's dragon spits fire into streaming sleet.

Who is this fae? Or . . . does it matter?

Not to the wraith.

The wraith slithers toward the small door left ajar. Leaves rise in hurricane spirals around the wraith as it makes its way through the opening. Thorny vines trail over the threshold and wind down the hallway.

The wraith pauses, what little heart it has left beating wildly. It is so close to having what it wants. What it longs for. Her.

Parts of her, the mechanical parts, lie at the bottom of the well. Parts of her, the organic parts, lie in the chest the wraith dragged to its hidey-hole. The wraith is ready to remake her, its love. But the part of her it wants the most is trapped inside that silver thimble, and the wraith needs great magic to free it.

This confluence of evil magic on Rookskill Castle—its own primal magic and the dark fae's magic—is the wraith's perfect dream.

CHAPTER 45

Moloch

Moloch strides through the castle. He's taken his own form again—that boy is too small. Uncomfortably tight for Moloch's overlarge ego. His leathery wings brush the walls and ceilings, raking the portraits. The subjects of those portraits cower and shut their eyes, and Moloch leans a little closer, just because.

He's frustrated that Isaac eluded him in this first encounter, but at least he knows now that it's Isaac that he seeks. And, in addition to carrying the key, what a powerful skill Isaac has. He can make magic stronger. Even Moloch's magic. This is a skill Moloch can use—will use—for certain.

Finding Isaac—capturing Isaac—will give Moloch power beyond even his wildest dreams.

He finds the hallway again where the boy and his dog and that mechanical monster lie spelled. Moloch doesn't need the boy's form any longer; he needs information. He leans over and puts clawed fingers on the boy's forehead to extract his thoughts and memories. The boy stirs in his unnatural sleep and moans.

The dire wolf grumbles and sniffs at the helpless dog and salivates. Moloch finishes his task and steps away from the prone bodies, saying, "No feasting yet, my new friend. But soon."

He makes ready to go when he senses a presence at the door that leads outside. A withered, once-human wraith stands in the doorway. It grins at Moloch with saw-blade teeth. It performs a small obeisance.

Ah.

This is the source of the ancient magic that has broken the castle wards. This is the source of much of the ancient power that fills the stones of Rookskill. This is the creator of the mechanical monster that lies at Moloch's feet. Moloch acknowledges the wraith with a respectful nod, one twisted soul to another, and then goes on about his business.

A few minutes later, Moloch catches his newest prey and manages to spell her before she can scream.

CHAPTER 46

Isaac

1942

Isaac didn't try to fly back through time, his mind was so full. Instead he let himself tumble. When he landed back in the darkened armory, he sat on the cold stone floor before his knight—Bedwyr—cradling the watch and trying to make sense of what he'd just learned. He pulled out the pendant from underneath his collar and examined it, the eternity knot.

The pendant that Isaac wore was the key to the Vault. The Vault, as Leo had cleverly surmised, was anywhere it was called to be, and Isaac knew all that was needed to make that magic happen was the pendant key and the symbol on a wall—any wall—and words asking the door to appear. Mistress Vivienne had said, "The Guardian requires you, door, here and now."

The armory was deathly cold and as silent as a tomb. Willow had vanished. Isaac looked up at Bedwyr as he contemplated the answer to his most pressing question.

Once, on a bright day when Isaac would have rather been outside, his father, trying to give a philosophy lesson to Isaac, was discussing logic. Isaac sat at the table drumming his fingers, looking out at the blue sky and listening to friends shout as they chased a ball through the street, all while his father kept repeating, "Occam's razor."

"Fine," Isaac said, thinking of a blade, not an idea. "May I go now?"

"It's the principle you can use to answer any question. Can you repeat it?"

"It's the, well, sometimes you have to . . . I don't know." Isaac was ashamed at having been so inattentive. He sat up and willed himself to listen.

Isaac's father began again. "This will help you whenever you're in doubt. Whenever you need to weigh evidence and come to a conclusion. Occam's razor states that the simplest solution tends to be the right one. It's not universally true— some problems in the world are complex. But if you break them down, generally, when you need to find an answer try for the simplest solution first."

Now, sitting before Sir Bedwyr, Isaac applied Occam's razor to his question.

The pendant was the key to the Vault of magical arti-facts. The key was carried by the Guardian.

Hypatia and the Incan man had worn the pendant and made the door appear, so they must have been Guardians in their times.

Mistress Vivienne, who had worn the pendant, was Guardian in her time and said, "I will not return. It's time for another, who is waiting for me even now."

Isaac's father, who wore the pendant, was Guardian in his time.

In the Incan city, Isaac had thought, *Please, door, appear and open*, and it had appeared and opened.

Isaac's father gave the key to Isaac because . . . The sim-plest solution to this question, to Isaac's question about why he was here at Rookskill, what was happening to him through all these time travels, and what he was supposed to learn along the way . . .

The simplest answer was that Isaac was the newest Guardian of the Vault of magical artifacts.

Isaac took a deep breath as he thought about this huge responsibility.

He shoved the pendant back down underneath his shirt and rose to his feet. He was following this time-travel puzzle so that he could learn how to become the Guardian. How to use magic. How to be the Isaac Wolf he'd always wanted to be—the hero of his own story.

But the best thing—the very best thing—was that he'd made friends along the way. In the diaries Leo had found in the library he'd read about the team—the team of Artifact Hunters that worked with the Guardian. How the team was crucial to success.

Guarding the Vault didn't have to be something he did alone. Defeating dark magic wasn't something he had to manage by himself. All the others had magical skills, too. He just had to amplify them, the skills of his friends. His new family.

The Artifact Hunters.

Right, then.

Isaac squared his shoulders and looked at Sir Bedwyr. "We're going to need a plan. But first things first. Can you, and the rest of them"—and Isaac gestured down the length of the armory—"can you all fight if I ask?"

The ghost knight lifted his head, and a blue light flashed through the visor. The flash was echoed up and down the line of knights, and Isaac heard a soft hiss that sounded like *yes*.

"All right, then," Isaac said. The knights could fight with weapons. Isaac would fight with magic.

He heard the familiar *pop* and Willow hung in the air before him. "There's been a bit of trouble," Willow said.

"Colin again?" Isaac asked.

"He's still missing. But no, this is new trouble. A very bad kind. We like Amelie the best, so it's really too bad."

Isaac sucked in a breath. "What do you mean?"

"It's not very nice," Willow said, and leaned close. "You'll have to see for yourself."

Isaac made for the door of the armory. "Fine. Let's go."

Willow said, their voice a sly wheedle, "Can we recommend a more direct route?"

Isaac paused.

"If you'll allow us, we'll magic you out," said Willow. "It's much quicker. We wouldn't do this for just anybody, but because it's Amelie . . ."

"All right," Isaac said. *After all*, he thought, *I've time traveled. What could be worse?*

Being magicked by a wight, as it turned out.

Isaac thought he was being squashed into a speck of dust, then exploded back to full size. "Ow!" He landed with a thud on the floor of a room he'd never seen. Every bone in his body hurt, as if he'd been through a tumbler with rocks. He lay flat on his back, trying to determine whether anything was broken.

"Honestly, you humans with your skin and bones and other whatchamacallit thingies. You are impossible."

"Those thingies are called internal organs. Which are fragile."

"Exactly."

Isaac groaned, sitting up slowly. "Where is Amelie?"

"This way," Willow said, pointing.

Isaac stood, clinging to the furnishings, one hand on the back of his pounding head. He staggered after Willow, who bounced along in the air ahead, humming.

The wight was humming. Off-key, too.

As was Isaac's brain, all of a sudden. That magical hum filled him and it was hard to control, it was so strong. He grabbed at the doorknob, thinking he couldn't feel much worse, until he saw what was in the room on the other side of the door.

Amelie was there, all right.

She was suspended, hanging in the air, high above his head, her eyes closed and her arms open and her hair and clothes drifting like seaweed around her.

CHAPTER 47
Isaac

1942

"Amelie?" Isaac said. Was she dead? If she was dead, he couldn't begin to . . .

"Ah," came a voice from the other end of the room. "Good. You're here at last. I thought this would do the trick."

A great tall creature (no, a monster), with leathery wings and a face bearing a white scar that ran from one earlobe up through one vacant eye socket and a remaining eye that glowed a burning red, rose from a chair.

A sluagh fae, Isaac thought, as he braced himself. Just like in the book. Just like he'd seen before.

A dire wolf next to the fae also rose to its feet, shook itself, and faced Isaac with teeth bared. Willow danced in the air next to Amelie.

"Thank you, Willow," said the fae.

"Willow?" Isaac asked, thinking the wight had led him into a trap.

"We didn't know they were here," the wight hissed. "We just wanted to help her."

"Now," said the fae, in a stilted but lilting voice, "I imagine you're trying to sort this out."

Isaac still hurt all over, and the hum of magic made his head throb. The fae was trying very hard to cast some kind of spell over Isaac, and he gathered as much of his newfound abilities as he could to ward off the spell. He steadied himself against the doorframe. "Is she dead?"

"Dead? Her? No. Not yet, anyway."

Relief flooded him, and he asked, "Why? Why all this? Who are you? What do you want?"

The fae answered with a short laugh. "Ah, my young friend. Isaac Wolf." He began to move toward Isaac. "My name is Moloch. Moloch of the fae." He tapped his head. "I now have Colin's memories. But his body was too . . . confining."

Isaac squared his shoulders. He put all the energy he could muster into resisting this fae, who was probing, pushing.

"I've been looking for you and the others before you, Isaac, for a long, long time." Moloch's words barely disguised a rich pleasure. The dire wolf uttered a rumbling growl.

Isaac couldn't tell whether he was unbalanced because of the wight's transport, or because he was worried about Amelie, or because he was fighting the dark magic emanating from Moloch.

"You want to know my story. How touching. Fine, then. Once upon a time, I was a respected member of the Seelie fae. Then humans decided to steal magical artifacts and lock them away in that infernal Vault, and I, well, I helped." Moloch shrugged. "It seemed like fun at the time." Moloch's one eye glowed bright as he paused and lowered his voice. "I was rewarded by being thrown out by my brethren."

"You betrayed your own kind just for fun," Isaac said, "and you have a problem with your punishment?"

Moloch's eye glowed hot, but his lip lifted in a slight, but distorted smile. "The Seelie fae only want to have a good time with their parties and music and dance and tricks and glamour. They are silly, the Seelie. For my, *ahem*, poor judgment, they banished me to live with the Unseelie host."

The sluagh, Isaac thought, not wanting to say it out loud.

"Yes, I know," Moloch said, reading Isaac's mind. "But I've

come to respect them, the sluagh." Moloch's voice dropped an octave with that word and Isaac shuddered. "They are much more focused than the Seelie. Not very bright, but focused. They have one desire. It's grim, but it's simple. And after all, light needs the darkness."

"What did you do to Colin?" Isaac asked.

"Nothing serious." Moloch waved his hand. "All fae can make a shapeshift. I borrowed him."

I can make a shapeshift. His mother could make a shape-shift. Did that mean that Isaac's mother was . . . a fae?

"Part fae, from a distant past relation," Moloch said, reading Isaac's thoughts again.

Isaac clenched his fists. If his mother was part fae, why, then, there was only one logical conclusion.

Isaac, too, was at least part fae. That was the magic his mother gave him. He felt sick, thinking he was in any way, however distant, related to Moloch.

"It would be so nice, Isaac, if we could be friends," Moloch said, sounding pleased, "since we both have fae blood." Moloch paused. "But I sense that you have a unique kind of magic. Even now I feel it."

Moloch was tapping, probing Isaac's magical energy, and the boy had to concentrate to resist the pressure Moloch put on him. Isaac's magic zipped up his spine, and he gave an involuntary shudder, then resisted again.

Moloch grimaced. "I'll find a way," he muttered.

"Let her down," Isaac said, as firmly as he could. "Bring Amelie back."

"I will, when we come to an arrangement," Moloch said. He moved closer to Isaac and said with urgency, "I could use your gifts, Isaac. And I need that key. I need you so that I can be what I'm meant to be. Listen, Isaac. I made a bad call, I'll admit. I should have been good, but they threw me out. I could be good again." Moloch turned his head, and Isaac could only see the side of Moloch's face that was beautiful and unscarred, and Isaac's breath caught.

Moloch was beautiful. So beautiful it was impossible to look away.

Moloch needed Isaac. Wanted Isaac's gifts and the key to the Vault—Moloch wanted access to the magical artifacts that Isaac's father had said were dangerous in the wrong hands—so that Moloch could be good again. Oh, Moloch was trying very hard to break through Isaac's resistance.

But . . . Isaac shook himself. If Moloch could go from being a Seelie fae to what he was now, could go from being beautiful to being a monster, then Isaac could slip from being an uncertain boy with magical gifts and a special, magical responsibility to being a monster, too. It wouldn't take much, would it?

Becoming a monster only takes justifying one little slip toward the darkness. One little thing that seems at the time like the right thing to do.

"So," Isaac said, "if I give you the key, you will let her go?" The pendant was cold against his skin. *Isaac, no one can take this from you by force, only if you relinquish it.*

"Of course," Moloch answered. "Once you let me inside the Vault, then the Vault is mine."

"I have to let you inside?"

Moloch stirred with impatience. "Yes," he said, with a hiss. "There's a little spell, just a small spell, yet to perform."

Aha. Having to let Moloch inside the Vault meant Moloch couldn't outright kill Isaac, which might give him an edge. "So, when I let you inside the Vault and give you the key and you perform the little spell, you will go back to your world and we will all live happily ever after?"

Moloch spread his clawed fingers.

"No?" Isaac said.

The dire wolf growled and bared his teeth. "The light can't exist without the darkness," Moloch said slowly.

"That's what I thought," Isaac said. He waited a moment. Then, "I'm sorry, but I will not help you. I am sorry you lost your place. I understand how you must feel, because I do not want to lose my friends. But the artifacts inside the Vault must be protected no matter what. So as much as I care about Amelie, I will not give you the key."

Isaac paused and glanced up at Willow, who still dangled at the ceiling. He bit his lip, hoping that the wight would understand what he was trying to say, and knowing that he'd use his own magical power to amplify Willow's. "If I could magic her out of here all by myself, I would. I would take her to safety. Anyone who cared about Amelie would do that. But I cannot."

Isaac straightened and stuck his hands in his pockets. His fingers found the Adder Stone cuff. "If I am a monster, I'm going to try and be a good monster. Not fall into evil. Not like you." He looked back at Willow, meeting (he hoped) the wight's eyes. "What do you think about that?"

Moloch snarled.

Willow took the hint.

Willow magicked Amelie away, and at the same instant, Isaac slipped the cuff up his arm, called on his power . . .

. . . and vanished.

CHAPTER 48

Isaac

1942

Isaac barely had time to register his relief.

Moloch gave an anguished scream, and it was all Isaac could do not to throw his hands over his ears. And then he had a horrifying thought. What if the dire wolf could smell him? He was invisible, not gone.

As it was, Daemon was staring straight at him. Moloch's red eye searched blindly, his great leathery wings expanding around him.

Isaac couldn't just wait to be found out. He had to do something. Now.

He leapt for the open door, just as the dire wolf leapt for him, then, hoping his long legs would not fail him, ran as fast as he could.

He had no idea where he was. He ran blindly, hearing the dire wolf panting and Moloch howling. Then, just ahead, an entire segment of wall pivoted inward, and Kat stood in the opening, waving both arms frantically and yelling his name. Isaac slipped off the invisibility cuff and put on a burst of speed and dove through the opening as Kat shoved the door shut behind them, shutting out the howls and screams of Moloch and Daemon. She threw an iron bolt across the closed door.

Isaac, bending over and bracing, saw that they were in a dim, narrow passageway. "How did you know?" he asked between panted breaths.

Kat held up the scroll with the map of Rookskill. "Leo had a vision. I hope you don't mind that I fetched the map from your room. Come on." She led the way down the passage. They were somewhere behind or between walls.

"Amelie—" he began.

Kat interrupted, "I know. Leo saw that, too." Tears welled in Kat's eyes.

"Got her away. Willow did it."

Kat grabbed Isaac's arm. "Willow?" she said hopefully.

He nodded, finally catching his breath. "Do not know where she is, but she is safe for now from that monster. Where are we?"

"Inside one of the castle's hidden passages. This map really helps." She waved the scroll.

"We must get to the others. Must find Colin. Must stop Moloch."

"I know," Kat said, her face grim.

"Where's Leo?" he asked.

"In the kitchen with Lark."

"Let's start there," he said.

She nodded. "Right, then. This way."

They ran down the passageway until they came to a small door, which turned out to be behind a wardrobe in one of the upper bedrooms. They shoved the wardrobe closed behind them.

They were making for the stairs when Kat grabbed Isaac's arm and they both flattened against the wall, peering from around the corner and over the balcony.

Three dire wolves paced the entry hall, sniffing, padding from doorway to doorway, their eyes gleaming in the low light. Behind them, through the great front door now open to the outside, vines moved inward, twining around the doorframes, climbing the walls, snaking toward the parlors and libraries and stairs.

Isaac and Kat backed around the corner as quietly as they could, hardly breathing. They slipped inside one of the rooms, locking the door behind, and stared at each other, wide-eyed.

"Beastly wolves!" Kat exclaimed.

Isaac nodded. The window was completely covered by thorny vines. "The map," he said.

They unrolled the scroll and set it on the floor. Kat ran one finger down an outside wall. The words that Isaac's father had written were gone but not the symbols of people, animals, and Willow and Lark, and other moving creatures.

"What's that?" Kat said, pointing to something on the lowest floor. It looked like a spider and was labeled MAGISTER.

Isaac shook his head. "I don't know that word. But there are those wolves." The three wolves slunk from doorway to doorway. "Look at the kitchen. Willow, Lark, and those must be Leo, and Amelie."

"I know a way down to the kitchen that'll avoid running into the wolves. Come on."

CHAPTER 49

The Wraith

The wraith is inside Rookskill for the first time. It licks what is left of its lips. It wants to find the bright, shiny thimble that sits inside the pocket of the girl Kat. The wraith's mechanical creation will help.

The winds screech around the wraith, bringing leaves and debris inside, and it peers through the whirlwind.

Ah. There it is, sweet mechanical, the wraith's creation. And there is one of the children, a small boy, and his dog. But the three are spelled, frozen and mute. Who? How?

The wraith squints and then sees who, how. The fae hovers over the bodies. The fae that appeared on his dragon. This fae has a wounded soul and a lovely white scar and large leathery wings.

Oh, what the wraith could do with those wings . . .

The wraith bows. The fae inclines his head, then vanishes down the passageway, a dire wolf at his side.

The wraith waves its hand and undoes the freezing spell, and its creature comes awake.

"Find her," the wraith commands. "Find the girl. Take the boy with you."

Yes, it thinks, find the girl. *Find the shiny thimble. Find the soul of the wraith's beloved. Find.*

CHAPTER 50

Isaac

1942

Kat led the way down a narrow back stairwell. The farther down they went, the more they saw that vines and branches and brambles had invaded the castle. By the time they reached the bottom, it was almost like hacking their way through a forest. And the sounds were disturbing—cracking against the aging stone walls, grinding over wood doorframes, the occasional thudding as a portrait was yanked off a wall.

"The wards are gone," Kat said, her voice a tremor.

When they reached the kitchen and thrust open the door, they came face-to-face with Lark. Her feet were planted wide beneath her huge orange petticoat, her bright pink hair standing up on end, her eyes wide as saucers. She brandished a pair of kitchen knives, one in each hand. Behind her, lying on the kitchen table, was Amelie with Willow floating above, flitting back and forth. Leo stood on the far side of the kitchen, and the ghost cat zipped from one corner to another.

"Thank the moonglow and starlight!" exclaimed Lark, lowering the knives. "It's been all we can do to keep the forest from strangling us."

Isaac went straight to Amelie, his heart in his throat.

"It's such a strong spell," said Lark. "Ghillies can reverse spells, but this one is terrible strong. Ghillies have lots of hidden powers," she added with a snarky glance at Willow.

"We are not without," Willow sniped.

"What if I helped?" Isaac asked Lark. "What if I amplified your spell?"

"Oh," said Lark, coming to his side. "Oh, yes, please."

Lark leaned over and began whispering, and Isaac felt the hum at once. He channeled it right through his heart. When he did that, he could direct it, an electrical charge over which he had control. He focused Lark's magic with all the emotion and energy he could manage.

"Wow," Kat whispered.

"Goodness," from Willow.

And then, "Hullo?" It was Amelie. "Isaac?"

Isaac grinned and she smiled back and he was warm all over. Everything around her—everything around him and

Lark, too—glowed blue as if they radiated intense energy. The magic buzzed inside Isaac, slowly fading away.

He had power. He used magic. He was part fae, but he didn't have to be a monster.

Amelie sat up slowly. "What happened? I only remember how it was so dark."

"Moloch," Isaac said. "That's his name. He's an Unseelie fae. He spelled you to get to me."

"But, why?" said Kat.

"Because I have the key to the Vault of magical artifacts."

"Yes!" said Leo.

"My father gave me the key, and, Leo, you were right. The Vault comes to the command of the Guardian who has the key. Which is what Moloch wants. When my father gave me the key, he made me the new Guardian."

"Oh, but, wait," said Leo, agitated. "That's not quite right. Not from what I read. Not quite."

"Um, but . . ." Isaac paused. "What is it, Leo?"

"This is important," Leo said, pacing. "You have to accept. You have to finish the spell."

"Finish the spell," Isaac echoed, remembering Moloch.

"Right. You aren't the Guardian yet, officially, until you finish the spell. This is a very dangerous spot to be in. If Moloch gets inside with the key before you finish the spell—rather like taking an oath, but it has to be done inside the Vault—then he'll be able to become the Guardian. And because he wouldn't hesitate to use the artifacts for whatever evil purpose, he could be the most powerful being in both the fae and human worlds."

There was a long silence.

Until something thudded against the door.

"Salt," Willow cried out. "Quick! Salt and iron."

"Oh," Lark cried. "Of course." She ran to a shelf and yanked at a burlap bag, then dragged it to the door and began spilling a thin trail of salt across the threshold.

Kat grabbed a great iron frying pan, wielding it like a tennis racquet.

The door shuddered, with a *boom, boom.*

"If we can get to the armory," Isaac said, "we'll have all sorts of iron in addition to reinforcements."

"What armory?" Amelie asked.

"Very, very deep," Willow said. "An ancient part of Rookskill. Now with bright swords buried there in the deepest part of the castle."

Thud! The door hinges began to work. A nail popped out and flew across the kitchen.

"Isaac," Kat said. "Look at the map. I think there's a stair-case behind the hutch."

Isaac and Amelie bent over the map. "Yes! It's there," Ame cried.

Bang! One of the hinges popped off the wall.

Isaac ran for the hutch and began to shove. "Leo, Amelie, give me a hand."

They pushed as Kat and Lark braced for whatever was trying to come through the door. The hutch budged an inch, when . . .

Bang!

Both hinges popped, and Kat and Lark leapt aside right before the door crashed to the floor of the kitchen.

"Oh," cried Lark.

"Oh, by all the saints," whispered Amelie. "How horrible."

"Miss Gumble?" Kat asked. "Oh, Miss Gumble."

The monster version of Miss Gumble, with blank eyes and pincer hands, stood in the doorway. Clutched tight in one of those pincers, dragging behind her like a sack, was the limp body of a still-unconscious Colin.

CHAPTER 51
Isaac

1942

"Push," Isaac said as he shoved at the hutch. "Now."

Lark stood her ground, armed with her kitchen knives. "Ha! Can't come over the threshold. Salt."

"Oh, Miss Gumble," Kat said again, her voice full of sorrow, and she lowered the frying pan.

"We've got to get Colin," Amelie said. She moved away from the hutch and toward the prone boy.

At that, Gumble took a heavy step right over the trail of salt.

Lark tripped backward. "No."

Kat bent and tapped her finger from the salt to her mouth. "Sugar, not salt!"

"Oh," Lark wailed. "I'm hopeless!"

"Push," Isaac cried, as the monstrous Gumble dragged Colin across the threshold. Isaac and Leo shoved as one, and the hutch opened to reveal a doorway. Isaac grabbed Amelie's arm, and then . . .

. . . everyone froze in horror.

Slithering behind the unconscious Colin was an even more hideous being than Gumble. Not human (at least, not any longer), not animal (except for horrible sharp teeth and long fingernails), the creature looked straight at Kat, raised one bony arm, and pointed. And gurgled.

Kat took a step away, dropping the frying pan with a clang.

Lark cried out and fled to the far side of the room.

Willow gave a shriek and retreated to the ceiling. "Wraith! It's the wraith."

The hum rose in Isaac, the hum of an ancient dark magic, and he wrestled with it, tried to contain it. He could read this wraith's tortured mind.

There was so much confusion, such hatred, in that miserable wraith, and it harnessed a magic different from Moloch's—older, deeper, more primitive. Isaac's mind filled with images of bones and sinew, pits of slithering vipers, giant spiders, and tortured creatures fused with wheels, pins, cogs—mechanical nightmares like the poor little mouse and Miss Gumble. The horror of those images chilled Isaac, froze him, made his knees weak.

But Isaac felt something else deep inside the wraith: longing and desire. Isaac sensed that the wraith wanted love, wanted the love of something it had created, wanted the love of the woman whose soul was locked inside Kat's thimble, had wanted that love for the longest time, had missed its chance at that love, and the sadness of this realization made Isaac want to weep.

He was frozen with sadness, with the wraith's terrible unmet desire.

Amelie grabbed Isaac's hands and forced him to look at her, forced him to look into her blue eyes. "You can stop it. Courage."

For the second time, Amelie's strength fed Isaac's.

He met her gaze and slowly nodded, turning as the wraith sidled toward Kat and took her right arm, and Isaac knew what it sought.

"It wants your chatelaine, Kat," Isaac said. "It wants the thimble. It wants what's inside. It calls itself *magister*, and it wants that trapped soul."

"I mustn't let it have it," Kat wailed, "but I . . . I can't . . . move."

Isaac reached into his pocket as he stepped toward the wraith and pulled out the watch, holding his hand open so the wraith could see the watch. The wraith paused, staring, mesmerized by the grinning Death's Head skull.

Isaac opened the skull to reveal the mechanism, and the wraith gave a tiny squeal. It fixed its eyes on the watch and dropped Kat's arm, just as Isaac had hoped. It moved toward Isaac, reaching.

Now if only Isaac could do what he must.

"I'm going to use the watch," Isaac said, not taking his eyes off the wraith. "For you, it will feel like no time at all. But I'll take this creature with me and leave it in another time."

"But, where?" Ame asked. "Where, and when?"

"I don't know," he said. "I'll just have to—"

A sudden noise came from somewhere outside the kitchen, a howl and then, most horribly, laughter. Diabolical, triumphant laughter.

"Moloch," Isaac whispered. His hand was extended toward the wraith, the watch open on his palm, and the wraith started at the noise outside and began to turn away.

Isaac had to act. He had to act now.

"Get ready," he said, speaking fast. "Make for the armory. Amelie, you and Lark grab some of the cast-iron pans to ward off Moloch. Leo and Kat, take Colin. But, Willow, you wait for me here."

Willow whimpered.

With his thumb on the crown, Isaac kept his eyes on the wraith, who looked confused, its head swiveling from the watch to Kat and back. "It's all going to happen very fast." He took a breath.

"Now."

With his left hand, Isaac grabbed the wraith's arm, and with his right hand he turned the crown of the watch a quarter turn and set the time machine in motion.

CHAPTER 52

Isaac and the Wraith in London

CIRCA 1870

Isaac and the squirming wraith swirl through space and time. The wraith makes squealing noises, as if it's in pain. Isaac, knowing what to expect, clutches the wraith's arm tight. When they land, they land on cobblestones at night. Isaac rolls to his feet, releasing the wraith.

Isaac's other time travels had been set by his parents. This time, he wasn't sure what to do so he focused on one thought: the inscription on the seal of the casket and the meaning of the watch itself.

Memento mori.

Which is exactly what he sees when his head stops spinning. Isaac turns toward a shop window, a photography studio. The mullioned window is filled with portraits, and painted on the glass are these words:

Memento Mori

Jos. Baker, Photographer

They've landed on the street in the middle of the night. The street is lit by flickering gas lamps, and the air is damp and thick with fog. The only sounds are faint and distant—a horse's slow clop, the squeak of a carriage, a foghorn. It smells fishy, smoky, and wet.

Isaac steps closer to the shop as the wraith still squirms and whines behind him. Some of the portraits are family groups, some individuals, all dressed in Victorian clothing. But they seem a little odd, and as Isaac stares in the dim light, he sees why. Even though their eyes are open, even though they all appear to be alive, in each of the pictures one of the people is dead. In some, a ghostly figure hovers in the background.

Isaac reads the card, printed by hand, that sits inside the window.

**Photographs of you and your deceased
loved one. Spirit photographs.
Together forever, never apart.
Mementos to treasure.**

Ugh. Isaac steps back. He must be somewhere in Victorian England—London, he guesses. He remembers reading that spirit photographs had been a popular notion in Victorian times. It seems an apt place for him to land with a monstrous wraith, the kind of monster memorialized by Poe and Shelley. Isaac will abandon the wraith in London not terribly long after the publication of *Frankenstein*.

The watch tick-tick-ticks in his palm.

He takes another step back and is suddenly thrown, hard, to the ground, a searing pain in his leg.

Isaac can't help letting out a yell. As he smacks the ground, his fist opens and the watch rolls away, with a *click-click-click* on the cobbles, coming to rest at the edge of a grated opening that leads to the sewer. The watch perches precariously, its skull mouth grinning at him.

This is *mori*, it seems to say.

The wraith has bitten into his calf, hard, and hasn't let go. Isaac kicks at it and tries to wrestle away. The pain is excruciating. He kicks harder, and the wraith finally jumps back with a snarl.

Tick-tick-tick from the edge of the sewer. If he can't get to that watch in time, or if it rolls into the sewer . . .

The wraith springs on top of him again. "Get off," Isaac yells.

He hears a whistle and a shout from the far street corner. Two policemen run toward Isaac and the wraith as they struggle on the ground. He remembers from the Alexandria library—in letting go of the watch, he made himself and the wraith visible.

The wraith pulls away, making for the watch in a quick crab-crawl.

"No," Isaac yells, and the policemen's footsteps grow louder.

"Here, you," one of them shouts. "Stop!"

Isaac leaps over the wraith just as the watch begins to ping its sweet but deadly chime. *One, two, three . . .*

How? Not enough time.

It must be short on time because Isaac didn't fully wind the watch. *Four, five, six . . .* He throws himself forward, over the wraith, reaching, his fingers just shy, and the wraith shoves Isaac from behind. His fingers brush the watch and it starts to roll down, down, but Isaac pulls and reaches until he can wrap his fingers around the skull—*ten, eleven, twelve*—safe in his fist.

As Isaac takes hold of the watch, the police arrive. The wraith scrabbles on the ground behind the vanishing boy, and the police reach to grab it. Isaac sees their bewildered faces as he falls back through time, now a ghost to them, while they are left to struggle with an abominable monster.

CHAPTER 53

Isaac

1942

Isaac fell right back into another commotion.

Everyone was exactly where they were when he left, but they sprang into action when he returned. Leo and Kat ran for Colin, hoisting him between them as they fended off the dreadful Miss Gumble, who reeled with confusion, having lost her creator. Amelie and Lark, carrying frying pans, made for the hutch and the door behind it while Willow hovered above Isaac.

"Willow! Wait," Isaac shouted. "Wait until they're all through the door."

Willow made whimpering noises as they zinged back and forth overhead.

From the shadows of the hallway outside the kitchen, surrounded by brambles, Moloch appeared, his single red eye piercing the dark. Ame and Lark were through the door, and then Leo and Kat with Colin, and Isaac put his shoulder to the hutch and shoved it shut just as they disappeared. Isaac grabbed the scroll map from the table.

Moloch grinned. "I don't need them, do I? I just need you." Daemon bared his teeth and growled.

Moloch looked up at Willow and pointed at them. "Don't you dare."

Willow zipped back and forth, faster and faster, saying, "Ow! Ow, that hurts! Ow!"

Isaac shouted, "Willow, now."

Willow screeched and magicked Isaac away. In the instant before disappearing, Isaac saw Moloch's expression change from triumph to anger, and he heard the dire wolf howl.

Isaac landed in the armory before the others had made their way down, which was good because being transported by Willow hadn't gotten any easier.

The bite on Isaac's leg throbbed with agonizing pain. He dropped the scroll and sat on the floor and gingerly pulled up his trouser leg. The deep bite into his calf bled, oozing thickly with a greenish tinge. Poison?

"Ow," Willow whimpered. "He can even hurt a wight. We don't like him. Not one bit. We don't like you, either, making us wait there."

"Oh, boy," mumbled Isaac as he examined his leg.

Willow lowered themselves to look. "Death bite," they said. "Maybe it serves you right for making us wait." Then Willow added, more quietly, "Or not."

"Wonderful," Isaac said. "Do not have time for this." He stood, exceedingly dizzy. Whether it was the bite or the Willow-magic, he lurched and went down again. "Sir Bedwyr," he said. "We need you."

From Bedwyr's visor came that quick blue flash.

"Wow." It was Amelie. She and Lark, with Kat and Leo supporting Colin, made their way through the heavy door into the armory. "I never knew this was here."

"Very magical place, this," said Lark. "Ancient. Those knights, of course, found their way here later but this part of Rookskill is old. Almost as old as the oldest magic."

Almost as old as the wraith, Isaac thought.

Kat and Leo brought Colin to lay him next to Isaac. Lark put her hands on Colin to revive him from his spell, and he sat up. "Where am I? Where's Canut?"

"Isaac?" said Amelie, touching Isaac's arm. "What's wrong?"

He gazed at her as if through a haze. "Lots of iron here. Safe."

"Show them," said Willow. "Show them what's going to kill you."

Isaac pulled at his trouser leg again. The bite foamed green, and his calf had swollen grotesquely.

"What is that?" Kat asked. "What happened?"

"Wraith bite," Isaac said. His tongue felt like lead.

"You need an antidote," Kat said.

"But where? Where's an antidote?" Amelie asked, her voice pitched high.

"I know," said Leo eagerly. "I know what he needs. It's in the Vault. I read about it in the history of artifacts. There's one called the Elixir. The Elixir of Life. One drop and it revives anyone close to death. More, and it can even bring back the dead."

"I remember it," Amelie said. "The Elixir of Life. We read about it when we were there, Isaac."

"All right," said Isaac. The air around him was fuzzy. "After a nap."

"No," said Amelie, her voice sharp. "Now, Isaac. You're going to call the Vault now. We need to get you the Elixir. Come on." She pulled at him roughly, and he staggered to stand, leaning heavily against her.

"What's going on?" Colin asked.

Amelie dragged the limping Isaac to a blank wall. "Right here. All you need is a wall, right? Just that and the key and the request?"

"I guess," Isaac said. *Was that right?*

"Get the key," Amelie said. "Now."

He fumbled with his shirt. That's where the key was, right? He thought so. He pulled at a chain. He tugged it out and wrapped his cold hand around the cold pendant at the end of the chain. "Cannot remember."

"You have to," Amelie said. She had him by the arms, holding him against the wall.

"Okay," he mumbled. "Um, hello."

Nothing happened.

Kat began to weep.

Then, with metal scraping on stone, Bedwyr moved toward Isaac, lifting his sword as he came. Isaac's head swam as he watched the sword. Bedwyr was going to kill him, right there.

Bedwyr raised the sword level with Isaac's neck, then pressed the point against the stone wall. He pushed, tracing with a slow *scratch-scritch*, as he made a mark on the stone.

The eternity knot.

Isaac remembered then. Bedwyr knew. Isaac needed the symbol to form the door. And the request. Images and words swam up in his memory—the woman called Mistress Vivienne—and he said, "Guardian. Requires you. Door. Here and now. Please."

He felt it then, the door, as it formed beneath his hand, and the other children gasped as he and Amelie tumbled into the Vault and the door disappeared.

The two of them were inside. Isaac had a profound desire to sleep.

"Come on," Amelie said. She dragged him toward the table with the ledger since he was unable to put weight on his injured leg. "We've got to find the Elixir."

Isaac fell against the table.

Amelie opened the ledger and leaned over it, scanning it quickly. "Isaac, there are instructions here. To become the Guardian, you need to recite that spell, like Leo said. It's all right here, in detail. I'm going to find this elixir."

"Right." He leaned his head on the table.

"Elixir, elixir," Amelie murmured, turning the pages. Turning and turning. "There. That's it."

She ran, disappearing in the low light of the Vault.

Isaac lay with his head on the table for what seemed like forever. The world had become very pleasant. Dreamy. His head swam and he couldn't see anything any longer, just an inky black. Nothing mattered.

He took the chain from around his neck and placed the chain and pendant on the table next to his cheek. Amelie could do it. She could be the next Guardian. There was no reason he had to stay any longer. He pulled the Death's Head watch and Adder Stone cuff from his pocket and put them on the table, too.

He felt Amelie's hands on his face, warm and soft. "Hmm," he said. "Take key. Be good. Be strong."

"No," she said. "You're going to drink this."

"'Kay."

"Isaac, open your mouth."

He tried, he really did, and then felt a cold liquid on his lips and he licked.

It hurt like nothing ever had before.

The pain shot from his mouth, down his throat, down through his whole body to his legs and then back. It was beyond pain—blinding, searing, hot and cold at once. His insides cramped, and he feared he would be sick and then all his muscles went rigid. He gasped, trying to suck in air, and sat bolt upright, eyes wide.

"Isaac?" said Amelie in a small frightened voice.

He saw her then, standing with a vial in one hand and the stopper in the other, her eyes full of concern, full of tears. He gasped, and then said hoarsely, "I think I'm going to live."

When Amelie put down the vial and threw her arms around him, Isaac felt hot and cold and knew his face must be glowing red. "Um, thanks to you," he said, looking at his hands. "Thank you."

"Don't ever do that again," Ame said a little angrily. "You're supposed to be the Guardian, not me."

He reached down to the wound on his calf, surprised that it no longer hurt at all. "I heard you say something about instructions?"

Amelie took him by the hand and pulled him to the ledger. "Right here. Read it."

In the ledger was the note from his father that Isaac hadn't been able to finish reading the last time he was inside the Vault with Amelie. He started reading, out loud, from the beginning:

Isaac, if you have arrived here, you have already made great progress. This is the Vault, which holds magical artifacts. You've been led here by one of those artifacts, and they are both useful and dangerous. They must be guarded at all times, for there are some who would use

*them for terrible purposes, to win wars or even
destroy the human race.*

*Your mother and I wish we could have
trained you properly, but it was not to be. You
must continue to piece this puzzle together.*

You, Isaac, now hold the only key to the Vault.

*Now that you are in Rookskill Castle, you
should know that your next set of clues can
be found in the library, in the volumes of
Guardians' diaries. They will tell you about the
Vault and your team of Artifact Hunters.*

Isaac looked up at Amelie. "That was Leo's find," he
said.

"I want to be one," Amelie said. "An Artifact Hunter."

Isaac smiled and read on:

*But there is one thing you must do to
accept your role. And yes, it is yours to accept.
I can no longer protect the Vault.*

*I'm writing this just before leaving the city
of Pumapunku. As your mother and I travel
again I will leave instructions for a future
Guardian to tell you the words to bring the*

Vault and enter it. I will ask that Guardian to add here the spell that makes you Guardian, because it is too dangerous for me to put this down all at once.

And I will give you the key when we meet during the last time travel that your mother and I will make.

Once you've said the spell and assembled your team of Artifact Hunters, you must seek magical artifacts around the world before they are found by those with evil intentions, and lock the artifacts in the Vault. That is your future.

Magic can be unexpected, so we hope to see you again one day.

Your loving parents.

Isaac paused and cleared his throat, suddenly thick. Amelie put her hand on top of his. "Okay," he said. "Here's the next. This one's from someone else."

From my vantage point, we have just met, Isaac. From yours, I have been gone many centuries.

These are your final instructions. It was

your father's hope that by the time you read these words you would better understand the scope of your duty. He and your mother had no choice but to send you through peril, for it is the duty of the Guardian to go into danger to retrieve and protect artifacts. It is in times of war, in times of catastrophe, in times unsettled that magic is most powerful and most vulnerable to the forces of evil.

The Guardian—you—must keep those artifacts safe. The Guardian—you—must collect your Artifact Hunters.

To become the Guardian, you must recite a simple spell. Standing inside the Vault with the key in your hand, you must say, "I accept" three times, and it is done.

From that moment, until you relinquish the duty to another, you are the Guardian as I have been in my time and your father will be in his. Being the Guardian will make you a target, but also give you extra magic.

I leave you in hope.
Vivienne

"She was there the last time I time traveled," Isaac said to Amelie. "In Camelot."

"Camelot." Amelie's eyes began to shine. "What I wouldn't give to see that."

"Maybe we can go there sometime," Isaac said. "To the happy Camelot. When all this is over."

The pendant lay on the table. Isaac picked it up in his fist. It was suddenly a heavy weight. He looked at Amelie and she nodded.

He clutched the pendant and said, "I accept."

The Vault echoed with whispers. He heard again the familiar hum in his brain, and the pendant grew unexpectedly hot in his fist. Amelie's eyes widened.

"I accept," he said, softer.

This time the whispers grew to loud mumblings, some sounding welcoming, some threatening. Isaac's hand tightened on the pendant, now icy cold. The hum grew to a zinging bolt of energy that coursed up his spine and back down, and he had to brace against the table with both arms.

He would become a target.

Be strong, Isaac Wolf.

He thought of Miss Rachel, sending him away when she was taken. Of Hypatia who sacrificed herself to save him, of the Incan man who showed him the Vault, of Mistress

Vivienne who left him these words, all of them past Guardians. He thought about his parents and what they had sacrificed to leave him the information he needed, and how they'd feel if they could see him now.

Isaac squared his shoulders. "I accept!" he shouted, and his voice echoed endlessly through the long and shadowy Vault.

I accept! I accept! I accept!

CHAPTER 54

Moloch

When Isaac vanishes before him for the second time, Moloch curses his miserable stupidity. How could he let a child get away with that ridiculous wight? He'd magic the hutch away and follow the children himself, but one of them left a pile of cast-iron pans up against the door and he can't get past those.

And the children have descended deep into the oldest part of this castle, into a bright place so rich with good magic that he doesn't dare follow—and speaking of iron, he can feel it, so hot and bright that it lights up the scar on his cheek with searing pain.

When Isaac disappeared with the wraith and then reappeared seconds later, why, that was disturbing. Isaac must have used the Witch's Watch to leave the wraith in some other time and place.

"Wouldn't dare do that to me," Moloch mutters. "Would. Not. Dare."

Without warning, a pain pierces Moloch's head like a driven spike.

Isaac—a child!—has just assumed the role of Guardian. Ach! He's spoken the words. Now he'll be even stronger.

The hideous creature on the floor behind Moloch twitches mechanically and makes a high-pitched whining noise as if she's experiencing some electric shock.

"What's wrong with you?" he says. He kicks her, to make her be still.

Moloch will make Isaac pay. He'll fix these foolish children for good. He can't stand losing to children, after all his searching.

The mechanical thing whines again.

"What in the world is that screech?" he yells.

He turns and waves his arms angrily over the creature, who stops twitching at once and falls as still as death. He steps over the body.

And then pauses and sniffs the air.

When Isaac took the wraith away through time and space, something changed. The powerful old magic that the wraith brought to Rookskill is beginning to fade. The creature on the floor has started falling to pieces, the vines have begun to wither and retreat, and even Daemon steps back as if he wants to slink away.

Enough, then.

Moloch raises his arms and calls on all fae magic. He's been holding back, but he's done with half measures. He'll murder them all, any who get in his way, whether human or fae.

He'll harvest their souls. Go full sluagh. He grins, his face twisting.

Becoming one with the Unseelie, forever a dark fae, forever harvesting human souls and preying on misery—becoming a true sluagh—requires a sacrifice. He pulls out a small knife made of glass.

Standing in this ancient castle with the magic that permeates the very stones, Moloch summons the most evil powers in the universe with a spell.

First he pierces his wrist and his fae blood drips onto the floor, hissing like acid. Then he raises the knife and cuts his face, a cut across his cheek to mirror the scar on the other side, and again his fae blood drips.

He is no longer a Seelie fae from any angle.

Moloch's skin tightens; his wings grow larger. His heart

shrinks and becomes hard, his remaining eye turns blood-red, his teeth sharpen to points. He was frightening before; he is terrifying now.

He wants humans and the Seelie to suffer.

As he says the last words of the spell, the room grows black as pitch and the wind whines through cracks and window jambs. The wraith's creature on the floor stirs, Daemon perks up, and the forest resumes its assault.

Moloch grows huge, terrible, a dread being.

With Daemon padding behind, Moloch strides through the castle toward the great front door, pushing aside the forest as he goes, his footsteps thundering against the stone.

Just as he reaches the door, Moloch catches from the corner of his eye the glint of gold, and he finds his way into what had been a library. A golden man is stuck in a spell, still alive, though as solid as can be and entirely covered by vines and leaves and forest litter.

Well, well.

He's part of this castle and that's enough for Moloch, who waves his hand, muttering a spell.

The golden man doesn't change outwardly, but Moloch knows he'll never be the same, and he grins, a lopsided, warped, sharp-toothed grimace as the fresh blood on his cheek still drips. When all is finished, Moloch will come back and release this new monster, with some added embellishments, into the human world.

He turns and goes outside and calls through the storm to Wyvern, who gives an answering bellow and blast of fire.

CHAPTER 55

Isaac

1942

When Isaac and Amelie walked through the door and back into the armory, the others swarmed to them.

"Is everyone here okay?" Isaac asked. "Colin, are you all right?"

Colin nodded and whispered, "I want to find Canut."

"We'll find him," Amelie said, patting his shoulder.

"What happened?" Kat asked. "Did you find the antidote?"

Isaac showed them his leg, and said, "If it wasn't for Amelie—"

She interrupted him. "Isaac is Guardian now. The Guardian of the Vault."

"Brilliant," said Leo.

"And I'm going to be an Artifact Hunter," said Amelie with a smile.

"What's an Artifact Hunter? It sounds amazing," Colin said. "Can I be one, too?"

"I am hoping we will all be part of the team, when we get through this," Isaac said. "There's a lot to talk about, but first we have one big problem still to deal with. Moloch."

"Tell us about Moloch, again," Kat said.

"He's the one that spelled me," Amelie said. "He's horrible. Evil."

"And he stole me," said Colin. "I can still feel him reading me. My memories. Thoughts. Feelings." Colin shivered.

"Leo," Isaac said, "what do you know about him?"

Leo shook his head. "He's not in any of the books."

Isaac said, "He told me he was banished by his own people to live with the Unseelie. It seems he has taken up Unseelie qualities."

"Well, if he's gone completely to the Unseelie side," said Leo, "it won't be easy to get rid of him. He could probably put us all in a spell and make us do anything he wanted. He might even, well, he might, um, take us. You know, like a true not-going-to-say-it. He might harvest us, as they say."

The armory was still, silent, cold as death.

Leo cleared his throat. "Except maybe you, Isaac. Your gift might hold him off."

"Maybe," Isaac said. *Maybe.* "But if we stick together . . . I think we need a plan."

"If you can help me, Isaac," Kat said, "I might be able to work a spell over him. I could possibly undo some of his power. Or send him back to the Realm of Faerie."

"I have an idea, too," said Amelie. "I can work with the ghost knights. They can give us some protection." She motioned to Bedwyr, whose visor flashed blue. The flash was echoed up and down the ranks of knights in the armory.

"I don't have any ideas at the moment," said Leo, and he shrugged.

"Leo," said Isaac, "I have a feeling you will come up with something when we need you the most."

Leo turned beet red.

"Well," Colin said, "I've been there, being possessed by him, and even though I don't want to go through that again, I'm with you. Maybe I can talk to that dire wolf."

Isaac nodded at small Colin, standing up bravely.

Kat murmured, "We've got to try," and Amelie murmured agreement.

"I'm in, too," said Leo.

"Moloch does have a dragon," Isaac said. "At least, the dragon appeared outside at the same time he did."

"Dragon," Colin said, looking brighter. "Ooh."

"Ahem," said Willow. "Not certain we can be of help."

Lark murmured, "Nor I," and danced in little bobbing movements beneath Willow, her full now blue skirts bouncing.

"I think Willow and Lark should stay behind," said Amelie. "You two can look after things in the castle. Willow, why don't you try and find Canut?"

"Yes, please?" said Colin.

"We can do that, as long as we don't run into *him* again. You always were our favorite, Amelie," Willow said, and blew kisses.

Isaac said, "All right, then. Let's find a way out of here that is a bit easier than those stairs, since we will be with the knights."

Kat unrolled the scroll and they all crowded around. "There." She pointed on the map. At the far end of the armory was an old door, shorter than Isaac was tall, that opened onto a long tunnel, which led away from the castle.

"Looks like it ends up on the edge of the cliff," Leo said.

"That will be perfect," said Isaac. He looked up at the others. "Are you ready?"

***

The knights, about two dozen in all, formed an orderly line and then began a slow march toward the door out of the armory. The children followed.

"Goodbye," Willow called. "Good luck. You might just survive. And if not, you can always become ghosts and join us."

"Well, that's comforting," Colin muttered.

"I'll make a beautiful pie for when you get back," Lark called.

"But don't eat it," Leo whispered unnecessarily.

The long, dim stone tunnel rose slowly upward. The air was close, and except for the soft clink of armor, it was still and silent. The faint blue light radiating from the knights guided them, and the walls of the tunnel closed in until Isaac had to hunch low and tilt his head. The knights were shorter than he was, even in their armor. They marched on and on, slowly, up and up. Isaac had to trust that the tunnel was leading them to a place where they could make a stand and face Moloch on their terms and not inside the confines of the castle that was overrun by forest magic.

Closer and closer, the walls of the tunnel drew on either

side until Isaac began to smell the salt air of the sea and hear the distant pounding of surf. Then cold air rushed in on them, and they emerged into the chill of early evening.

They were on the cliff edge far from the castle, which they couldn't see—the forest had overgrown it and crept down to the very edge of the cliffs. The air was damp and foggy, and Isaac was at once chilled to the bone. The others rubbed their arms for warmth.

"Now what?" Kat asked.

But before Isaac could answer, they heard it: a terrifying screech from overhead. A blast of flame arced through the dark sky, the dragon a darker blot above them.

They turned as the dragon descended to the rocky ledge and Moloch and Daemon both slid from the beast's back. Moloch unfurled his own huge leathery wings, turned to face them, and smiled. "My dragon is a very good hunter," he said. "And now we've found you."

CHAPTER 56
Isaac

1942

Isaac gasped. This Moloch was not like the Moloch he'd met earlier. This Moloch was terrible. This Moloch radiated menace and anger, exuding evil.

His teeth were sharpened to sharklike daggers. His single eye burned like fire. He stank of rot, and he was dreadful: bloody face, claw hands, huge leathery wings, skin stretched over cheekbones sharpened to points.

The pendant on Isaac's chest vibrated so that it was all he could do to stand still. Moloch pulled hard at Isaac, forcing him to enhance the magic that Moloch wanted.

And Moloch wanted darkness. The darkest kind of magic. Isaac could not resist him.

Moloch waved a hand, and everyone except Isaac and the knights fell to their knees and cried out. Isaac staggered, trying to hold himself together.

The wind howled and stinging sleet pelted them. Even the earth beneath their feet seemed to heave. The hum in Isaac's head was so loud it drowned out the sound of the sea pounding the cliffs, and he tried to fight, tried, but it was so difficult . . .

"Now you understand," Moloch said. "Now you see what you're up against." His single red eye gleamed, and the scar that ran up his cheek to his empty eye socket puckered as he grinned. A new gash, slashed across the other side of his face, dripped blood.

Moloch was using Isaac to amplify dark magic and Isaac couldn't stop him, as hard as he tried. The raw power that emanated from Moloch was overwhelming. Isaac's legs buckled as he fought to stay upright.

Leo pushed himself to his feet. Isaac hadn't seen him take a sword from the armory, but there Leo was, waving one wildly and hollering, "I'll fight you . . ."

But Daemon flew at Leo, knocking him flat and standing with front feet on Leo's chest as the sword skittered across the ground. The wolf bared its teeth in Leo's pale and frightened face.

"Let's see what happens when I take away that boy's mind," Moloch said, and Leo began to cry out.

Amelie yelled at the knights, and Bedwyr came to her

side, but the other knights, turned evil at a command from Moloch, surrounded Amelie and Bedwyr with swords drawn, as Moloch laughed and waved his hand. Snakes emerged from the empty ghost armor, slithering toward Amelie, who screamed in terror.

Colin yelled commands at Daemon, but Wyvern lifted into the sky, dove at Colin, plucked him off the ground, and flew into the clouds.

Kat, holding her right arm out with her fist clenched, began to chant, "Freeze with winter. Freeze with winter."

"And you, you think you're so powerful." Moloch thrust his arm in her direction, and she froze, her spell backfiring on her.

"You see? I have them all under my power," Moloch said.

Isaac went down on one knee, bracing against the wind and Moloch's energy.

Isaac was alone, and the evil magic that Moloch mustered was running through Isaac, channeled through him, becoming stronger by the second, as he knelt before the dark fae.

The sky was a swirl of black clouds. Trees groaned and cracked in the forest.

"Give up, Isaac," Moloch called. "I'm using you anyway. I'll take the key and the Vault."

Moloch moved close to Isaac and stretched one clawed finger out and hooked it under the chain around Isaac's neck. He was helpless, frozen.

But the chain holding the key became welded to Isaac's throat. *No one can take this from you by force.*

Moloch couldn't take it. And though Isaac couldn't tell, the chain must have emitted a shock to Moloch, who yanked back his hand with an angry growl.

"Give it to me, Isaac, and maybe I'll spare them. And you."

Only if you relinquish it.

Moloch continued, "Fine. I'll take you with me. Yes. Think of what we can do together. With your abilities, why, you would be a prince of the Unseelie. You are part fae." Moloch paused. His red eye glowed brighter. "I'll not only spare your friends, you can bring them. Make them your pets."

Isaac was silent. The wind howled and sleet ran down his cheeks.

Moloch moved closer and his voice became a purr. "Isaac. You can stop this human war. You can stop all wars, forever. Be the first hero of a new world. If we unite and take over the realms—both faerie and human—imagine." Moloch's red eye gleamed. His huge leathery wings expanded. "You'll command armies. We'll slaughter all who stand in our way."

Spare his friends. Become a prince in a fairy-tale realm.

Stop the war. He could stop the Nazis. Isaac Wolf could stop the Nazis, could chase them out of Prague, could chase them off the face of the earth. He could find all the stolen people—Miss Rachel, her brother, all his vanished friends and neighbors. He could repair all that had been lost, prevent more atrocities. Isaac could see it—how glittering the new age was that he'd begin. How everyone would revere him. He'd be a true hero, a new kind of hero for a new world, a world right out of great tales.

Except that it would really be a world of darkness. An Unseelie world.

Which you must not do.

Magic was powerful. And the temptation to become someone of power, whether that power came from magic or not, would always lead down a dangerous pathway.

Those who wish to win wars will stop at nothing to use magical artifacts for evil purposes.

Isaac knew the consequences of giving in to Moloch, as clearly as if he'd been gifted with Leo's foresight. As clearly as if his father was there, lecturing him yet again on right and wrong. Or his grandfather on making a choice.

Because the right thing is not always the easiest.

He knew what he, or anyone given such power, could become. He must not relinquish the key. He must become a hero, but not the kind that Moloch wanted.

Isaac needed to be the kind of hero who stands up for what is right and not for what is easy, or self-gratifying.

Moloch said, "Come, now. It's all over for you and your friends anyway. Come with me. The fae realm can be . . . lovely."

"Then why don't you go back?" Isaac said with effort. "Stay with your Unseelie friends?"

Moloch narrowed his one eye. "They aren't my friends," he snarled. "They are my servants."

Ah. Servants.

Not friends.

Isaac fought against the power of Moloch and remembered he was supposed to have some kind of special knife, a knife he would have picked up on his first time travel in the ring of stones had he not botched it. Maybe if he tried again now . . . He reached in his pocket for the watch.

But the watch wasn't there. He'd left the watch in the Vault. Another mistake.

Colin was somewhere up in the night storm in the claws of the dragon. Amelie and Bedwyr were at the mercy of the knights, with poisonous snakes surrounding Amelie. Leo was flat on his back under the weight of the wolf, and Kat was frozen, her hand outstretched, fist clenched, a blue light slipping from between her fingers.

A blue light.

At the same moment that Isaac saw the light, Leo said, in a strangled voice, "Chatelaine. Use the—" before the wolf growled and snapped.

The chatelaine. The chatelaine held dark magic. A witch's soul was imprisoned inside the thimble. The chatelaine held dark magic, so maybe, just maybe, since he was already channeling dark magic, maybe he could turn it on Moloch.

Isaac concentrated all the power he had on Kat's chatelaine.

But it was more than all, because he also felt a surge of energy from his friends, a positive energy. Isaac used it against the dark magic, channeling the bright, good magic through his heart.

He knew what was needed to win over the darkness. The power of good magic. The bright energy of friendship.

Isaac, unlike Moloch, had friends.

And then, instead of shifting out of fear, Isaac realized

he could make a shapeshift from this combined bright goodness, and he pushed up to his feet and became taller and
stronger even than Moloch.

Isaac moved to stand with Kat, holding her arm out and
holding her up, frozen as she was.

The knights around Amelie dropped their swords, and
the snakes vanished. Daemon slipped off Leo with a whim-
per and ran for the woods. The dragon descended without a
sound onto the cliff edge and let Colin go, and Colin together
with Amelie and Leo joined Isaac to support Kat.

Kat's fist began to glow, then her fingers opened.

"What are you trying now?" Moloch snapped, but there
was a tremor of fear in his voice.

The chatelaine was bright with blue light, and as Isaac
concentrated—as he willed the dark magic he channeled
into the chatelaine, as he willed the bright magic he channeled from his friends into his heart—a shot of blue light
came from the thimble on the chatelaine, a light so bright he
had to squint.

Something emerged from the thimble, and then a figure
formed before Moloch, a ghost-witch woman. Isaac concentrated all his energy through her and against Moloch.

The blue ghost-witch stretched her arms toward Moloch.

Moloch's red eye widened. "No! You can't . . ." as she embraced him with a burning blue fire.

Moloch, in the arms of the ghost-witch, was consumed. He vanished with a strangled cry into a thread of smoke.

Before Isaac could react, Kat woke from her frozen state and fell against him. He still held her arm out as she clutched the chatelaine, and she cried, "Catch the soul in silver old." The ghost-witch turned and became a wisp that fled back to the thimble as Kat closed her fist around her chatelaine again, and Isaac and the others kept her from collapsing.

The magical storm around them fell to silence, the sleet stopped, the trees stilled, and the clouds broke apart, swift and silent in stringers and bands, to reveal twilight stars.

The night stars filled the sky, the entire Milky Way a fat ribbon of light.

"His name's Wyvern," Colin said, as he patted the snorting dragon on the neck. "And he actually didn't like Moloch at all."

Kat shook herself, the chatelaine back in her pocket. Amelie and Leo had pulled themselves together, and there were hugs all around.

"Moloch knew that I hate snakes," Amelie said with a shiver.

"He tried to take my mind," Leo said.

"It's horrible, being spelled," said Kat.

Isaac looked from one to the other and managed a weary smile.

"You've grown," Amelie said to Isaac, tilting her head. "You were always tall, but you've grown even taller."

Isaac's face grew hot. "All of you," he said. "I couldn't have done this alone. But you gave me your energy." He paused, then pointed at Kat's fist. "You're going to have to show me how you control that thimble. Especially if we have to hunt artifacts like it."

"She always wanted one thing. Just one," Kat murmured. "All the bad she did to us, she did for that."

"What?" Isaac asked. "What did she want?"

Kat said, wistful, "She wanted love."

"The wraith," said Isaac, remembering, "it called itself magister. It loved her, too. That's what I felt when I saw into its mind."

Amelie looked up into the sky. "Now that I think about her, and even it, that way, it's terribly sad." She sighed. "That makes it easier to understand."

She exchanged a glance with Colin, and he nodded. They were all silent, except for the snorting dragon.

"So. We're going to hunt artifacts," said Colin.

"We'll travel through time and space," said Amelie.

"It won't be easy," Isaac warned.

"But we'll be the Artifact Hunters," said Leo with a grin. "Brilliant."

CHAPTER 57

Isaac

1942

The first task for the children after they dispatched Moloch was to find MacLarren and see what they could do for Gumble.

Kat worked at spells to return the forest to normal (or as normal as an always-enchanted-although-not-usually-evil forest could become) and send the dire wolves back to wherever they came from.

Wyvern allowed Colin and Isaac to fly on his back so that they could search the forest for the teachers.

The moon, once it rose, was halfway to full, so it was bright enough to see as the dragon circled the castle. They spotted MacLarren first, but when they landed they were astonished to find Gumble, too. Both were a mess of filth but in fine fettle, though maybe Isaac and Colin were not as surprised to see the teachers as their teachers were to see the boys riding a dragon.

"We thought you were a goner," Colin said to Gumble.

"We were strung up like two coneys in a snare," growled MacLarren.

"Yes, it was quite unnerving," said Gumble, removing debris from her hair.

"Beatrice was the clever lass, aye," said MacLarren. "Before that creature was able to do its worst, she created for herself a doppelgänger so that's what it played with. We got out of the trap but couldn't escape until it was gone. It were an awful sight to see it with Beatrice's look-alike and the things it done to it. Knives and mechanical replacements and all."

"Angus was very helpful by working out how to free us from the creature's trap and we hid in the upper branches of its tree," Gumble said. "It was a bit chilling to see myself cut to ribbons. Now, what about this dragon? What's been going on here? All we could tell was that a storm had the castle under siege."

Colin and Isaac exchanged a look. "We have much to tell," Isaac said.

Wyvern flew to the castle tower and curled his great

green body around it and settled down comfortably, after dislodging a few loose roof tiles.

The other children were jubilant to see Gumble. Her mechanical double was removed from the kitchen—"Easy, now," said MacLarren. "She be a tad too familiar"—to be buried in a far corner of the castle grounds.

Willow had found Canut and Lark had unspelled him, and Colin rolled on the floor with his giant dog as Canut slobbered happily.

Baines was the worst victim. They found him still spelled in the small library. A bird had begun to build a nest in his outstretched hand.

Kat whispered in his ear, "Return."

A shimmer surrounded the man as the gold misted away. He blinked, then blinked again, looking at the partially built nest he held. "I had the most interesting dream," he said vacantly. "Magic is wonderful. Don't you believe in magic?"

The others exchanged surprised looks.

"Excuse me. I must fulfill my mission. Off to destroy the world."

"Oh dear," said Kat. "My spell wouldn't have done that to him."

"I do believe," Miss Gumble said, "a little trouble is brewing."

"I bet Moloch had a hand in it," said Leo.

"Lark?" said Kat. "Can you help him?"

"I can get rid of the bad parts," Lark said, and she mumbled.

Baines paused, and said, "Ah, but wait. I am a tree. Must go outside. A bit of fresh air, that's the ticket. Must put down roots, that sort of thing. Use magic to make new leaves. Jolly good." He turned and shuffled for the door.

Willow chortled.

"I'll see to it that he doesn't wander off," said Leo.

Repairing the castle would take effort. The stone walls, portraits, and tapestries were damaged, and dead leaves littered the floors. Amelie worked with Willow to magic some brooms but it would take time to repair everything.

"Well," said Gumble as they listened to the *swish, swish* of the brooms, "we have plenty of kindling for the fires."

Lark danced around the dinner table, trying to get them all to try her special celebration pie. Gumble must have been still a bit woozy because she took a big bite. And then froze, eyes wide.

"Lark," said Amelie sweetly, "sugar? Or salt?"

"Oh, dear," Lark said. "Or maybe baking soda? They all look so much alike."

When he went to his room, Isaac opened his pack to retrieve the casket that had held the watch and was surprised when not two, but three, books tumbled to the floor.

There was Shelley's *Frankenstein*, and Grimms' *Tales*, of course, but a third slim volume in a red leather binding was unexpected. He opened it to the title page.

A Personal Account of the Craven Street Monster,
London, 1873

by Sergeant Winslow Fifer

as Witnessed by the Sergeant and His Fellow
Officer Peter Ramsey in 1870

Isaac turned the pages to several hand-drawn images. One was of the street on which he'd landed with the wraith— complete with the photographer's storefront. Another was a very good likeness of the wraith itself.

Isaac turned to the final pages to read.

> We do not know what became of the monster once
> it disappeared after the near-fatal bite Officer
> Ramsey suffered, but we fear it to be still at
> large. Yes, there are monsters in this world, and it
> behooves the casual person to shutter his windows
> and lock his doors at dusk, lest he should encounter
> such a vile beast in the darkness.

Isaac leaned back against his bed. He had possession of a book he'd never seen before, with a story that grew out of his time travel to Victorian London. How had he engaged the law of unintended consequences when he'd left the wraith in nineteenth-century London?

Would the wraith return to Rookskill still seeking Kat's chatelaine?

Mistress Vivienne had said the Death's Head watch carried a promise and a curse. Isaac didn't want to have created an evil out of what seemed like the right thing to do.

On that score, Isaac thought with a bit of irony, maybe only time would tell, but he resolved to ask Kat, who knew about science.

CHAPTER 58

Isaac

1942

In the days that followed there was much to do. Gumble and MacLarren resumed their lessons in magic with renewed fervor. Baines went back to MI-6, where the children later learned he'd been given a new post tending to the gardens around the buildings, "since he appears to be under the misapprehension that he is a tree." Gumble added, "His superiors are not surprised."

MI-6 was pleased with the progress with Rookskill's Special Alternative Intelligence Unit. Leo forewarned them of a planned German invasion in the northernmost Shetlands. Amelie and Colin mustered various ghostly and animal spies to discover the movements of men and munitions on the eastern front. Kat created spells of protection around Allied troops on the western front. And Isaac enhanced all of their magical abilities, making them each stronger, day by day.

Isaac also practiced his shapeshifting and found that he could begin to take specific forms, and even better, with practice he could change those around him, too. He began to master the art of disappearing at will. All of this would be invaluable to them as Artifact Hunters, and work on that important task began right away.

Isaac took careful inventory of the items in the Vault, and he and Leo also made a study of the diaries of the Guardians that were collected in the small library.

"My father knew these diaries were here," Isaac said one evening.

"That's why your parents sent you to Rookskill," said Leo. "There's another thing. Look at this." He fetched another huge volume with faint lettering. *History of Rookskill Castle, From the Oldest Times Until the Present*, the "present" turning out to be the middle of the seventeenth century. Leo read, "'The rocks upon which Rookskill Castle stands today held the ancestral home of one of the Order's early communities, later to become known as the Order of the Artifact Hunters. Rookskill contains deep magic.'" Leo added, "I'm sure your father knew that."

As all five children studied the roles of Artifact Hunters,

they learned that many artifacts had fallen into the wrong hands in the past and caused havoc. Apollo's Arrow could cause either famine or good health, and had done both. The Shirt of Nessus was poison and responsible for several unexpected deaths.

"Heaven forbid that the Nazis should get their hands on any of these," said Kat.

"Or the fae," said Amelie. "Listen to this."

> The fae lost magical artifacts when humans created the Vault. Humans did so to prevent mischief and misuse of the artifacts, whether by human or fae. Of course, the fae, being fae, are lazy and prone to give up rather than pursue a task, for they dearly love to party.

Isaac sat up straight, and said in his most serious voice, "I must have much more human blood than fae blood." He paused. "Don't you think?"

"I think," said Amelie with a big smile, "that we're all going to like being Artifact Hunters with you, and that you'll be a brilliant Guardian of the Vault."

Isaac blushed right to his toes.

The power of the Death's Head watch continued to haunt Isaac. He and Leo searched the library for information about it, trying to determine whether Isaac had unleashed any of the curse. They did find one scrap that related to his travel to the circle of stones, which he now knew was the Ring of Brodgar.

The user of the watch may envision, through time travel, the end of a civilization. Blessing or curse?

"That's cheerful," said Leo.

"Yes, but maybe that's it," Isaac said. "In the Ring of Brodgar I witnessed people fighting one another and then the Unseelie fae came to take them. It was the end of their world."

"So, it's *don't fight, or else*?"

"Well, I guess. War could be the end of the world, right?"

"Then what we're doing as Artifact Hunters and the SAIU is even more important," Leo said. "For more than just king and country."

And then there was the other aspect of the watch. The law of unintended consequences. Isaac told Kat about finding the book about the wraith. "I had never seen that book before, so it didn't exist until I took the wraith back in time. Would the wraith come back to find itself?"

She tapped her chin. "I've been reading up. The wraith would be caught in a predestination paradox. In a time loop. It would come back to this very same place and time to have this very same set of experiences happen to it, over and over. And what it was before, the magister as you called it, that still exists, too, and we have to hope that the two never meet, as some think that could create a time implosion. But as the wraith, it catches up with itself, just to repeat its time loop forever."

She finished, "Fortunately, we don't have to participate again. That we realize."

He scratched his forehead. "Okay. I don't really understand, but all right. So, what about my parents? And the time stream?"

"That's different. A time stream is neither a time nor a place. Time is like a river and there are eddies. Your parents are caught in an eddy. Unfortunately, it's an eddy that's unreachable, especially since we're already downstream of them."

"Can I go back to them?"

"Not without changing everything," Kat said. "Getting yourself caught in a time loop maybe. Or worse."

"So, there's nothing . . ."

Kat pressed her lips together before saying, "I don't think so. Sorry."

"But," said Amelie, peeking over the edge of the chair in which she sat reading, "I remember seeing something else in the Vault ledger about an artifact that might let you talk to them. I can't remember exactly what it was, but . . . You should go look."

Isaac spent a couple of hours scouring the ledger before he found it.

Item number K-127. This object looks to be a snow globe, but it is in fact a time warp (a suspension of time). On the bottom is the trigger. The user can set the trigger and identify the persons and time in the past the user wishes to visit and then enter and eventually leave the time warp.

This time warp is a charming place—a small cottage in the woods in winter. It's a way to visit old friends or family who have passed on without changing the future or the past (as with a time machine).

This entry was written in his father's hand, and his father's usually straightforward hand slanted as if he was betraying emotion. Isaac found the snow globe, and yes, it was charming. He smiled.

He could see his parents, and maybe even his grand-father, from time to time, even if only for a little while.

CHAPTER 59

The Wraith in London

CIRCA 1890

Tales tell of a creature—or numerous creatures—that roam the foggy streets of London during the waning decades of the nineteenth century.

Jack the Ripper. Spring-heeled Jack. The mad roving tiger. Ghosts and demons and glowing-eyed beasts. Wild tales from a city that is growing fast, that suffers thick pea-soup fogs, that is captivated by the wondrous findings of a certain Mr. Charles Darwin. The nineteenth century is a time that has spawned a collection of writers—Poe, Shelley, Stoker, Dickens, Stevenson—who pen some of the most frightening and fascinating stories written in the English language.

Perhaps that's why a wraith can make its way through the city and then out, moving only at nighttime, wandering the countryside, ever traveling north. Perhaps that's why this wraith survives, through the energy of grim nightmares and dark magic. Perhaps that's why this wraith lives a very long time as it slinks ever closer to its great desire, drawn as it is, over and over, to a castle far north in Scotland.

This wraith has a skill for making, and it does so as it moves through the countryside. It makes small mechanical monsters that follow it like children follow the Pied Piper. They follow it north, from glade to glen to rocky burn, to a place that becomes known as "the place of the elves."

Every so often a child wandering off by herself will hear a small noise and see something in the bracken. Something hunkering low, fearful, watchful, having a tiny hedgehog body with gigantic eyes and peculiar ears, or a bird body with baby-size cat legs. But no one can catch these little beasties, so the myths around them grow and become fanciful stories of elvish hybrids that were made by a wicked magician—whom some called magister—who has turned into a wraith.

A wraith who desires a tiny object, shiny and magical: the thimble that holds the soul of its beloved.

CHAPTER 60
The Artifact Hunters

1943 AND BEYOND

On a full-moon winter night in 1943, five children and one giant dog materialize in New York City's Central Park on Gapstow Bridge, one by one, from thin air, with a soft *whoosh*. They stand silent for a moment, gathering their thoughts and making certain that their arrival has not been noticed. A black cat, who moments earlier was washing his paws on the bridge rail, slinks into the shadows and watches the strange children with unblinking eyes.

The very tall boy at the center of the group greets the others with silent nods and pockets the Stone of Recall, an artifact that gives him the power to transport his Hunters from place to place.

Isaac Wolf, Katherine and Amelie Bateson, Leo Falstone, and Colin Drake have been using magic to help with the war effort and so much more. They each have code names now.

One, the Librarian, has informed Allied commanders of the best places to land on the beaches. Another, the Diviner, has rallied certain unseen but benevolent spirits to carry out acts of sabotage on the enemy. A third, the Dragon, has learned from animals where bunkers lie hidden and prisoners are held. A fourth, the Professor, has generated strong spells to protect innocents when possible and glamour their captors.

And the fifth, their leader, the Wolf, can create their disguises, amplify their gifts, and inform them when he needs their help to seek out a potentially dangerous magical artifact or perform some other task for the benefit of the human race, as Artifact Hunters have done for millennia.

"If you find it," the Wolf says in a low voice, "send the signal to the rest of us."

The others murmur assent.

"I'll bring the Vault to"—he pulls out a folded map— "the Museum of Natural History, Central Park West and Seventy-Ninth Street. I've been there before. In the Hall of African Mammals, there's a lion diorama. We'll meet there."

"I like lions," says the Dragon. The cat raises its head, gazing at the boy fondly. "What's it called again? The artifact?"

"Tablet of Destinies," the Wolf answers. "About so big. Black. Actually makes pictures, like at the cinema." He makes a rectangular space with his hands. "Amazing. But don't be tempted to read it."

The Professor nods and says, "Law of unintended consequences."

"And after we find that one, back to Rookskill for a bit?" asks the Librarian. "I'm in the middle of reading volume seven, and it's quite exciting."

The Diviner adds, "And I need to get back to have a few words with Lark. Apparently, the new recruits are starving."

The Wolf smiles. "Yes. Back to Rookskill for a bit. Right, then. Ready? I'll make disguises."

If you were watching and looked away for an instant, when you looked back you'd see five elderly people, bent and shuffling, and one seeing-eye dog.

The Wolf nods to his friends, who nod back, and they separate and slip away through the moonlight, ready to use their strange magical gifts for the good of all.

Acknowledgments

This novel went through many iterations, and without the support of my brilliant editor, Kendra Levin, I could not have brought it to life. Patient and thoughtful, she knew how to help me reach more deeply into characters and plot and pry the story's heart—and Isaac's—wide-open.

Much of what became the central concepts of both time travel and the Vault of Magical Artifacts was hatched during brainstorming sessions with my son, Kevin. He has the makings of a master storyteller, and I'm proud to say (and not only as a mother, but as a fellow writer) that he's pursuing that career path in earnest. His imagination is dazzling, and he knows what it means to tap the emotional core of a character. As the saying goes, watch this space.

I lucked into a collaborative critique partnership with one of the best writers in the kid-lit world, Jen Cervantes. Jen was with me from the very start of this story, and I thank my lucky stars for that! She's an amazing editor. Not only did she read every word of this manuscript, she read every word at least twice—and she read a lot of words that ended up on the cutting-room floor—with nary a complaint, and often with the most constructive detailed criticism a writer could wish for. I owe you so many abrazos, mi amiga. ¡Y hasta la próxima vez!

My agent, Erin Murphy, not only vets my work before submission, she edits my work before submission, and that is truly a gift. And she provides the strongest shoulders, warmest smiles, sincerest hugs, and the most intelligent observations and determined support—honestly, I don't know what I would do without you, Erin, and the entire EMLA team and family.

Aneeka Kalia, assistant editor at Viking, stepped in to provide invaluable oversight and guidance. Kate Renner is the talented designer and Jen Bricking did the brilliant cover and illustrations. Thank you all.

And where would I be without Janet Pascal, easily the best copy editor in the business? Thank you, Janet, for making time for my book! And to Anne Heausler, whose sharp eye caught so many extra words and exclamation points (ahem), and who gave Wyvern a bit of new life, so many thanks.

Our longtime friend Lee Freeman gave me Michael Gruenbaum's moving memoir about his life as a Jewish boy in Prague who was sent to Terezín internment camp during the Nazi occupation. My husband patiently accompanied me to Prague and to Terezín. Let me just say that as beautiful as Prague is, Terezín is equally or more heartbreaking. While *The Artifact Hunters* is not a story of the Holocaust, it is a story about survival, friendship, and the choice to do good. I hope that the underlying message I've conveyed to young readers—to all readers—is that it is possible to stand up for what is right and good in the face of evil.